INAPPROPRIATE

By Sherry Morris

This is a work of fiction. Names, characters, places goods services
and incidents either are the product of the author's imagination or
are used fictitiously, and any resemblance to actual persons, living or
dead, businesses, companies, products, events, organizations or
locales is entirely coincidental.

Edited by Diane Parkinson
Cover by Bojan

ACKNOWLEDGEMENT
I couldn't have written this book without the giggles of my critique group (Alleyne, Diane and Robin) to keep me chuffing down the track.

DEDICATION
To Sandra, Andy and Mom
With love to Mikie, Andy and Olivia

Chapter One

I hate discovering dead bodies.

I shook my head and slammed on the brakes. While leaping out of the golf cart onto the smooth Cocoa Beach sand, I wiggled my fingers into a pair of nitrile gloves. A shiver of fear convulsed up my spine as a fishy dead-human stench wafted through the dawn. I tiptoed over to a bloated young black man face up in a drenched United States Navy uniform, matted with sand.

"Sir, do you need some assistance?" *Please roll over and puke or something.* "Hey, buddy, you okay?" Nothing. I gave him a little nudge in the ribs with my sneaker. He felt squishy. I shuddered.

The June sun rose pink on the horizon. Red sky was good luck for sailors or something like that. Not for this guy.

This is so not the way I want to begin my last shift before vacation.

I loosened his tie, unfastened a button and placed two of my fingers on his carotid artery. No pulse. He stared past me, big brown eyes with long eyelashes frozen in a peaceful expression. No, not peaceful. The curl of his lips looked as though he had been up to something mischievous. I lowered my face and put my ear to his nose to listen for breathing as I studied his chest. I didn't see or feel respirations. Up close he smelled like chlorine bleach.

I wasn't a coroner but it was obvious to me that this guy had been dead for quite some time.

I struggled with the gritty wet material, unbuttoning the rest of his shirt exposing his hairy chest and a gold Star of David necklace. I didn't find the dog tags I was searching for.

"Rest in peace, unknown sailor."

I whispered a little prayer for him and pulled off the gloves as I hurried back to the vehicle. After slipping them into the black plastic trash bag, I exhaled, flipped open my blue cell phone and punched nine on speed dial. I glanced at my simulated diamond Tinker Bell watch and wiggled my wrist to make the pixie dust dance under the crystal.

"Cocoa Beach Department of Public Works. What is your complaint?" asked Igor the grouchy dispatcher.

"It's Sandra Faire. I've found a military floater washed up in front of the Copacabana. He's dead."

Within ten minutes I was surrounded by three hotel security guys in gray trousers and blue blazers; Andres, the perpetually hung-over lifeguard; Eagle, the hotshot volunteer beach patrolman who always startled the sunbathers tearing around the sand in his ATV; *Bicep Betty* in the yellow polka dot bikini and matching support hose; six uniformed City of Cocoa Beach cops. And Lieutenant Hottie Hernandez, homicide.

Okay so his first name was William, and not that he was my type...anymore...but my temperature sure soared whenever he met my gaze. I needed to figure out how to reroute those errant hormones. I was through with hot *uber* good-looking alpha males. Especially this one. No man of mine answered his cell phone during a romantic interlude. Just because there was a category five hurricane looming was no excuse for him to run off to work and leave me panting on the kitchen table.

Well, yeah, we had some other issues. William and I weren't compatible except when we were making out. His kisses sent me to nirvana. Perhaps it's just as well the hurricane interrupted us. I had nothing to regret.

We didn't have anything in common. I was eighteen the first time he kissed me. And the last time. Now I'm twenty-three and he would be thirty soon. I didn't like cops. They were paranoid, manipulative drama kings. Well, most of the ones in my family tree were.

Hottie was dressed in a black tee shirt, way too tight. I could see the outline of his chiseled abs and the ripple of his deltoids. A badge on a chain hung around his neck, a service weapon and handcuffs tucked into the rear of his deliciously form fitting Levis.

The lieutenant swaggered down and looked over the deceased from a distance as the tide lapped the sailor's mucky dress shoes. He paced off an area for the uniforms to seal the death investigation scene. Hotel security assisted, offering hot pink umbrellas to shove into the sand to wrap the yellow police tape around.

The lieutenant stopped and squatted before approaching the body, shining his flashlight on the sand with a slow sweeping motion. He led the crime scene photographer to the areas he deemed important. After the initial images were shot, forensics arrived.

The CSI team deployed different colored lights and donned

goggles. The photographer changed out the filters on his camera to match the colors the forensic team used.

The lieutenant had a lengthy conversation with the lifeguard then shook his head, scribbled on a notepad, ducked under the police tape and made a beeline for me.

I leaned casually against the umbrella rental stand, twisting an errant strand of pale hair around my finger, determined not to let his deep testosterone voice move me.

He looked down and rubbed his clean shaven chin. His eyes lingered on the finer parts of my anatomy as his gaze climbed to my face and he asked me, "You discover this one?"

I sucked in a deep breath trying not to remember his erotic whispers.

"Did you discover the body?" He repeated.

I nodded.

"Anyone in the area at the time?"

I looked into his smoldering brown eyes and shook my head.

"How long ago?"

I checked Tinker Bell. "About forty-five minutes now. I called in the find at six-thirteen."

"Did you notice any footprints around the body before you approached it?" He cocked his head to one side and gave my sneakers the once over.

I kicked up one foot so he could see my treads. "Sorry, I forgot to look…"

He frowned and gave me that *you've disappointed me again* look. "Did you disturb anything?"

"I unbuttoned him with gloves on. He was all buttoned up to his chin. I felt his carotid artery. I couldn't find his dog tags. Oh…and I kicked him in the ribs."

"Left or right side?"

"Left."

He scribbled in his note pad. "Have you noticed anything out of the ordinary on the beach in the last twenty-four hours?"

I shook my head. This was why I hated discovering dead bodies. It forced me to collide with the most inappropriate man for me in the whole darned universe. I didn't want things to get stirred up again. I couldn't get things stirred up again. *On account of what I did during the hurricane.*

6

"Do you know him from anywhere?" he asked.

I shook again, exaggeratedly slow with a wide-eyed expression.

"Thank you, ma'am. I'll be in touch." And with that formal tone, he strutted over to the hotel security guards kibitzing near my golf cart.

I smoothed my bright white Department of Public Works tee shirt down over my red uniform shorts as I passed them. They were discussing the evangelical Christian service held last night in the Copacabana ballroom. Pastor Eugene Donaldson was a modern thinking, feel-good preacher very popular with the locals and tourists alike. He had led prayer breakfasts at the White House during both Slick Willie's and Dub-yah's terms.

I chimed in, "The sailor was Jewish. There is a Star of David around his neck. He wouldn't have attended."

William rolled his eyes and glared at me.

I hated when he did that. Just because I wasn't a cop didn't mean I couldn't solve crimes…or sort out which leads were dead ends.

I climbed back into the golf cart and waved to Andres, the lifeguard. He smiled and waved back. I guess the guy was good looking if you liked suntanned guitar playing Euro-blonds without muscles. I didn't. I didn't like his sing-song German accent either. And I especially didn't like guitar players anymore…because of Hurricane Alfredo.

I went on about my job, puttering down the beach, stopping to pick up a piece of petrified palm trunk, a glass grape juice bottle and a deflated football. I plucked them with a mechanical snatcher device. I don't know if it has an official name but I called mine Monkey. After two years at this job I was pretty efficient. I could do it all from the driver's seat. Snatch it and drop it into the trash bag and go along my jolly way.

The theme to "The Pink Panther" jazzed from my shorts. I stopped and dug my phone out. My mother's picture smiled on the caller I.D. I inhaled and answered. "Hi, Mom."

"Sandra, are you still intending to climb aboard that train of fools?"

"They aren't fools, Mom. They're very nice people."

She sobbed, "You're being kidnapped by that cult and I'll never see my baby again." She launched into one of her motherly speeches about how everything I do is inappropriate.

Mom was so disappointed in me. My four brothers were cops working under my dad, the police commissioner. But I toiled as a sanitation engineer and public relations specialist for the Department of Public Works. Translation: I picked up the trash left on the beach and told the tourists where the public restrooms were located. At least the uniform was cute.

What Mom didn't know was by day I collected garbage but by night I was an infamous cozy mystery author. I wrote under the pen name of Dixie London. And I didn't have a thing published. I had written almost twelve books...well, the first three or four chapters of twelve different books. Okay, so I was more like an infamous cozy mystery author wannabee. But I had fun. I belonged to the Global Order of Scribes pronounced "goose" for short. The international convention was transpiring in Morocco this week.

Rosemary Donaldson, wife of televangelist Eugene Donaldson, was the president of our local chapter. I couldn't stand her, the snobby fakey flake. She arranged to have a little writers conference of sorts aboard three private railcars hooked onto the back of her husband's crusade train, which was hooked onto the back of a regular North American Passenger Railroad train.

Of course I could set my feelings for her aside and grace the authors with my presence long enough for a two week free vacation aboard the private rail cars. The Donaldsons' were wealthy so I knew this would be a first class to-do. The Agatha Christie birthday shindigs she hosted at her mansion were always loaded with fat shrimp, alligator tar-tar and a white chocolate fountain. Maids and cabbage roses everywhere you turned in her gaudy museum. Even the ceilings were painted with rose murals. Last time I tucked two pieces of her toilet tissue into my pocket to show Mom. It was printed in full color, embossed and scented with roses. Mom wasn't impressed. She told me it would cause bladder infections.

"Mom—Mom—Mom!" I finally got her to stop ranting. "I told you it's not a cult. I'm not going as one of the devout followers of Pastor Donaldson. Rosemary invited our mystery readers' book club to tag along. We'll be segregated from the fanatics. We have our own private cars and we'll be reading and discussing books...and knitting."

Mom loved knitting so I just threw that in.

"Really, knitting?"

"Uh-huh. A couple of the ladies are involved in the knit-a-scarf-for-a-serviceman charity. We'll be knitting up a storm for those brave Americans." I was great at making things up.

"Oh, well why didn't you tell me? What time do we leave? I'll need to finish the laundry…"

"No!" I cleared my throat. "No, Mom. You can't go. The train is already filled to capacity. You needed to reserve a compartment ahead of time."

"Nonsense. I'll bunk-in with you."

"No can do. I have a roommate. Dina."

"Oh…Dina. How is she? Is her Aunt Beverly recuperating as well as can be expected?"

Dina Devers was the only friend I had who Mom approved of.

"Dina and Aunt Beverly are doing just fine. I'll let her know you asked about them. I gotta go, Mom. Got to finish up by noon today."

"Come see me before you leave."

Yeah, right. So you can jump in the backseat and stow away. "I'll try. Gotta run. Bye." I closed my phone and stuffed it back inside my pocket.

I drove along the beach. Two guys stood knee deep in the surf, fishing. An early jogger trotted by. I smacked my forehead and took my foot off the gas. If Lieutenant Hottie had any follow-up questions for me I wouldn't be available. I should have told him I'd be leaving on the *GOOS Express* this afternoon. Could this be a dilemma? He didn't tell me not to leave town or anything. And I just reported the body. I wasn't technically a witness…or suspect. And besides, it was a routine death investigation. I was confident the autopsy would show he had drowned. Poor guy. He had looked so young and fun loving. I resolved to live like every day was my last and chase my fondest dreams.

The sailor probably was on shore leave, rented a speed boat with his buddies, got drunk and fell overboard. Yeah, that's it. He seemed really happy by the smirk frozen on his face. I ought to open a detective agency. And I could hire my writing pals as operatives. An all woman force. Nobody would suspect us of spying on them. We'd make a killing. I giggled at my pun.

I peeked at Tinker Bell, shook up her pixie dust, looped around and did a U-turn. It was time to stop by the dumpster and then check-in with Igor.

A crowd of tourists had gathered at the crime scene as the police carted off the corpse. I sighed. Great, they were noshing donuts and drinking Starbucks. More trash for me to collect later on.

The lieutenant stood down along the shoreline running his fingers through his short dark hair. Perhaps I should stop off and let him know I'd be leaving town. I slowed down and threw my hand up. He didn't notice me so I kept going. I decided to call him from the train.

Part of me was relieved not to have to talk to him face-to-face. If Lieutenant Hottie were to make a late night visit to my little studio apartment...to discuss the case, I wouldn't be home to answer the door...wearing something entirely inappropriate.

* * *

At exactly 1:47 P.M. I checked-in at the Orlando North American Passenger Railway station and dragged my huge cerulean blue rolling duffle bag outside. Missing one wheel, it fought me the whole way. I set my chambray blue hard plastic cooler on top of it and looked around the platform.

The crusaders sported primary and pastel colored leisure suits and church appropriate dresses. The African, Asian and Cuban-Americans carried the style off well enough. However, the European-Americans who had baked thousands of hours in the Florida sun, resembled shriveled dates.

Rosemary Donaldson waved me down to the rear of the train. My tummy jittered with excitement. And hunger. I couldn't wait to gobble the fancy food. I took a deep breath and plodded through the throng of elderly passengers.

"Hi, Rosemary."

We fake kissed the humidity near both cheeks. I tried not to cough in the perfume haze engulfing the raven haired, liposuctioned, botoxed pastor's wife dressed in white patent leather boots, striped over-the-knee socks, a ruffled plaid fuchsia miniskirt and an orange low-cut sweater. She had the body for the outfit but at her age and considering her husband's holy profession...jail bait tart was not a good look.

"We can board any minute now. Here's our itinerary," she said in her high-pitched nasally voice and offered me a floral motif pocket folder with a thick stack of papers inside. I let go of my suitcase handle and accepted it. The suitcase plopped down onto the concrete with a resonating thud. The cooler's lid didn't dislodge, thank goodness. I squatted to pick them up.

"Sandra, I'm so glad you talked your mother into joining us," said Rosemary.

I shut my eyes tight, scrunched up my face and clenched my fists, hoping I hadn't heard correctly. Before I stood I asked, "Pardon? What did you say?"

"Your momma stopped by my house this morning with a trunk full of yarn and knitting needles. She volunteered to teach the crusaders to knit."

Chapter Two

As I rose and repositioned my belongings the crowd of writers and crusaders parted. Mom propelled her luggage cart toward me stacked with a green steamer trunk, a three piece Pepto-Bismol pink luggage set, travel ironing board, portable DVD player and a box of groceries. She was dressed in her signature over-sixty-Floridian-chic: a knit twin set embroidered, beaded and sequined with flamingos; matching green Capri's with bugle beading at the hem and pockets; wedge-heeled lime leather sandals; wraparound sunglasses and a lime green visor. She had pulled her blonde hair into a ponytail.

I looked just like Mom with the only exception being she carried a voluptuous extra thirty pounds. The outfit would be very cute on her, if she were over sixty. But she was only forty-six. She had married my dad when she was eighteen and they had five kids in five years. Two sets of identical twin boys then singleton me.

I couldn't think of anything to say that wouldn't get me sent to my room so I just smiled really big.

Mom blew me a kiss.

"All aboard!"

I turned my head to see my brother Andy dressed in a navy blue conductor's uniform. He was a member of the Central Florida Chapter of the National Railway Historical Society. I had forgotten he had volunteered for this adventure. Out of all my brothers, Andy was the kindest to me so at least I wouldn't have to worry about our sibling bickering drowning out the train whistle.

I was sure he wasn't any happier than I that Mom had tagged along.

New York Times bestselling horror author, Hazel Hatchet, a.k.a. *Hack 'em Up Hazel*, shoved past me, her ample hip bumping my arm as she adjusted the straw cowgirl hat over her close-cropped afro. Her long amber and sterling silver earrings swung heavily to and fro. Hazel grabbed the handrail on the green iron steps and grunted. Andy gripped onto her arm and hoisted her aboard.

I stepped back closer to the station and took my first good look at the train. The last three cars were painted or more likely wrapped in a cabbage rose print. Pink orange, yellow and white everywhere. In front of them were several cars plastered with Pastor Eugene Donaldson's toothy face. "The Crusade of Peace" was painted in gold leaf.

Ahead of those cars were tired brown and gray North American Passenger Railway baggage and passenger cars. I couldn't see the diesel locomotives.

I marched toward the train dragging my duffle bag.

"Hi, Sandra," sniffled *Weepy Wendy*, an anorexic trauma nurse practitioner who had wallowed in the throes of woe the entire time we'd been acquainted. She wrote romantic comedy. "I had such a bad night at work. There is this really mean Dr. Fruiterman and he kept yelling at me. I knocked over a tray of sterile instruments and–"

"Hi, Wendy! I'm so sorry you had a rough night. Life is just not fair. Can't wait to hear all about your latest work-in-progress." Oh shoot! Why did I say that? I always found it very uncomfortable conversing with her. I never could come up with the right words to help her feel better. Some people must want to be miserable.

Staring at her hair, my brother helped Wendy up the steps. Once she had boarded he shook his head. Wendy's frizzy locks were dyed black with thick stripes of white woven in. Think Cruella DeVille on a bad hair day. I shuddered, imagining accident and heart attack victims opening their eyes to see Nurse Wendy standing over them.

I was so excited and anxious to ride the rails again. Andy always invited me along whenever there was a special steam train excursion in the region. He invited the whole family but they all were too caught up in their own egos and imagined troubles to be transported to a gentler time. Even his twin, Matt. They were identical in looks but not personality. That's how I told them apart. Matt was the 5'10" blond with the sneer. Andy was the 5'10" blond with the twinkle in his eye.

A North American Passenger Railway employee sashayed by with a big brown take-out bag from the Olive Garden. I wanted to mug her. I was so hungry. Maybe I could chat her up and she'd offer me a breadstick.

A loud whistle and thunderous roar sped by on the other track. Must've been a freight train though I couldn't see it because our train was blocking the view.

It was my turn to climb onboard but I backed up and beckoned

13

the next writer to go on before me. I didn't want to be caught in the aisle behind *Weepy Wendy* and have to hear about her latest bad luck. She'd make a perfect mate for Matt. What was I thinking? No, please no. I didn't want to have her sniffling around at every family gathering.

I rolled my eyes as Andy turned on the charm for exotic Matilda Irwin, a.k.a. *Tabloid Tilly,* an Aussie photo journalist here on some kind of youth working visa. Matilda was of Chinese, Aborigine and *probably English prison camp* origin. Men seemed to find Matilda irresistible. I couldn't stand her. *I'll think up a reason later.*

I enjoyed an evil grin while she flirted and finally wiggled aboard.

Andy shuffled luggage around, shoving it further away from the door. I was fascinated by the stacks of crap people brought with them. Suitcases and snacks I could understand. But the step ladder, potted Norfolk Island pine tree, fireplace tools, bird cage, litter box, cushioned toilet seat, laundry detergent and chlorine bleach were a bit quirky.

"Sis, why didn't you tell me Mom was coming?"

"I didn't know! Honest! She just showed up. This is going to be a miserable trip." I whined.

"Why? I mean other than the obvious."

"She doesn't know I'm a writer," I whispered. I left my luggage with him and climbed the three steps.

Everyone made a right so I followed them and took a seat midway down a highly polished cherry conference table. I counted sixteen leather chairs.

As the remaining passengers flitted in, no one sat next to me on either side.

Elderly body builder *Bicep Betty,* of yellow polka dot bikini fame, reposed directly across from me snapping her black bubble gum. Every book she wrote was full of kink and husband homicide. No wonder she was an old maid...and had a cult following.

Most of the faces were familiar to me and I looked forward to becoming acquainted with the newbies.

My best bud, Dina Devers, a moderately successful eBook author, stumbled in last. She wrote steamy romance. I found her books to be hilarious but didn't dare let on.

The gossip around the beach was that Dina didn't get enough

14

oxygen at birth and as a result, while her intellect was normal, she was freakishly happy and strangely giddy at inappropriate times.

Dina tripped over the hem of her long leaf-green broomstick skirt and grabbed the back of a chair to catch herself. It rolled out and spun to one side. She plopped down in it and giggled, finger fluffing her cute strawberry blonde curls.

I thought it was so weird to find free rolling chairs on a moving train. Somebody might be seriously injured.

"Welcome to the *GOOS Express*," Rosemary announced. "I'm so delighted we all could take this little working vacation along the rails."

The ladies applauded and thanked her profusely. Very excited about the chance to interact with other writers, learn from the speakers and pitch my books to agents and editors, I smiled and clapped.

The whistle tooted twice and the train lurched forward. The chairs jerked sideways. Some of the ladies gasped. I stuck my arms over my head and enjoyed the ride.

A voice broadcast over the public address system: "Good afternoon, ladies. This is your conductor Andrew Faire. We have departed exactly on time at 2:57. Our scheduled arrival in Washington, DC is at 8:46 tomorrow morning barring any unforeseen glitches. You'll notice the train stop from time to time to allow freight traffic to pass through or to make a regularly scheduled stop for the North American Passenger Railway. Please do not place anything in the toilets but the supplied toilet paper as the plumbing system is very sensitive and if one clogs then all toilets in the car will back up. In the evangelists' lounge there are over-the-counter pain relievers, sleeping aids, cold and allergy formulas and motion sickness medications available for purchase as well as a limited selection of toiletry items. If we can be of any assistance please don't hesitate to contact me or my fellow volunteer crew members from the Central Florida Chapter of the National Railway Historical Society: *Big Marc* Clinger and Jimmy Tamales. Enjoy your conference."

"Ladies, if you will open your folders you'll find the packet with our speaker schedule," said Rosemary. "Unfortunately, our keynote speaker Tony O'Rourke, the *New York Times* bestselling author of sixteen police procedurals including *The Naked Detective*,

15

has been unavoidably detained. He hopes to join us later in the trip, although that shall pose a problem with sleeping accommodations. We only have allotted room for two speakers per day. They each travel with us until the next big hub stop."

I perused the schedule: Orlando to DC to Chicago to Albuquerque to Los Angeles. I couldn't wait to dip my big toe in the Pacific Ocean for the very first time.

Rosemary opened a cardboard box and passed hardcover copies of Tony O'Rourke's latest release down the table. I nearly squealed. My favorite author. He was the reason I became a writer. I took one and flipped to the back and searched the last few pages then the first few. No photo or any *about the author* page.

I envisioned a white-haired portly recluse clad in a golden smoking jacket with leather patches on the elbows. He relit his pipe as he navigated the narrow path to the desk through a jungle of ceiling-high crumpled white paper. He hunted and pecked on an old Remington typewriter in his family's dank Irish castle. *Tony O'Rourke, gifted genius. My idol.*

"Nevertheless," Madame President Rosemary continued, "Our first speaker is aboard, Anna Deerstalker. A science fiction author and online writing coach. She will present a workshop on the richness of conflict, precisely at 6:00 P.M."

I glanced at Tinker Bell. It was nearly 3:30. I shook the pixie dust as I flung my hand in the air and waved.

"Yes, do you have a question?" asked Rosemary.

"When is dinner served?"

"There is not time to prepare and serve a formal meal this evening. There will be hors d'oeuvres available throughout the trip in the parlor car at the end of the train. Feel free to indulge yourselves."

My stomach burned. I hadn't ingested anything today but the three Hershey's Kisses I snatched out of the candy jar on Igor's desk. That's what I get for skipping breakfast, and then the darned floater set me behind schedule so I didn't eat lunch. *I should call the lieutenant about that soon…*

"Ladies, we have a few rules here. No smoking, alcohol or recreational drugs allowed. No wireless internet devices. No cell phones," said Rosemary.

Dina raised her hand.

"Yes?" asked Rosemary.

"What about our portable word processors?"

"Of course you can keep whatever technology you use to write. Laptop computers, netbooks, word processors, etc. Just be sure you disable any wireless connections. We have much work to do."

She held the cardboard box up. "I'll pass this along. Empty all banned items into the box."

I watched incredulously as the ladies sucked up to her and thought it such a good idea to help us focus on our craft. No way would I store my phone in the box. I'd just pretend I didn't bring...

The Pink Panther jazzed from my shorts pocket.

Everyone looked at me. I sighed and pulled my phone out. I missed the call. *Mom.* I switched it off and gingerly placed it in the box. Just as well, I didn't need Mom pestering me.

Then I remembered what had happened that morning. Waves lapping the happy corpse crashed in my mind. As the box slid down the table past me, I said, "No, wait. I need my phone. I discovered a dead body today and the police may need to contact me."

The business car fell silent except for the chug-a-chug of the train.

Bicep Betty blew a big black bubble, popped it with her pen then whispered to *Tabloid Tilly.* Tilly locked eyes with me as she fondled her camera. There was something witchy about that girl from down under and I didn't trust her. I kept my composure, glanced down at Tinker Bell and shook some pixie dust.

"Sandra, you really do need to get a proper job and stop cavorting with the underworld." Rosemary voiced what some were no doubt thinking.

"That poor lost soul. I'll bet no one stops to think about how terrifying it must be for the victim in the horrific moments before being murdered," *Weepy Wendy* boo-hooed.

"Of course we do," *Pat-the-Pirate* squawked. "We all do. We're writers."

Pat was a popular historical adventure novelist with a ruddy wrinkled face, wooden leg and a glass eye.

Dina kicked back her chair and clopped over to me. "Who, what, where, when and how? Do tell!"

"I discovered him washed up on the beach this morning. In front of the Copacabana—"

"It was Ricco!" Dina blurted.

"Ricco?" I asked.

"You know, Tony shot him because he was jealous Ricco had made a move on his girl Lola at the Copacabana."

I grinned and shook my head. "I didn't find any yellow feathers in the sand. You should audition for the show where you need to know the correct song lyrics."

I turned toward the others. "Anyhow, he was a good-looking young sailor and I've probably revealed more than I should have."

Clear packaging tape screamed like fingernails on a chalkboard as Rosemary sealed the box. Chico, her Cuban-American pool boy/hairdresser/paid companion, carted it off. With my phone inside. My plea hadn't impressed her.

"Ladies, please begin your daily writing. If you did not come prepared, or if your writing apparatus is packed in your luggage then help yourselves to one of the journals on the credenza. Pens and sharp pencils, too. No more chit-chat please. We need a silent and peaceful atmosphere for our muses to run wild and free."

I plodded over to the credenza and selected a very high-end journal bound in pink leather. I decided to use a pencil so I snatched a metallic gold number two. I gazed out the window at the cumulonimbus clouds layering themselves in the sky. It looked like rain.

I returned to my seat, opened the journal and wrote on the inside of the cover:

The Case of the Adorable Plumber
By Dixie London

At the top of the first page I wrote:

It was a dark and stormy afternoon in Fredericksburg, Virginia. More American lives had been lost here in the Civil War than in any other town in any other war. As I climbed out of my old brown pickup truck, thunder exploded like a Union soldier's cannonball...

I was surprised how easily the words spewed forth. I had no life-long interest in the Civil War and had never visited the battlefields and cemeteries of Fredericksburg, but I had done my homework. I loved learning new things, which I passed along to others through my books. Well, I would pass them along once they were published. But I had to finish one of them first. Perhaps *The Case of the Adorable Plumber* might just be my break-out novel.

The clickty-clacking of the train, the white noise of the air circulating system and the sound of some of the other ladies typing orchestrated a very stimulating melody.

I was way into chapter three when my stomach began growling out loud. I really needed to get to those hors d'oeuvres. I glanced at Tinker Bell. 5:41. I shook her pixie dust as I stood and pushed my chair under the table. "Do we select our own rooms?" It felt good to stretch my legs. I wiggled my toes inside my sneakers.

Rosemary and the other writers looked up and then checked their watches. "My, how time flies when you are lost in your own little personal writing bubble. All right, ladies, I think we should wrap it up now." She sorted through some papers on the table. "I have a list here. The crew has delivered your luggage to your compartments." Rosemary shuffled papers. "Sandra Compartment A. Wendy is in B. Betty you get Compartment C. Pat..."

Great! We each get private rooms. Or broom closets. I wondered how large and opulent they were. As Rosemary droned on with our room assignments, images of fairytale castle bedchambers danced in my mind. Yeah, I knew we were on a train and only so much can be done in limited space but still I had high hopes.

"Your rooms are right through the door near where you came in." Rosemary motioned toward it. "Make sure you grasp the handrails in the vestibule between the train cars. We don't want anyone getting injured here on the *GOOS Express*, now do we...?"

When she finally finished, I blurted, "Where are the hors d'oeuvres?"

"They are in the last car. In the parlor area next to the restroom. Help yourselves. I do hope you like the selections." Rosemary flashed her porcelain white teeth stained with fuchsia lipstick.

That was the cue for everyone to give her their deepest gratitude. We did. Then we headed for our compartments.

I stepped into mine. Darn. It wasn't a fairytale castle bedchamber. But the retro Art Deco opulence was very tasteful.

It had mahogany paneled walls, a brass sconce and a little oscillating fan up in the corner near the ceiling. There was a small wash basin and mirror near the pocket aisle door. A wall-length oval window on the outside wall was flanked with a plush red velvet arm chair and a large red velvet sofa which apparently converted into a bed at night. The light scent of roses wafted in the air. Rosemary was great with details.

My duffle bag was stuffed almost under the sofa. I noticed an unfamiliar tapestry carpet bag stowed upon a shelf above the chair my cooler was tucked under. A newspaper stood crisply folded in a vertical holder on the window and two bottles of water glistening with condensation beckoned in the cup holders.

I counted three doors.

I smiled and tried the door apparently leading into the next compartment. Locked. Good. I didn't need *Weepy Wendy* boo-hooing in at all hours. I opened the closet door. There was a stepladder folded inside. I shut the door.

I rubbed my arms and glanced up at the little fan. I'd have to figure out where to switch it off.

I pivoted and opened the bathroom door. And screamed.

So did the lady sitting on the toilet.

Chapter Three

I retreated to the corridor and checked the lighted sign above the door. Compartment A. And that sure did look like my suitcase and cooler.

I reentered the room, leaned down and tugged my duffle bag out. Yep, Sandra Faire was clearly written in blue gel pen on the luggage tag.

The bathroom door opened.

"I'm so sorry. I didn't know anyone was using the bathroom in my compartment," I said, blushing.

A beautiful little woman…and I mean little…the shortest little person I'd ever met stuck her dark-chocolate hand out. "Hello, I am Mary Agnes Starr. You must be my roommate, Sandra Faire. Jesus loves you," she said in a sweet southern accent.

"Yes he does. Thank you. And Jesus loves you, too."

Mini Mary Agnes wanted to shake. I kept eyeing the bathroom and the sink near the door. I didn't want to shake until she had washed her hands so I tugged the cooler out and then opened the lid.

"I brought iced teas. You want one? Go ahead and wash up. There is a little bar of soap and a fluffy hand towel on the sink. I'll make us drinks."

"Caffeine is blood from the devil," said Mary Agnes as she climbed into the chair. Her fluffy cloud-white dress could have fit one of those Just My Size Barbie dolls. She was very small boned and thin. Like a living breathing doll. The eyelet lace billowed over my cooler. She swept the angelic fabric aside.

I replaced the lid on the cooler. "I should empty this water in the sink and find some fresh ice."

"Close the compartment door," her voice cracked.

"Why?" I asked, creeped out. I wanted to run. We would just see about this. No way would I share a compartment with a complete stranger with poor personal hygiene. There must have been some mix-up. Dina and I had signed-up to room together. We were going to brainstorm three novels for each of us as we drifted off to sleep lulled by the rocking of the locomotive.

"Close it," Mary Agnes whispered with an air of desperation.

I did. But I made sure not to clasp the latch and opened the gold silk drapes on the corridor window fastening them to the wall with Velcro.

As I turned toward the frightened woman, I asked, "What's wrong?"

"Mobsters are here! I spilled my purse in the parking lot and my marbles rolled under the tire of a red limousine." Mary Agnes wrung her hands. "I was crouching down to retrieve them...and I heard their plans."

She'd lost her marbles all right.

"I heard this one muscle-headed guy say, 'We'll take care of *Donaldson...*'"

"What makes you think there is anything sinister in that?"

"Because as I quietly dropped my marbles back into my purse a bunch of receipts and candy wrappers rattled. They jumped out of the car and the muscle guy pointed a gun at me and growled something like, 'You didn't hear anything, girlie.'"

"This is a scene in your W-I-P, isn't it?" I grinned.

"What?" Mary Agnes asked.

"You're a writer. Your work-in-progress. The book you are writing."

"Miss Faire, I am no purveyor of fiction. I read only of the scriptures. I am on a mission from God to save your heathen soul."

I felt faint. My vacant stomach wailed. "I have to eat. Now. Low blood sugar." *Lord Jesus, save me from this kooky missionary. Amen.*

I exited the compartment and dashed down the aisle not stopping until I entered the Victorian parlor car where my chapter mates were noshing. It contained four oxblood leather arm chairs flanking two small tables and a round stuffed sofa at the end. The kind I had seen in hotels. The peach paisley upholstered center was solid and you could walk around it and sit anywhere and lean back on the coordinating peach chenille cushions.

Windows on three sides offered panoramic vistas. I noticed the emergency brake and a fire extinguisher clearly labeled on the wall near the door. I peeked outside and saw a sheltered observation deck. Rain poured down beyond it. This was the last length of the locomotive. Nothing but tracks behind us.

In time with the cadence of the train I walked to a credenza near the restroom and grabbed a plate. Unfortunately, the other writers had scarfed nearly all of the hors d'oeuvres. A small amount of pâté and caviar remained. No crackers. I had an aversion to liver and fish eggs. I sagged in grave disappointment. I would have thrown up from malnourishment had I anything in me to actually come up.

"Captain Sparrow, bring me my rum!"

I snapped my head around to see *Peetie-the-Parrot* perched on *Pat-the-Pirate's* shoulder. She always brought him to our meetings. He was a Solomon Island Eclectus, a medium sized parrot. Lime green with red and turquoise under his wings. All males of his species looked like this. The females were red with purple and turquoise. His beak looked exactly like candy corn. *Boy would I love to jump inside a giant bag of candy corn and eat my way out.* My tummy screeched.

I made myself a cup of hot tea and plunked in four sugar cubes. I took two in a napkin to munch on.

I weaved through the crowd, looking forward to chatting with Pat and Peetie but *Contest Carly* was petting the parrot by the time I got near them.

Carly, a tattooed late twenty-something Philippine-American award winning unpublished author, was coming close to snatching Rosemary's contest-slut tiara. Neither was published but at least Carly's three novel length manuscripts were complete. Rosemary had only penned one chapter which she had paid a high priced New York editor to critique. I resented her gall, entering professionally edited work in contests for unpublished authors.

I noticed Dina pacing by the back door. I couldn't wait to switch rooms with whomever they had erroneously paired her with.

Sniffling approached. My shoulders hunched, I wished myself invisible. Harry Potter could do that with his invisible cloak. He could also cast spells. *Boy would I enjoy casting a few.* I popped a sugar cube in my mouth and sucked.

"Do you know Hazel just received an eight digit contract with Fathom Publishing?" *Weepy Wendy* asked me.

"That's wonderful." I half turned to her, smiled and made my way over to Dina.

Wendy followed me. I tried not to groan.

"It's just not fair. The top writers get all the money. I'll never be discovered."

This was my cue to hug poor pitiful Wendy. Instead, I said, "You'll do it, Wendy. It's your turn next. You are a very brilliant author. Just wait…and as a matter of fact since Hazel is here on the train what a golden opportunity…"

"What do you mean?" She sounded timidly hopeful.

"Stick to her like glue. Study what Hazel does. Her methods. When does she write? What inspires her? What does she do to stimulate her muse? Trail her. Stick by her side."

"You really think that might help?"

"Absolutely," said Dina. "Now don't waste a minute. Why, I'll bet you'll learn her secret! Don't forget to keep it to yourself…until you're bumping Hazel off the bestseller list!"

Wendy smiled for the first time in my memory. She trotted over to *Hack 'em Up Hazel*, who was slurping an oyster out of its shell.

"Dina, I've got to get something substantial in my stomach. Somebody has to have something edible on this train. Follow me."

She did.

We headed north past our compartments and crossed the threshold into the business car.

"I have the roommate from Hell. We have to switch," I whispered over my shoulder.

"Mine seems delightful. A lovely little old lady called Norah. She's napping."

I grunted. "Must be nice." I was so tired.

"Are you jealous of Hazel?" Dina asked.

"Nope. She's a very sweet lady. And talented, hard working and I hope she enjoys every penny they'll give her. I just love how she writes her guys. It's almost like she has secret inside information on how the male psyche operates."

After we dodged the rolling chairs in the conference room we made it to the dining car. It had been prepped for breakfast with little boxes of cereal perched on each table.

I plopped down in a booth, grabbed a box of Special K, ripped it open and gobbled it using my fingers. I washed it down with the tea.

"My mom asked about your Aunt. How is she?" I inquired.

"Working me day and night. I'm so glad her friend Marvin is moving in to help her while I'm away." An evil smirk morphed onto Dina's face. "He has no idea what he's getting himself into. If you ever have to have surgery for carpal tunnel syndrome *do not* have

24

both wrists repaired at the same time."

"Why not?"

"Because she's absolutely helpless with both hands and arms bandaged. She can't get the dressings wet and she's in a lot of pain. I have to wax her moustache, shave her pits and wipe her nether regions."

My brother the conductor appeared. "The cereal is for tomorrow."

"I'm starving. What did you eat?" I asked.

"The crew had pizza."

"Is there any left?" I devoured it in my mind.

He shook his head. "Sorry. Hey, I'll bet Mom brought snacks. She's two cars ahead. Walk through the baggage car and then she's in the next sleeper car, Compartment H."

"Thanks!" I was halfway down the aisle before Dina caught up with me.

"Don't get so far ahead. Do you think we should tell your brother about the red limousine?"

I stopped and whipped around. "You saw the limo, too?"

"Yeah. And those guys looked sinister. They were yelling at a midget."

"She's a little person. Midget is an insult. Jeeze, Dina, don't you know anything about being politically correct?"

"Whatever. How do you know about the midget?"

"She's my roommate, *Mini Mary Agnes*. She is really upset. Said they threatened Donaldson."

"The reverend or Rosemary?" Dina asked.

I shrugged my shoulders.

"Let's tell your brother."

"My brother since he's the conductor or my brother since he's a Cocoa Beach cop?"

"Yes."

"I don't know. I guess so. He'll probably poo-poo it away."

We entered the baggage car and squeezed down the aisle cluttered with boxes of *Bibles* and crates of food. I crinkled my nose. This car smelled like a sour mop. I stopped and scanned the area but didn't see a crow bar. It figured. I was standing in a refrigerated food Mecca yet couldn't access even a crumb.

I scraped the side of my ankle on a crate of cantaloupes and groaned. Mom's green steamer trunk was next to it near the door to the sleeper lounge car. We turned the doorknob, stepped through the vestibule, opened the opposing door and entered.

This car appeared to be the mirror-reverse of ours. I heard Christian rock music accompanied by acoustic guitars. My stomach churned as my pulse raced…remembering. I wished every acoustic guitar in the world had washed away with the hurricane.

The silver silk drapes were drawn open on all of the compartments. They were empty. I shoved Dina in front of me and reluctantly headed for the tunes.

Joel Donaldson, the surly nineteen-year-old son of the reverend and Rosemary, played piano. His dad and *Andres the lifeguard* strummed guitars as Rosemary sang. Surprisingly, they sounded pretty good. Mom clapped to the rhythm. I caught her eye and cocked my head toward the door.

She popped up and rushed us back to her compartment. I slid the door closed. The air conditioning drowned out the music.

"Sandra Marie Faire, where have you been? Why didn't you tell me you discovered another dead man? I forbid you to work at that job one more day. Do you hear me? Why haven't you been answering your phone? Did you lose it again? You had it this morning…"

When her interrogation let up so I could get a word in edge wise, I said, "Rosemary confiscated all of our phones and electronic devices which contact the outside world."

"Why on earth would she do a thing like that? Will it disturb your reading? Have you been talking loudly on the phone again disrupting everyone around you? I've told you time and again. You don't realize how loud you are speaking into the phone—"

"Mom, no. It's not me. I have no idea what gets into Rosemary's craw with her rules but since she's footing the bill we all complied with Her Highness."

"Wash your mouth out. Speaking of such a beautiful, good woman that way."

"Mom, do you have any food? I'm starving."

She touched my chin and looked my face over. "Sandra, you really need to eat regularly. You are going to get constipated and that will lead to diverticulitis and heart disease."

"Mom, the food?"

"Sit down. You too, Dina. Hello, by the way."

"Hi, Mrs. Faire." Dina smiled and sat next to me on the royal blue velvet sofa.

Mom flipped open a suitcase and placed a cloth napkin on each of our laps. Then a hard unbreakable white plate. She dealt low-carbohydrate pumpkin seed bread, lean turkey breast, Muenster cheese and romaine lettuce slices. Then she pulled out a baggie with balsamic vinaigrette and snipped the corner with her manicure scissors. She drizzled the dressing.

I was already eating my top slice of bread before she finished.

As we gobbled the sandwiches, she said, "Lieutenant Hernandez phoned me. He was unable to reach you and has further questions regarding the homicide."

I swallowed hard. "So the medical examiner has ruled it a homicide? Not an accidental drowning or suicide then?"

"Yes. How could you run off and not tell the police where you were going?"

I finished my sandwich and burped. Mom handed us each a bottle of water. I cracked the lid and guzzled half.

"The police commissioner and four of his officers know my whereabouts. The lieutenant found me. No biggie."

"Sandra. That is such an immature, cavalier attitude. You are an adult. Act like one." She took my napkin and wiped some dressing from my chin.

I handed her my plate and she gave me a banana.

Dina finished her sandwich and rinsed her plate in the sink. My mom took it and dried it with the white terry hand towel. "Did you get enough to eat? Would you like a piece of fruit? I have blueberries, oranges, apples and bananas. The bananas need to be eaten before they go soft. None of my kids will eat soft bananas. I always have to make banana nut bread with them."

"You make the best banana nut bread, Mom." I wished I had some now.

Dina looked at her watch and said, "It's after six! We're late for our first workshop."

I stuffed my banana peel in the chrome trash slot under the sink. It pinched my finger. I kissed Mom's cheek. "Thanks for the snack. Love you."

She kissed me back. "I love you, baby dumpling."

27

How embarrassing. She called all her kids baby dumpling. It was fine in private but it embarrassed me in front of Dina.

Mom followed us to the baggage car. I needed to persuade her to return to the crusaders. She thought I was in a book readers club. She didn't know this was a conference for writers. She would never approve. Not that she approved of much of anything I did anyhow.

"Mom, we've gotta go. We're late."

"I heard you. Hold on a minute." She stopped at her steamer trunk and popped the lid open. "Pick a color. Both of you."

We looked at the sea of crayon colored wool. I selected a multicolored rainbow skein. Dina plucked out a shimmery black one.

Mom handed us each a set of small wooden needles. "These should be perfect for the scarves. Let me know if you need more. Now I must go back to the crusaders. They are starting a rummy 500 tournament."

"Good luck, Mom. Have fun." I hurried down the aisle.

"Thanks for the food, Mrs. Faire…and the yarn and needles."

"Tootles, girls."

Dina whispered, "What's with the yarn?"

"I told Mom we were reading and knitting scarfs for the military."

"Why?"

"Because she'd have a cow if she knew I was a writer." I heard the door to Mom's car open as we entered the conference car. I exhaled.

I quietly slipped into the first available seat at the table and plunked my yarn and needles into my lap.

The end of Dina's yarn had snagged the door latch and pulled her back. She stumbled. Everyone looked. "I'm fine. It's nothing. Go on."

I trotted back and untangled her. We took our places at the conference table. The writers passed us the handouts and I found the spot the speaker expanded on.

Anna Deerstalker said, "Exterior conflict can be as simple as a husband lamenting, 'Cereal again?' This could set his long-maligned wife off on a murderous rampage."

I glanced around the table. Everyone was taking notes. Including *Hack 'em Up Hazel*. This made me very curious. Why would a bestselling author need pointers in conflict? Odd indeed. I feigned a sneeze and tossed my pencil down the table. It landed on Hazel's notes.

"God bless you," said *Weepy Wendy* and *Contest Carly*.

"Gesundheit," said *Pat-the-Pirate*.

I thanked them, begged their pardons and walked over to retrieve my pencil. Hazel flipped her notes over before I could read them. *Drats*. I returned to my seat.

Anna Deerstalker droned on, "There is also internal conflict in the cereal example. The husband knows he shouldn't eat the sugar laden carbohydrates but he has a powerful sweet tooth…"

I doodled little moons and stars on my conflict worksheet. The cadence of the train rocked my body. My eyes glazed over. I tried to focus on the conflict—I really did but all I could think about was evicting the mini-missionary, stretching out in my bunk and sleeping soundly all night.

The train blasted its whistle through a grade crossing. The engineer really laid on the horn as he applied the brakes. My eyes flew open.

Anna Deerstalker asked, "Who would like to share her conflict diagram with us?"

I must've dozed off. I hoped I hadn't snored. *Please don't pick me.*

Bicep Betty stood. Her gnarled hands gripped the table for support. "Midge would be rid of her poor excuse for a husband before the night was through. She held him at gunpoint with a shotgun, forcing him to lie naked face down on the floor where she had broken a case of wine bottles and tied him spread eagle between the radiator and the coffee table…"

I shook my head and cringed. I didn't want to hear the rest. Make her stop. All of her stories unfolded like this. She didn't need help with conflict. She needed help with her twisted mind.

Dina worked on the tangle of black yarn, rolling it into a ball. I removed mine from my lap, fished out the end from the inside of the skein and circled the yarn into a precise tight little sphere. I loved the colors. Red, orange, yellow, green, blue and purple. Just like the rainbow. I tuned *Bicep Betty* out.

Rosemary rushed in. "So sorry, ladies. I'm wearing two hats on this retreat. The crusaders insisted I sing for them." She took a seat at the end of the table.

Tabloid Tilly read her conflict next. My ears perked up until I didn't hear any juicy celebutante gossip. She finished quickly. Fine by me.

Anna Deerstalker asked for questions. Nobody had any. Rosemary thanked her profusely for her time and wonderful information. The ladies and I applauded. My yarn ball rolled off of my lap. I set the skein on the table and chased after it. Unfortunately, it had wrapped around the shoe on *Pat-the-Pirate's* wooden leg as she tried to rise. She tripped onto the floral carpet.

"I'm so sorry, Pat! Are you all right?"

Contest Carly and *Weepy Wendy* helped her into a chair. I extracted the yarn and she pulled her black polyester pant leg up, adjusting her wooden leg. Yep, it really was wooden. *Pat- the-Pirate* indeed. No, that wasn't nice. She was a lovely lady. Poor thing. Life wasn't fair.

I skulked back to my seat re-rolling the ball as I went. The skein fell to the floor. I gave it a good yank to hoist it up. A metal ball chain slithered out of the end. *What in the heck?* I flopped it onto the table and extracted dog tags.

Dog tags?

Chapter Four

Holy smoke 'em if you have 'em. Dog tags were hidden inside my skein of yarn. The dead sailor's tags were missing. These are his. I just know it. Why are dog tags stuffed inside my mother's yarn?

As I flipped them around to read the name, I heard the clang and whoosh of the doors opening behind me. I stuffed the dog tags back into the skein, picked up the ball, knitting needles, my handout and pencil and glanced innocently at the reverend and my brother. They were walking and whispering and didn't acknowledge me. I jumped out of my seat. It rolled back, bouncing off the wall and back to the table. I slipped past them and made a dash for compartment A.

I arrived and fastened the door behind me. Good, *Mini Mary Agnes* was gone. I heard the toilet whoosh. Oh poop. Now what?

I flipped the lid off my cooler and shoved the yarn inside, stuffing the loose tangle down into the water. I replaced the lid just as the bathroom door slammed into my back. I winced and rolled out of the way as best I could in the confined space.

Mary Agnes huffed and offered her unwashed hand to help me up.

I instead grabbed the ladder on the converted bunk bed and hoisted myself up, kicking the cooler under the chair all in the same swift movement. I heard the water sloshing.

"God punishes those who sin."

"Excuse me? Are you saying I got hurt because I'm bad? And furthermore, you are the one who injured me. Do you think you are Lady God or something?"

"The holy Mrs. Donaldson paired you heathen writers up with us chosen ones to save your wicked souls."

A knock at the door caused us to look out the corridor window at the reverend and my brother the conductor.

Mary Agnes glanced in the mirror, primped her hair and then opened the door.

"Sandra. Leave," said Andy.

"What?" *Was this be-mean-to-Sandra-night or something?*

"We need to speak with Miss Starr privately," said Pastor Donaldson.

Whatever. I squeezed past everyone and loped down the hall and into the parlor car. It was empty. I could see *Tabloid Tilly* out on the vestibule with her camera snapping away. I wondered how she could take pictures with just the little light outside.

I poured myself a cup of hot water and plunked sugar cubes and a teabag into it.

Settling onto the rounded sofa, I stared out the window into the blackness.

"You can't go back to your room," said Andy.

He had startled me. "What?"

The reverend will be staying with Miss Starr for the rest of the night."

I shook my head in incredulity. "That's too twisted. Do you mean that Reverend Donaldson is taking my place?"

"Yeppers."

"That's kooky. He and Rosemary surely have a huge suite. What is going on, Andy?"

"The body you discovered this morning. He was her brother."

The train pitched hard to the left. Scalding tea slopped onto my lap. I whimpered.

Andy pulled a handkerchief from his breast pocket and tossed it to me. I blotted and waited for a believable explanation.

"Mary Agnes Starr is a regular member of Donaldson's congregation and he says she's a little bipolar but rarely takes her meds. So with that information Hernandez decided not to interview her until morning."

"Wait. William is on the train? Or will he get on in the morning? Why didn't they just take her off the train? Isn't this a bizarre way to conduct an investigation? What do they think she knows?"

"I don't question the brass. Just do as told. But this seems quite irregular to me, too. Anyhow don't disturb them."

"So where am I supposed to sleep then?"

"Curl up here. I'll find you a blanket."

"My back will be all out of whack in the morning. It's injured anyhow. Mary Agnes slammed the bathroom door on me. Let me stay with you."

"Jimmy Tamales is snoring in my bottom bunk."

"Fine. I'll go to Mom's room."

"Her top bunk doesn't have a mattress."

"Why?"

"Gross story from the last crusade. Believe me you don't want to know…"

I sighed and pursed my lips. "Hey, the other speaker didn't get on yet. I can take his room." Thank goodness I remembered. Cool. I'd be in Tony O'Rourke's room before he was. Maybe there was some sort of telepathic muse waiting.

"The lieutenant is holed up in there. Made it into a mobile command center."

"Of course. Lieutenant Hernandez is the ever efficient investigator. Always leaving me in the lurch." I wished I hadn't said that out loud.

"I'll be back with a blanket." Andy exited toward the sleeper.

The back door clanged shut as *Tabloid Tilly* stomped inside. I flinched. She shuffled past me in a haze of cigar smoke. Her huge camera dangled around her Olive Oil neck.

I opened my mouth to greet her but she didn't meet my eye. I don't think she'd ever spoken to me before. An odd one, that Aussie. An air of *I'm better than you* about her. I'd noticed that with Australians. The women I'd encountered were aloof and the men were really cute but took stupid chances.

When I was fourteen Mom had an Australian e-pal come to stay with us for three weeks. They'd met in an internet knitting room. The woman was visiting North, Central and South America one winter. She was ping-ponging her way across the continents cheaply because she invited herself to stay with other online knitters. Well, okay so I never figured out how they knitted online but apparently Mom enjoyed it.

Anyhow the woman ate nothing but the disgusting black vegemite and plain unflavored gelatin she brought with her. And she practiced Riki and played ukulele at all hours of the night. Oh, did I mention she didn't like teenagers?

* * *

I kicked off my sneakers and sat Indian style on the sofa. Andy shook a thin white synthetic blanket out and tossed it on me. I sat there like a ghost. He clattered plates, cleaning up the hors d'oeuvres remnants and then said, "Hey you."

"Hey what?"

33

"If you need something, *Big Marc* will be walking the train every half hour. I'm going to bed."

"Night-night!" I waved under the blanket.

The room became darker. He must've switched the lights off. The train seemed to pick up speed as it jarred from side to side more rapidly. I could see flashes of light every now and then through the thin blanket. It smelled pretty good. Like fabric softener. I checked Tinker Bell but I couldn't see her. I shook the pixie dust anyhow. I decided it was close to midnight.

So the dead sailor was allegedly murdered. Poor guy. Or did he have it coming to him? Did the murderer do it in self-defense? Was it a woman? Or another guy?

His poor grieving sister, *Mini Mary Agnes*. I should have been nicer to her. But she was kooky and judgmental. Wanting to save my heathen soul. How dare her. My soul was not heathen.

I was a good girl. More or less. More than less.

I attended church for weddings and funerals and Christmas Eve and Palm Sunday. I loved passing the light through the congregation from candle to candle and I had fun with the palm fronds.

I did not lie or…well, except for fibbing a little bit to Mom sometimes but you know, that's allowed.

I did not cheat. I did not steal. I did not drink…technically. Those blue Jell-O shooters during the hurricane didn't count. I did not drink them. I slurped and chewed them, pretty much.

I had never smoked. Well those few times behind the skating rink with Dina and Al Dente didn't count. I couldn't figure out how to inhale anyhow.

And I did not fornicate. I had never done so, thanks to Lieutenant Hottie and darned old Hurricane Alfredo.

Just great. I was wide awake now with my meaningless life flashing before my eyes. All on account of the holier than thou little person who commandeered my room. My nice soft bunk. My tooth brush. My polka dot pajamas. My cuddly little stuffed wolf I always slept with.

I yanked the blanket off of me and tossed it on top of the center of the sofa.

I plodded over to the credenza to make a cup of tea in the dark. Not a good idea. I stubbed my toe. I jumped around holding it and repeating "Oww! Oww! Oww! That hurts!"

When the pain subsided, I fumbled on the wall until the lights came on. "Cookies!" Andy had set out cookies. And fruit. Oranges, apples and bananas. "I love you, Andy." I stuffed a hard mass-produced sugar cookie in my mouth and dispensed hot water into a foam cup. I dunked in a tea bag, threw the wrapper out and grabbed a handful of cookies.

I sat at the nearest table and arranged the five cookies neatly on a large floral cloth napkin. Two chocolate chip cookies, two sugar cookies and I bit the odd one. Oatmeal, yum.

The door squealed opened and in stumbled *Big Marc*. He was a member of the National Railway Historic Society. And a Pearl Harbor survivor. Nearly seven feet tall and close to four hundred pounds, he was dressed in a navy blue conductor's uniform like Andy's. *Big Marc*'s liver-spotted hand grasped onto the credenza as he bent close to survey.

Using the rag he pulled from his rear pocket, he wiped crumbs into his hand and then shook them into the trash can in the cabinet below.

"Hi," I said.

He whirled around. "Who's there?"

"It's me, Sandra Faire. Andy's sister."

"Oh, hi-dee-ho there, Miss Faire. What are you doing up so late making messes?"

I frowned and tried to hide the four remaining cookies with my arm. "I was kicked out of my room so I have to sleep in here tonight."

"Why?"

What could I say? *Big Marc* wasn't a cop. I couldn't very well divulge any details because who knows why and, *oh my goodness*, the dog tags I found must be the dead guy's so, oh my gosh, maybe the killer is on the train! Why didn't I think of that before?

My head was spinning.

"You look pale." He adjusted his Coke-bottle thick cataract eyeglasses and doddered closer, peering into my face.

I tried to sit up straighter to make some personal bubble space. He smelled like root beer.

"Why were you kicked out of your room? Did you mess it?"

"No. I did not mess it. Reverend Donaldson is ministering to my roommate."

35

"Oh, yeah. They'll probably be a lot of that going on. Those evangelists pray at all hours."

Good. I had told the truth. Enough and not too much. I could tell Lieutenant Hottie about the dog tags in the morning. I hoped they did not rust in the cooler. Surely they were stainless steel.

Shoot! Any finger prints will be compromised in the water. He'll be disappointed in me again. As usual.

"Me, I'm Jewish. We don't do that entire hubbub. But back when I was in the service we had to put up with it. I retired from the Navy in 1960."

Wow, he retired before my mom was even born. What a geezer. I found him fascinating. I loved old WWII movies. I wanted to write a mystery set in the White House during Roosevelt's administration. Franklin's. FDR's son Elliott had penned a very enjoyable series casting his mother, Eleanor, as sleuth. I was so disappointed when I found out Elliott had passed on. There would never be anymore Eleanor Roosevelt mysteries…*unless I wrote one…*

"I was only at sea for the first three years while I was still a bachelor. Every ship I was assigned to sunk. I traveled the world. Loved Australia and Brazil the most. My kids were all born in different countries…"

Poor guy, blown up on every ship. He must have nightmares. Traumatic Stress Disorder or whatever they call it. Australia? I wondered if he thought the women there were cold, too. Wait a minute. What was the Navy doing in Brazil? "Why were you in Brazil?"

"After the war we got rid of a lot of our vessels by selling them to Brazil and we had to keep a small contingent there to oversee. I was a petty officer. I did secretarial work." *Big Marc* peered out the back door and then shuffled toward the vestibule. He returned to me and whispered, "That was just my cover. I was really in Rio de Janeiro to refuel our submarines…enroute to the Bermuda Triangle…"

I got a creepy feeling. One of those scary women's intuition thingys. Every nerve in my body prickled. Actually, it was about time.

The train pitched hard to the left, sending *Big Marc* running across to the other side of the car. I jumped up and lunged for him as he hit his head hard against the window breaking the pane of glass out. Wind and rain whooshed in.

I grabbed under his arms and hoisted him into a chair. I pulled a muscle in my side.

His mouth gaped open and his green eyes looked huge in those glasses. He had a big gash on his cheek.

"Are you all right? *Big Marc*?"

He slumped over the side of the chair.

"*Big Marc! Big Marc!* Are you all right?"

His eyes rolled back in his head. I thought I was going to faint.

I could hear my Advanced First-Aid instructor's Yiddish voice in my head. "Lay the victim down. Check for airway obstructions, respirations and pulse. ABC. Airway – Breathing – Circulation."

I threw him onto the floor and he hit his head hard again.

"Sorry!"

I unbuttoned his vest, placed my cheek next to his nose and watched his chest. No puffs. No rises. I felt his wrist. Good. He had a pulse. I should start rescue breathing.

"Help!" I hollered.

"Good girl," said my instructor's conjured voice.

I maneuvered *Big Marc*'s head into position, lifted his chin to open the airway and detected a breath of root beer. What a relief.

"If the face is pale raise the tail. If the face is red raise the head," prompted my instructor.

Hmm…His complexion always looked like the mottled walking dead. Not really red though. I stuffed a throw pillow under his head. No. Wrong. His cheek was bleeding. I yanked the pillow out and he clunked his head again.

"Sorry!" *First cause no harm…* That was the Hippocratic Oath.

I stuffed the pillow under his feet, yanked the napkin from under my cookies and pressed it on *Big Marc's* wound, applying steady pressure. I felt the crumbs under my fingers. *Shoot! I hope he doesn't get an infection.*

"Elevate the wound higher than the heart," said the little voice.

Wait a minute! I had it right the first time. I yanked the pillow out from under his feet and gently placed it beneath his head and shoulders. No, that raises his heart. I dragged him over to the sofa and propped his head and shoulders up against the seat cushion.

"Yell loudly for help," my instructor urged.

"Help! Somebody help me! We have a medical emergency!"

Wendy was a nurse! Which room was *Weepy Wendy* in? "Wendy! Wendy! Help! I need medical help! Is there a doctor in the house?"

"Keep reassessing the victim's condition and administer aid," said the little man who wasn't there.

Broken bones! I needed to check for broken bones. I placed one hand under and one over each limb and slid them down their lengths. Other than *Big Marc's* bow legs, I was pretty sure everything else was kosher. I pressed hard and felt his ribs. They weren't broken yet. They would be if I had to perform C.P.R..

"Cover the victim to prevent shock," said my invisible professor.

Darn it. I couldn't remember exactly what shock was. I probably got a C on that quiz. I stumbled across the train, grabbed my blanket and threw it on him. Now what? I placed two fingers on *Big Marc's* wrist. I couldn't feel a pulse. I began panting in panic.

"If no one responds try yelling 'Fire!' That might bring someone curious," suggested the guy from back in the day.

"Help! Fire!" I screeched. "Fire!" "Fire on the train!" "Fire in the hole!"

"If absolutely necessary leave the victim and go for help," the voice told me.

I couldn't leave *Big Marc*. I needed to start C.P.R.. I grabbed his feet and pulled him back down onto the floor. Boy did he hit his noggin hard that time. I tilted his head back, pinched his nose, gave him two quick breaths and tried yelling one last time. "Help! Police! Help! Free chocolate!" Nothing. Wait, I know! *"Glory be to God! Jesus Christ our savior has risen!"*

Come on all ready, somebody has to hear me. "Help! Random House Editor taking appointments! Help! Please help me!" Why wouldn't anyone come to my aid? "Mommy!" Somebody help me. Anybody. Please. Don't let *Big Marc* die.

Oh, the heck with it. I ran to the end of the car and pulled the emergency brake.

Chapter Five

A thunderous squeal, flashing lights, the crashing of stowed luggage and sleeping people resonated in slow motion. Screams and curses filled the distant air.

My head hit the bathroom door hard as it was jolted open. Peetie-the-Parrot flew screeching toward me. My world went dark.

* * *

I felt myself being dragged backwards. Voices. Cuss words. Male voices. A blow to my stomach and all the blood rushed to my head. Forward propulsion. I opened my eyes and saw a great male caboose. Upside down. Clad in dark wash jeans. Handcuffs dangled. My hair hung down near my arms. I was upside down. Somebody was carrying me. Over his shoulder. I noticed a Glock tucked into his waistband. I grabbed cop handcuffs. He threw me down on a bed.

I brushed the tangled hair from my face and looked into Lieutenant Hottie Hernandez's big brown smoldering...*make those angry eyes.*

He snatched his handcuffs from me and returned them to their holster. "Did you stop this train?"

Train? Train...oh, yeah, I was on a train.

"Sandra, did you pull the emergency brake and stop this train?"

"Well I didn't do it by dragging my foot."

"Why?" he demanded.

"Why?" I repeated.

"Yes, why?"

I watched his nostrils flare and his eyes bulge. I would have rather looked at something else bulging.

He got right in my face. "Why did you stop this train?"

I remembered. I needed a nurse. "I needed a nurse."

"What's wrong with you?"

What's wrong with me? "My back hurts. *Mini...Minnie Mouse* hit me with the potty door. Oww. My side hurts, too. And I stubbed my big toe." I put my hand up and felt a huge goose egg on my forehead. "What happened to my head?"

"You obviously bumped your head."

"How do you know somebody didn't conk me over the head?"

"Did they? Who?"

I propped myself up on my elbows and wondered how that toilet paper became wrapped around my leg.

"Who conked you over the head?"

"Huh? I don't know. But they could have. Then again, I probably did hit my head on the bathroom door. Or toilet or something... I remember! Peetie!"

"Peetie hit you? Who is Peetie?"

"*Peetie-the-Parrot. Pat-the-Pirate's* pet."

"Oh, for the love of— Have you been drinking?"

"Drinking? No. I'm a good girl. You know that."

I remembered *Big Marc*. I bolted upright and nearly passed out again.

Hottie caught me. "Careful! Lay back down."

Under different circumstances I'd love to obey but... "Oh! *Big Marc*! Pearl Harbor! Old guy working as a car attendant. He stumbled and clocked his head, breaking out a window as he passed out in the parlor car. He had a heart attack. That's why I pulled the emergency brake. I kept yelling 'Help!' but no one responded. I didn't know which compartment *Weepy Wendy* was in."

"Weepy Wendy?"

"Nurse. Nurse with scary hair."

Hottie snatched out his cell phone, commanded something into it then turned his attention back to me.

Damn, he was so good looking when he was mad.

"What time is it? How long was I out? Where are we?"

"Oh-one-hundred hours, Thursday. I don't know. Dillon, South Carolina."

I realized everything was quiet. The train had stopped. The air conditioning wasn't whirring. I didn't like this silence. I tried sitting up again. This time, slowly. He offered his hand to help me. Oh, his hand. His hot, strong hand. His touch sent shockwaves of pleasure through my body.

He let go, reached his arm across to the cup holder by the window and grabbed a small water bottle. The lid made a little peep noise as he cracked the seal and offered it to my lips. I let him pour the sustenance into my mouth. Of course it dribbled cold all down my neck. I pulled away.

"Sorry," he said.

I wiped the water with the corner of his blue covers.

Andy came to the door. Hottie jumped up and talked to him in hushed tones. He turned to me and said, "I'll get your mother to sit with you. I've got to go."

"Where? And why are you onboard anyhow?"

"*Big Marc* Clinger is missing. I am conducting a murder investigation."

"*Big Marc* is dead?"

"That's not what I said. I'm investigating the murder of David Starr, the sailor you turned up on the beach."

"Why aboard the train? There aren't any suspects—"

He was gone before I finished. I remembered the planted dog tags. Shazam. The killer is on the train! And messing around with my mom's yarn. Why is he...*or she* hiding evidence, or are they planting clues? Does the killer want to be discovered? Is this a murder mystery weekend?

No nothing that fun. Nobody is writing a murder mystery dinner party play. Well, I don't know. Maybe *Contest Carly* or Rosemary might be. But if it is Rosemary we would never find out whodunit because she would only write the first act.

I was really tired. And boy did my head ache. Throb, throb throb. I just wanted to take two Extra Strength Tylenol's, lie back and go to sleep and wake up in DC in time for Tony O'Rourke's presentation.

I was just about to doze off in Hottie's comfy covers, which smelled so good like he does, when Mom swooped in.

"Wake up! Wake up! Sandra Marie Faire!" She slapped my cheeks.

I pushed her back. We wrestled until I was sitting up. She placed a cup of tea to my lips. I pulled back. "Too hot!"

"Fine. I'll put some ice in it." She ran out into the corridor.

I had looked forward to an inspiring and relaxing excursion. Just my luck.

Mom reappeared with a pewter ice bucket and tongs. She plunked two small cubes in my mug and stirred them with a peppermint stick.

Leave it to Mom to pack peppermint sticks.

"What did you hit your head on this time, Sandra? I think you need glasses. You're always walking into things." She placed ice cubes inside a floral napkin and then stuffed it inside a plastic Wal-Mart bag. She twirled it three times tied a butterfly knot and pressed it on my head.

"Oww!" I tried to pull it away. She pressed harder. I squirmed. She won. I held the ice to my head.

I picked the toilet paper off of my leg and handed it to Mom. She huffed, threw it in the little stainless steel trash shoot and washed her hands. She came over and soaped up my hands with a wash cloth, rinsed it out then returned to wipe the soap away. I just rolled my eyes and compiled. Mom gets into these hyper-mommy jags and it's better not to challenge her.

"What were you doing in the parlor car in the middle of the night? Do they have an internet connection in there? Were you surfing for inappropriate photos of Johnny Depp again? Sandra Marie—"

"I got kicked out of my room."

"Why? Did you and Dina have a fight over another boy?"

I would always be twelve years old in Mom's eyes. "No. Dina isn't my roommate. They decided it would be fun if they paired up the writ—umm—book readers club with the missionaries or crusaders or whoever they are." *That was a close one.*

"Why on earth?"

"I have no idea."

"So who is your roommate then? Where is she?"

"Mary Agnes. She's in our room with Pastor Donaldson. I was booted out for the night and had to sleep in the parlor car."

Shoot. Too much info. Now I was going to have to tell her the rest of it.

"Why? What did you do to her?"

"I didn't do anything to her. Why do you always assume… Mary Agnes is grieving. Her brother died."

"Oh, how terrible. I'm sorry. Was it expected or sudden?"

I removed the ice pack, inhaled and stuck my tea in the cup holder. I swung my legs over the side of the bunk and propped myself up with Lieutenant Hottie's two pillows.

She was going to find out so I might as well get the lecture over with. "Her brother is…was the dead guy I found washed up on the beach yesterday morning."

Mom shuddered. A full body shimmy.

"Mom, are you okay?"

"That is too creepy and coincidental. You discovered his body and she is your roommate that very night. I think something is going on here. Something very fishy. And scary... She fumbled in the rickrack trimmed pocket of her pink chenille bathrobe. Pulling out her cell phone, she flipped it open.

"Who are you calling in the middle of the night?"

"Your father. We'll just see what's going on here. I don't like it one bit."

No. Not Dad. He would stop the train. No, wait. I already stopped the train. Now Dad would dispatch a local yokel squad car to take us home. I would be grounded for the rest of my life.

Mom huffed and shoved the phone back into her pocket. "No service." She pulled a ball of mint green yarn and knitting needles from her other pocket and plopped down in the chair. "Put the ice pack back on your head."

I did.

* * *

I woke up to the dark Thursday dawn. Mom was drooling in the chair, her lap draped with a green coverlet. She must have knitted all night.

I heard the chug-a-chug of the locomotive. Good, we were moving again. I quietly slipped out of bed and into the corridor. I hurried down the hall and I peeked in the curtains to my room. No reverend. It was dark but I would have seen him if he were there. I stepped inside and closed the door and flipped on the light. Mary Agnes wasn't in her bunk.

I was still in my uniform from yesterday. I really wanted to brush my teeth and take a shower but not until I retrieved the dog tags from the cooler.

The lid was off of it. The dog tags were gone. The floor was wet. The yarn led into the bathroom. *Oh, no. Mini Mary Agnes had found her brother's dog tags.* How horrific. I thought I was going to throw up. I felt guilty but then again she shouldn't have been snooping in my cooler. Maybe she was really thirsty... No. She didn't drink tea. I remembered her scolding me.

I knocked on the potty door not knowing exactly what to say. "Mary Agnes? Are you in there? Mary Agnes, it's Sandra. Sandra Faire, your roommate." I knocked again, louder.

43

No answer.

I opened the door and screamed. She was hanging from the shower rod. Trussed up in the yarn, dog tags and the belt from her white dress. I climbed up on the stepladder, grabbed her legs and tried to yank her down but it only seemed to tighten the yarn. I jerked hard and the dog tags broke off in my hand, but Mary Agnes didn't. I shoved them in my pocket as I ran out in the hallway screaming, "Help!"

Hack 'em Up Hazel and *Pat-the-Pirate* galloped to my aid. Hazel wielded a fireplace poker. Pat had a patch over one eye. She must take the glass eye out at night. I tried to tell them what had happened but my words were unintelligible. I kept jabbing my hand in the direction of my room. *Tabloid Tilly* shoved past me and entered the compartment. An Aboriginal scream permeated the car. Then all was quiet.

Weepy Wendy stumbled down the hall. "In there. Help." I got the words out.

Wendy entered.

Matilda exited.

An agonizingly long moment later the nurse reappeared. She closed the drapes. And the door. "It's too late. There is nothing we can do for her now."

Strangely, *Weepy Wendy* wasn't crying.

I was.

My brother shoved through the crowd of ladies in their nighties. "What's going on?"

"Mary Agnes Starr hung herself," I choked out.

He entered my compartment. A nano-second later Lieutenant Hottie joined him. And Reverend Donaldson and the North American Passenger Railway crew chief. It was getting awfully crowded in my room.

I started feeling woozy so I stumbled down the hallway and through the vestibule to get a drink of water. I entered the parlor car, grabbed a bottle and plopped down in a chair. I snapped open the lid and took a big long drink.

I had discovered dead bodies before. But they were all strangers to me, washed up on the beach. Not someone I knew. Not in my room. I said a little prayer for Mary Agnes Starr. I hardly knew ye.

So that's why she brought the stepladder. She'd planned to kill herself.

As I swallowed I remembered the dog tags. Pulling them from my pocket I leaned over the table to read them in the light. My hands shook.

Dente, Alfredo P.
555-09-1947
BLOOD TYPE: AB-
ROMAN CATHOLIC

I was stunned. I had to be dreaming. Please wake up Sandra. Please wake up.

Al Dente joined the Navy? His dog tags hung the dwarf?

Lieutenant Hottie was on the train. *No, no, no! He must not find these and link me to Al Dente. No! This is not happening!* I ran into the restroom, locked the door, lifted the seat and flushed them.

Hurricane Alfredo.

Here he blows again.

Chapter Six

I needed air. I needed to jump off this train of ghouls and find peace. I missed home. Palm trees, sun and cake with gobs of buttercream frosting. A vision of Cocoa Beach flashed. And the dead sailor. I shook my head, trying to shake away the whole awful conundrum. I spied the door on the rear of the train and ran for it. I flung it open and stepped out on to the observation deck. Rain and wind pelted my face as I leaned over the metal railing.

No, no, no. I didn't need the sobering reality. I needed comfort and fantasy. Tears dripped from my tired eyeballs. Again. I let them. I didn't care who saw. Not that I wanted anyone to see me. I needed to disappear.

. As the train slowed I stepped to the side and thought about jumping off. Tuck and roll is what you are supposed to do when you jump from a moving vehicle. I think. I'd loved all of the Worst Case Scenario guidebooks. What did they advise to do when you're trying to identify a murderer; you discover your roommate has hung herself; your Mom is disappointed in you and you have just destroyed evidence, and what in the heck did it mean anyhow?

A clap of thunder preceded a heavy downpour.

The door squeaked open and then banged shut.

"Salutations marionette of mystery. What is the status of your comeliness? It has been light-years since our souls last collided."

No this can't be happening to me. Closing my eyes, gripping the rail tight, my stomach recoiled.

He nicked my neck with his fingernail as he clumsily brushed my hair back. I felt his hot breath on my skin and tried to pull away.

He whispered, "Your valiant minstrel of melody has returned. No longer an apprentice, I shall pedestal you to the heavens in the richness you deserve."

Al Dente had just blown back into my life. Hurricane Alfredo.

I heard the squealing of the brakes and the blowing of the whistle as the train stopped. Great, just great. Why was it stopping?

My fingers found the gate latch, swung it open and I jumped down. He wrapped his arms around my waist as I moved and I lost my balance. We tumbled head over bottom down a prickly embankment, landing in a car graveyard.

I landed on top of Al Dente. My legs straddled his meek chest. Even with a short military hair cut he still looked like a scrawny nerd with a huge honker of a nose. I looked into his innocent blue eyes and all those old feelings rushed back.

"Where in the fettuccini have you been for the last five years?" I shouted, not waiting for an answer. "I woke up on the mildewy bathroom floor in a cheap motel way off the Vegas strip. Alone. You left me nothing but a joint checkbook, a marriage license and regret."

Rain pelted my face.

"Lovely marionette of mystery, I can explain. If you will please remove your languid legs from my ribs and allow me to rise like the hallowed phoenix...I think I came to rest on a radiator."

I crawled off of him and grabbed his hand. I jerked him up.

I heard footsteps approaching. I didn't want an audience. I'd been waiting a very long time and I needed answers.

"Turn around and put your hands in the air!" ordered Lieutenant Hottie.

I cringed and turned toward him. He had his gun drawn. I threw my hands up high. "Don't shoot! I—"

"Back away from her!" Lieutenant Hottie commanded as he ran over to Al Dente and shoved the gun barrel under his chin.

I shrieked, "Don't! Don't hurt him."

"Who's the geek?" the lieutenant demanded.

"It is I, Alfredo Dente. Husband of the discriminating marionette of mystery."

Oh God. My secret was revealed. Strike me dead and open up the door to Hell.

"And so we finally meet," said Lieutenant Hottie.

"What?" I asked. He said that as if he knew all about Al Dente.

"You have a lot of explaining to do, Dente," said Lieutenant Hottie.

"Have you been wanting to meet Al Dente because you like his music? Or has he done something illegal? Or is it who his uncle is?" I asked.

"I've been waiting to meet your husband," said Lieutenant Hottie.

Thunder clapped. The brightest bolt of lightning I had ever seen

47

lit up the sky. Trembling, I wrapped my arms around myself.

How did he know? Is this why he had been so cold to me all these years? Is this why he had rebuffed all of my flirting?

Andy and a couple of North American Passenger Railway cops swarmed us. They cuffed Al Dente and hauled him up the hill.

"You okay, Sis?" Andy asked as he shoved Al Dente past me up the steep incline.

I couldn't bring myself to speak. What could I say? I'd been outed. Alfredo Dente was the guy I had married in a moment of teenaged stupidity because he was in some sort of trouble he couldn't tell me about. Little did I expect my groom to disappear the morning after our nuptials.

He and Dina and I had been best friends since we met in Kindergarten. Some time in the seventh grade Al Dente and Dina became step-cousins.

My dirty little secret was now irrevocably out in the open. It could only get worse if…

"Sandra Marie Faire. What have you done this time?" asked Mom. She goose stepped down the hill in her blue thong kitten heels. Today she wore an indigo chambray crop pants set with a lime green tee peeking out from under the indigo Peter Pan collared jacket.

I groaned.

Mom held a green polka dotted umbrella and awkwardly toted a package wrapped in plain brown paper all tied up with string.

"Sandra, this package came for you special delivery. I signed for it. There is no return address. See if there is a note enclosed."

This was so surreal. I jumped from a train, monkey tangled with my guitar playing mobster's nephew nearly gone long enough to be declared legally dead secret husband of a few drunken hours. The guy I've yearned for all these years shoved a gun under my husband's chin. I discovered my dead dwarf roommate hanging in the potty. And now my mom is delivering a package to me in a junkyard in the rain.

It was at this point I realized I needed to step back and figure out just how my life became so whacked. Why couldn't I be a normal girl and find a nice little office job and a nice little house and a nice little cat and a nice little boyfriend in a nice little bowtie?

No not a bowtie. A nice hot boyfriend.

I know. The heck with the cat, house and boyfriend, I'd move to

Ireland and work as the confidential secretary to Tony O'Rourke, fabulous mystery recluse. I'd host magnificent charity events in the ballroom and dance with all the heads of state and exotic rich guys. Yeah, that's good enough. I didn't really need a boyfriend.

What was Al Dente mixed up in? Why was he arrested? Where had he been for the last five years?

* * *

My brother hustled us all back to the train. I looked up at the U.S. Marine helicopter whooping overhead. Pretty low, enough to help me make up my mind to obey and climb back aboard the train of fools. Now I would just concentrate on learning the craft of writing. After all that was the whole purpose of this trip.

Freezing rain pelted the windows as we chuffed down the tracks. I saw the helicopter take off from a clearing in the junkyard. Very odd indeed. I'd file that in my imagination and my muse would have a go at it some day. What was it doing? Who was in it? What was so special about landing in a junkyard before an ice storm? I'd come up with something very clever indeed.

There was too much chatter in the parlor car. The evangelists were one upping each other with some sort of scripture trivia game. *Bicep Betty* was showing off her latest erotic romance anime complete with illustrations, which I did not want to see.

I didn't know if the other writers were being polite to Betty or if they had a morbid curiosity. They say people have that about death, too. Fascinated with all the little mundane details. Not me. I would prefer to do without it.

The window had been replaced. I wondered if *Big Marc* had turned up and I hoped he was all right. And I hoped I hadn't given him a concussion.

My pinky finger grew numb. I looked down at the hemp string constricting it. I'd forgotten about the lightweight package Mom had delivered to me. I had no idea what was in it nor who could have sent it. And for that matter I didn't realize they had special deliveries to a train. What in the heck?

I parked myself on the round sofa. Dina shook a blanket out on top of me and plopped herself down. "So do you wanna swap rooms?"

"Yes!" This was just too great. I had been dreading reentering the scene of the crime. "Are you sure? I'm really freaked out about

49

Mini Mary Agnes. I'll probably see her face in every bathroom mirror from now on."

"I just adore ghosts. I'm hoping she'll haunt us."

I rolled my eyes. Dina had loved the Ouija board when we were little. She told the scariest ghost stories around the campfire at Girl Scout camp.

"Do you think *Napping Norah* will mind switching, too?" I asked.

"I couldn't ask that dear little lady to move. She's so comfortable in her bunk. She doesn't even snore."

"Fine. I'll swap one evangelist for another. Do you really want to move into my room?"

"Please." She smiled.

I pulled the blanket off of me and stood to fold it. Dina grabbed the other end and assisted. It was really warm in this car. My wet clothes and hair weren't bothering me and I was usually always cold indoors.

My brother set a fresh pot of coffee on the credenza. I jumped up and steadied myself to the rhythm of the train. I swaggered across the car to him.

"I'm switching rooms with Dina. From A to H. Will you please retrieve my cooler and duffle bag?" I remembered the wet yarn and said, "No. Just the duffle bag is good. You can throw the cooler out."

"I'm busy now."

"Please?"

I got in his face and gave him the pouty lips.

"Fine."

He took the empty coffee pot and disappeared.

* * *

At 10:00 A.M. I was surprised *Napping Norah* was on the top bunk. Surprised and annoyed. That meant the ladder would be in the way day and night. What a nuisance. Oh, well the bottom bunk sure looked comfy. I settled on to it, kicked off my shoes and switched the little reading light on. I set my attention to the mysterious package. First I shook it. Sounded like nothing. I listened. Nope it wasn't ticking. So I picked at the knot. Other than breaking my only long nail, that didn't get me anywhere. So I wiggled and stretched the string until I was able to pry it off the box at the corners.

I ripped open the package to find a red cardboard box. I opened

50

it. White and Navy blue tissue paper cradled an empty single-use size bottle of chlorine bleach. The kind you get from machines at the Laundromat.

I pressed down and twisted the lid off. It was empty.

I stuffed it back in the box and tried to stuff it under my bunk, but the box wouldn't fit. Fine. I took the bottle out and dashed into the bathroom and flushed it down the toilet.

The dead sailor had smelled like bleach. Why was somebody gas lighting me?

Shoot! Sandra you are retarded! You just destroyed evidence! Why didn't you turn it in to Lieutenant Hottie? You dunderhead.

Because William was really mad at me. And he really hated Al Dente. And just what did Al have to do with the dead sailor? Or his sister? Oh, my goodness, say he ain't the murderer? I'm married to a murderer!

I needed my mommy. I stuffed my feet back into my sneakers, except my heels were not inside. I hustled through the business car and into the baggage car.

I was stopped by an Amazon woman in a blue suit with a listening device in her ear.

"You cannot go in there. Return to your quarters."

"My mom is in there. Mrs. Faire. Mrs. Terry Faire."

"No admittance. Do as told."

"And just who do you think you are? I can go anywhere I want to on this train. I'm a friend…guest of Mrs. Rosemary Donaldson."

"I'm with the Special Investigator, and if you don't return to your quarters immediately you will be detained and interrogated."

"Why?" I asked.

"It's none of your business."

"This is kooky. What are you talking about?" *This must have to do with Al Dente's arrest!*

"There are sensitive matters going on here that must be kept secret."

Okey dokey then. That would explain the helicopter in the junkyard. "Fine."

I grumbled my way back to the business car and plopped down in one of the rolling chairs. It slid across the car and slammed into the wall. Fine.

* * *

51

Around noon Dina stumbled in with a bag of Cheese Doodles and two Cokes nestled in her knitting.

She plopped them down on the end of the table and said, "Hi."

"I love you," I said, my mouth watering for the doodles.

"Love you too, bud. How are you taking all of this?" She clopped over and pushed me and my chair to the snacks. Plopping down in the seat next to mine, she slid a can of Coke my way and struggled to open the doodles. When she was about to stick the corner of the bag in her mouth I intercepted and yanked the top seam apart. Doodles and orange dust flew. We laughed. It felt so good to laugh. Tears poured down my cheeks.

"What's wrong?" she asked.

"Nothing. Everything. Too much. Not enough. My mom is right. Everything I do is inappropriate."

"Don't let other people judge you, Sandra. Well, okay so she's your mom and knows you better than anyone in this world and has expectations and dreams for you because she knows how high you can achieve if only you would believe in yourself."

I glared at Dina. I opened my mouth and closed it. I opened it again and she threw a Cheese Doodle inside. I rolled my tongue around the delicious cheesy puff as it melted in my mouth. I chewed and swallowed.

"You can't say anything because you know I'm right."

"But I am not my mother and I certainly don't want to be or to ever turn into her."

"And she doesn't want you to." Dina guzzled her Coke. "What do you want to be when you grow up, Sandra?"

"I don't know anymore. I used to want to be a bestselling author. And the owner of a private investigation firm. And to be one of those volunteers who decorate the White House Christmas trees. And a groupie for a rock band."

"Which one?" Dina asked.

"Not his," I said firmly.

"Not who's?" Dina asked again as if she didn't know.

"You know." I didn't want to say his name.

"My cousin Al's band."

"My husband Al's band." I slunk down in my chair.

"So why have you brought him up after all this time? Oooh…has it been seven years since he vanished without a trace?

52

Can you have him declared legally dead and start dating again?"

"I wish. It's been five years, eight months and six days" I glanced at Tinker Bell. "Four and a half hours more or less." I half-heartedly shook the pixie dust. "And I'll never date again."

"Sure you will."

"Nope. The only guy I've ever wanted to rock my world hates me."

"Oh. William again."

"Again? No. What we had never was. It was only in my imagination. And at least now I know the reason he dumped me. Froze me out."

"Why?"

"He found out about Al Dente."

"How?"

"I don't know. *Did you tell him?*"

"I can't believe you asked that," Dina balked.

"Sorry."

There was a long uncomfortable pause. Dina blew her nose.

"Back at the last stop we were uncoupled from that big old long North American Passenger Railway train and now it's just the crusade cars hooked on the back of two North American Passenger Railway diesel locomotives." She sweetly tried to change the subject.

I looked over her shoulder and out the window. We were whisking by a station. The sign was painted *Cumberland*. That was in Maryland.

"No! We didn't stop in DC and pick up Tony O'Rourke! No! No! This is just not fair. This sucks." I was so disappointed.

Dina kicked some chairs out of the way and launched herself down the car peddling with her feet. She grabbed her yarn and knitting needles and propelled back to me.

"Stop feeling sorry for yourself. Start making your dreams come true."

"How can I? I have a sucky job. I keep finding dead bodies. And my dream man arrested my husband. And I need some of Mom's banana bread really bad. But Al Dente was just arrested and some Special Investigator is here.

"Back the train up Sandra. Al is alive?"

"Lieutenant Hottie arrested him when I hopped from the train."

Dina paddled down to the conference table again, grabbed a yellow legal pad and pen and peddled back up to me. She shoved it in my hands. "Begin at the beginning."

"The beginning of what?"

"You want to write a great book."

"So." I pursed my lips and shrugged my shoulders. "As if that would ever happen."

"Fine. Do you want to open a private investigation firm?" Dina asked.

"As if," I said.

"Do you want to be a White House volunteer?"

I gave her the evil eye.

"Well, do you still want to be a groupie?"

"Not really anymore. I think I've outgrown all of that stuff. I want to be like Copernicus or even better, Galileo."

"Come again?" asked Dina.

"Copernicus defied popular thinking by reasoning the universe did not revolve around us peons on planet earth. He thought for sure the universe must revolve around the sun but he couldn't prove it. Then Galileo invented a telescope and did prove the earth and everything celestial revolves around the sun. It got him into all kinds of trouble with the church."

"Do you want to get into trouble with the church?" Dina asked.

"No. If you asked *Mini Mary Agnes,* I'm already in trouble with the church. Oh, great. And now I have to get a divorce. I'm sure she'd roll over on the marbles in her grave if she knew all about that."

"I'm not computing, pal," said Dina.

"Sorry. My mind is a wild lava flow spewing and turning and bending every which a way. What I'm trying to say is that I want to do something to change the world. Something good, something smart and logical. I want to leave a mark on planet earth. I don't just want to pass through life being one more mundane ho-hum human who did nothing but create a big old wasteful green footprint."

"How did you remember all of the ancient Greek stuff from school?" Dina's brow furrowed.

"Ancient Roman stuff. I loved history class. You slept through all the movies."

"It was right after lunch. I carb crashed. It wasn't my fault."

54

"Well, I think about it sometimes. On Saturday morni
eating breakfast while watching the fashion show on *Have
Deal for You*, I flip to one of the science or history channels on T v.
It makes for some very vivid dreams. And plot ideas for books. And
it also makes me realize how uninspired my life is. I really need and
want to do something spectacular. Not for the attention, though I
wouldn't mind accepting the Nobel Peace Prize or the Presidential
Medal of Honor or whatever it's called. I want to change the way we
do something. Something we are doing wrong. There are so many
mysterious parts of our brain that scientists don't know what they do.
Maybe if I try hard enough I can tap into some fantastic heretofore
unused part of my brain and put it to good use."

Dina nodded. She sat quietly as if taking it all in.

"Fine. I think we can make every dream you have ever had
come true in a small way. Some in a bigger way. But you have to
take the first step. Write!" she said.

"Write what?"

"Begin with the first thing that happened to you to set off this
latest calamity, the latest inappropriate thing you've gotten yourself
mixed up in."

I wrote:

1. Discovered dead body on the beach.

"Clues?"

2. Sailor uniform
3. No dog tags
4. Star of David
5. Old *Bicep Betty*
6. Two fishermen
7. Early jogger
8. Squishy
9. Death Scent
10. Mucky shoes
11. Face up
12. Mischievous smirk
13. Dwarf's brother
14. Dwarf my roomie on train
15. Dwarf missing her marbles
16. Dwarf upset by mobsters
17. Red limo

18. Dina saw red limo mobsters yelling at a dwarf
19. Dwarf ministered to by Rev. D.
20. Dwarf hung by my yarn and Al's dog tags
21. *Big Marc* clinically dead yet missing
22. Nobody heard me yelling for help
23. Toilet paper wrapped around my leg
24. Al Dente in the Navy?
25. Al Dente showed up
26. William knew about Al Dente
27. William Arrested Al Dente for what?
28. Junkyard
29. Helicopter
30. Special Investigator
31. Mean suit lady
32. Train shortened
33. Train didn't stop in DC
34. Tony O'Rourke didn't get on
35. Mom gave me box
36. Bleach
37. Sailor smelled like bleach!
38. Dog tags
39. Who sent the package?

"I need to talk to mom to see who delivered the package."

Dina's steady crunch, crunch, crunch along with the clattering of her knitting needles orchestrated a percussion to go along with the locomotive's forward drag then catch up drag then catch up.

Catsup? I'd love a big pile of waffle fries. "What time is lunch?"

Right on cue Jimmy Tamales, a pudgy, bald fifty-ish conductor friend of Andy and *Big Marc*'s, pushed in a cart. We scurried the chairs out of the way. He dealt a boxed lunch at each table space as Dina and I replaced the chairs. The Global Order of Scribes filed in, chattering away about Contest Carly's new story. Something about a Viking adventure.

Rosemary took her place at the table and asked us to bow our heads. She selected me to say grace.

"God please rest Mary Agnes' soul in everlasting love… God, thank you for our food and love and friendship. Amen"

"Amen," was echoed around the table.

We dug into the boxes. A ham and Swiss croissant sandwich,

potato salad, a green apple and two small ginger snaps for dessert. Bottled water to drink.

Hack 'em Up Hazel taught us an index card system for plotting. We were to take a package of pastel marbled index cards and write one thing on each that needed to happen in a story, one that we hadn't started writing yet. Well, if this worked for a bestselling author then it was worth the effort. I embraced the challenge.

I began writing. She encouraged us to jot down the obvious such as they meet, something bad happens, they kiss and they live happily ever after. Then she told us to write whatever popped into our heads no matter how silly it seemed.

My story was about a woman who had been kicked out early from the ladies' version of the French Foreign Legion. She was set up in a new life posing as the wife of an Australian plumber. He was in the witness protection program.

So I began writing whatever popped into my kooky head.

Plumber is short, plump and bald with bad knees. I was picturing loveable old Jimmy Tamales to model him after.

Next door neighbor is hot. Pining over his missing fiancée.

Fiancée is not coming home. Heroine knows this because she dug her grave.

Neighborhood block party

Bake sale

Shrimp on the barbie

Hot guy doesn't have curtains on his bathroom window in the front of the house

Dog fight

Cat fight

Rain storm

Okay, I was stuck

"Lay your cards out, shuffle them around until you get a good rhythm and throw away the stupid ones. Over your shoulder. Then pick them up and file them in the back. When you get stuck on the story go back and take a look at them. They won't seem so stupid—"

My brother's voice interrupted on the P.A. system:

"The toilets are not working in the parlor car or in the last sleeper car. Please, ladies and gentleman, I beg of you. Do not place anything in the toilets except human waste and the provided toilet paper. No tampons. No paper towels. We will not be able to snake these out until Chicago so it's going to be a very long day and night. You may use the toilet in the business car. It is the only one in working order. Please keep it so."

Chapter Seven

I cradled my head in my hands and groaned. The dog tags and the bleach bottle had ruined our trip. Not only that, they surely would be discovered in Chicago when the plumber arrived. So I had until then to come up with some sort of plausible denial story. No wait. Nobody would be able to prove I was the one who had flushed them. Surely forensics couldn't lift my fingerprints after they had been swimming in the mucky sewage. Then again with all the crime scene investigation technology advances I would be fingered for sure.

I have until Chicago to figure out if the dog tags and bottle of bleach are linked to the dead sailor's death. And if so...then how so? And where is Lieutenant Hottie? Why did he arrest Al? Maybe when everything gets cleared up, Hottie and I might be able to begin again.

I smiled, remembering his hot hungry tongue in my mouth.

I inhaled, sat up and straightened my back. It cracked. I felt like one big boo-boo. I longed to be back home and in a killer Yoga class at the YMCA. At least then I'd know I was sore for a good reason because I had challenged my body. Not sore because a judgmental dwarf slammed me in the back with a door. Or because I pulled a side muscle heaving an elderly giant and no one would come to help me. Or because I stubbed my toe on a train in the dark. Or because I tumbled down a prickly embankment monkey tangled with my wayward husband.

I turned my head and winked at Dina. She smiled and nodded knowingly. I wondered what she thought she knew. It probably had to do with the potato salad. So I scraped the last bit of mine from the plate and ate it.

"Ladies, I suggest you retire to your rooms for a little shut-eye session with your muse," said Rosemary in her nasally voice. Today her teeth were stained with coral lipstick to match her floral patterned tube top. Chico had done a magnificent job at piling her raven hair in ringlets atop her head.

"When you wake don't be surprised if your characters are ready to line themselves up on your manuscripts. First though let's give a big thank you to Hazel Hatchet for sharing her wonderful inside secrets. Bravo, Hazel."

We clapped and cheered.

I really enjoyed the workshop and looked forward to giving Hazel's technique a whirl.

I let the car clear out and used the ladies room before returning to my new compartment.

* * *

At 4:00 P.M. Compartment H was toasty warm. I had hated freezing in Compartment A. It was dark with the drapes drawn and the lights out. Jeeze, *Napping Norah* was still dead to the world. If only I had not a care in the world like her. Oh, well, goody for her. We hadn't even introduced ourselves yet. I didn't know what her face looked like. I hoped she wouldn't be upset Dina and I had changed rooms. I would just explain to her Dina had a thing for ghosts. There was a holy ghost so Norah might understand. Oh, no. Did she know that *Mini Mary Agnes* was dead? Had they been friends? A picture of the hanging replayed in my mind. I shuddered and then shook it off. Life goes on for the rest of us. God bless Mary Agnes and her brother. What did Andy say his name was? David. David Starr.

I plopped down on the bottom bunk and kicked off my shoes. I climbed under the gold blanket and lay my head down on the soft fluffy pillow. I closed my eyes. What was that smell? Oh, it was so gross. I covered my nose and mouth. It must be the backed up toilet. And that was my entire fault. How could Norah sleep with that stench? It was so disgusting.

* * *

I dreamt about a trio of witches. They were frolicking in an enchanted forest with cute little chipmunks and chimpanzees scampering and swinging through the autumnal maple trees. I could hear the turtle doves singing in harmony. A wise old owl perched rigid on top of the hat of the fat witch. She was stirring and stirring and stirring. Her incantation resonated melodically. "I dedicate this spell to all the guilty people who will soon be sentenced to die a shameful death inside this vat of blue Jell-O."

I woke up pulse pounding, sweating and whimpering. Remembering the blue Jell-O shooters. Vegas. The disco chapel of love. Al Dente and I were drunk from slurping Jell-O and got hitched by a Super Freak look-alike as the disco ball spun and I puked on a Manx cat.

I nearly gagged and puked again because of the foul odor saturating the air. Wait a minute. That was not just the plumbing. I recognized that odor. *Death.*

I jumped up.

"Norah? Norah? Are you well, dear?" I knew the answer. I picked up my sneakers and poked her in the back with one. It didn't press in. She was rigid. Oh no. Not again. I slipped on my shoes and climbed the first wrung of the ladder and felt her neck. No pulse. *Not again.*

I jumped down, ran into the hall and screamed, "Help! Help! Somebody please help!"

This time the responders emerged from their compartments at a leisurely pace. *Pat-the-Pirate* and *Contest Carly* quietly walked my way. *Hack 'em Up Hazel* trudged along behind them with her fireplace poker. Dina came running, tripping on her skirt. *Weepy Wendy* pushed them aside and gave me the evil eye and a smirk as she entered my room and then quickly exited, drawing the gold silk drapes.

"What did you do to this one?" she accused.

* * *

After dinner the train stopped in Pittsburgh. The local authorities removed the "possible death" victim. That was how the railroad had to report it. They didn't have the power to declare someone dead. Needless to say I was never setting foot in Compartment H ever again.

Much to the ladies' vehement protest there was no Pittsburgh plumber standing-by to unclog us. Just as well by me even though it was a double edged sword. I hadn't aligned the clues together the right way yet. I stared out the window in the parlor car. The rain whooshed down in steady sheets. A freight train was whizzing by. It looked like a trash train. It probably didn't smell as bad as Compartment H did.

My mind began clicking. What did Al's dog tags and the bleach bottle have to do with the dead sailor? And who planted them? The minstrel of melody, Alfredo Dente? *Mini Mary Agnes?* She was dead when the package was delivered but who knows when it was mailed or dropped off at the courier…I really needed to talk to Mom to see how it had arrived.

And who had access to my mother's footlocker with the yarn inside? When were the dog tags planted in the rainbow skein? Could Mom have been the one sending me the clues? She certainly wasn't the murderer any more than Al Dente was. He had no backbone.

But Al was supposedly in the Navy and the dead guy was a sailor. Or was he? I shouldn't assume anything. After all he wasn't wearing dog tags. I could ask *Big Marc* if wearing dog tags 24/7 was mandatory. If I could find *Big Marc*. Where could he be? Did someone steal an old man? Was he ejected out the window of the train when I pulled the emergency brake? Could crotchety *Big Marc* be the murderer?

Big Marc certainly had access to Mom's footlocker when he helped load the luggage. Could he have hung *Mini Mary Agnes*? Was her death a homicide? What time did Reverend Donaldson leave compartment A?

And how is Al Dente all mixed up in this? It was such an odd time and place and method for him to reappear after five years of absence. But I guess he had to show up some place some time.

I remembered that Many Agnes' brother, David Starr, smelled like bleach. Did the murderer try to remove his or her DNA evidence off of the victim's body with bleach? I closed my eyes and pictured him lying on the sand. His blue uniform didn't have any white bleach spots on it. So very odd.

Someone had sent me a bottle of bleach as a present. Anonymously. Gift wrapped patriotically in red, white and blue. Then wrapped in plain brown paper and tied up with string… *a few of my favorite things…*so the song goes. From *The Sound of Music*. Al Dente loved musicals. So did Dina and I. We were so nerdy. Or cultured. I giggled. Yeah, right.

Who was patriotic? *Big Marc*. Who liked red, white and blue? Mom had several outfits coordinating with that theme. One with a flag and fireworks, one with bees and one with a big red sequined anchor. Nautical. Navy. Sailors. David Starr, Al Dente and *Big Marc* Clinger were in the Navy. Who else was?

Someone had brought a gallon of bleach on the train! I remembered seeing it on the pile of crap waiting to be carried on board. I needed to find out who brought it.

I paced in the parlor car walking the length of it as three crusader ladies sipped iced water in holy silence. I smiled at them and said, "Hello. Do you think the rain will stop soon?" I tried to make polite conversation.

Two glared at me with their noses stuck high up in the air. The oldest woman, about sixty-five and dressed in a tan ruffled moo-moo buttoned to her three chins said, "It shall rain for forty days and forty nights and all the sinners of the world shall drown in shameful stench."

I could feel them willing God to strike me dead with lightning but I didn't care. I did not kill *Napping Norah*. Nor *Mini Mary Agnes*. Nor her *Starr of David*.

Lieutenant Hottie had been right rolling his eyes at me on the beach when I was trying to tell him the deceased wouldn't have attended the church service because he was Jewish. *Jeeze, Sandra. You can be so tunnel-visioned sometimes. He was wearing that necklace because that was his name, David Starr.*

It wasn't my fault that for some horrible reason it was my charge in life to discover the dead. I certainly didn't want this creepy job. I didn't want to go back to my job with the Department of Public Works either. Nope. It was time to change my destiny by gosh by golly. By goody gumdrops. I wished I had some green spearmint gumdrops to bite into.

I fished around inside the credenza drawers and found a pencil, ivory railroad stationary and a matching envelope. There was also a thick pack of Juicy Fruit gum. Yum. I didn't know how so many people could chew the sugar-free stuff that was so popular these days. I enjoyed the old Fruit Stripe gum and Juicy Fruit and Big Red.

I left the sweet stuff, closed the drawer and walked with purpose across the car. I sat erectly in a comfortable leather chair next to an end table. I licked the tip of the pencil and immediately crinkled my nose. It wasn't my pencil. Yuk. I wondered who else might have licked it. Johnny Depp perhaps? Did they have pencils back in pirate days? *Sandra, focus. You have an important task at hand.*

By the light of a nice little lamp with a green glass shade I wrote my resignation letter.

Dear Mr. Ishkabibble,

I hereby resign my position with the Cocoa Beach Department of Public Works effective two weeks from your receipt of this notice.

I crossed that out. He could say he never received it. I took a clean sheet of stationary and started again.

Dear Igor,

I quit.

With Warm Regards and No Regrets,

Sandra M. Faire

I slipped the paper into an envelope and licked it shut. Now if only I had a stamp.

Oh well. I stuffed the letter into my back pocket and returned to pacing and sleuthing.

I spied with my little eye two potted plants in one corner. I'd never noticed them before. A dracaena and a Norfolk Island pine. Low light lovers. Dracaenas were London's palm trees. They grew them in parks on the top of buildings. Yep. That sounds peculiar but I saw it on the travel channel. I wondered where Norfolk Island was. Somewhere in Virginia? I shrugged my shoulders. Norfolk, Virginia had a Naval Base...

There was a Norfolk Island pine tree stacked with the luggage when we were waiting to board in Florida. Who did it belong to? Did it matter? I'd find out.

Well now that I was almost officially unemployed I had no reason to return to Cocoa Beach other than to retrieve my belongings and to tell my landlady goodbye. My lease was up at the end of next month anyhow and since I'd paid a month in advance I was hoping we were even. I could just take off and start a new life. *Away from all the dead bodies.*

The church ladies sashayed up to me. "You stay away from our congregation. Do you hear me?" asked *Mrs. Moo-Moo.*

"What have you got against me? I don't even know you." My stomach flip-flopped. Why was she ordering me around?

"You do not want to know us, girlie. We can take care of your kind. An eye for an eye. A life for a despicable life..." She

64

interlocked her arms with the other ladies and waddled hip to hip until they had to walk separately around the corner.

I shivered. No one had ever threatened me. Well except for that prissy cheerleader in tenth grade because of that rumor I started about her boyfriend... I enjoyed an evil grin.

Man, I wish I had a stamp. I remembered stuffing my mail in my suitcase as I was leaving for the train. Maybe I could soak a stamp off of one of the letters if it didn't have the cancel lines through it. Hey, it was worth a shot. *Where was my suitcase anyhow?*

I spied it on the opposite side of the potted plants. Andy probably stowed my duffle there. I'd been evicted from yet another room. It was now another death investigation scene. With yellow police tape across the door. Now there were no vacancies left.

I walked over to my pretty cerulean blue duffle bag and unzipped the top outside pocket. I yanked the mail out, ripping the corner of a Victoria's Secret catalog as the zipper bit into it. I tossed it in the trashcan under the credenza along with a postcard from the dentist reminding me it was time again for another cleaning. My teeth were pearly white and in fine working order. He could find a new sucker to overcharge. And I didn't need any new bras and it wasn't like I was shopping for steamy lingerie to tantalize Lieutenant Hottie. He wasn't interested in me anymore.

Drat. Only one letter and it had a metered postage barcode not a lickable soak-offable stamp. It was from SunTrust Bank in Las Vegas, Nevada.

This was something else that needed to be taken care of. Now that my wayward minstrel of melody Alfredo Dente had returned I could divorce him. Or annul him. I wasn't exactly sure if the marriage had been consummated. I didn't have those kinds of feelings for Al Dente. To me we'd always be five years old, giggling on the monkey bars on the playground. I will never eat Jell-O again. It had made me so sick. Okay so the Jell-O wasn't the culprit. It was the alcohol they mixed it with. What kind? Vodka? Rum? Hooch?

I didn't even remember checking into the Dew Drop Inn. I woke up alone on the cold red tiled bathroom floor. Ghastly hung-over with a pillow under my head. My tangled hair was matted with stinky puke.

It didn't really matter to me if the marriage had been

consummated or not. It wasn't like I was saving myself for my second husband. Lieutenant Hottie wasn't the marrying kind and I was pretty sure Johnny Depp was in love with someone fabulous.

At least after the divorce or annulment I'd finally have closure.

I never touched this money before. I was in denial about the marriage. And now I knew why those automatic deposits from the federal government had been so small. My husband was in the Navy. However, it was a joint account and it mattered not that he made all the deposits. I figured half of all assets were mine. And this was what I'd use for seed money to launch my new life. Let's see, six hundred and something bucks deposited every month for five years was roughly $35,000. Halved, that was nearly $18,000. Almost enough for a down payment on a little house somewhere normal. In Middle America. Yep. I'd just get a house and a cat and a fun little quirky job to pay the bills while I wrote my novels and saved the world.

Jimmy Tamales strolled through the car straightening up the newspaper strewn on the sofa and checking to see if the rear door was properly latched.

"Hi, Jimmy."

"Good morning, Sandra. Can I get you anything?"

"Do you have one of those memory eraser thingys they used in *Men In Black*?"

"Sorry. But we can learn from the tragedies and move forward." He tipped his conductor hat and waddled back down the car.

I turned the envelope over and slipped my fingertip inside one end of the flap. As I ripped it open it ripped my skin open. "Oww!" I shook the statement out as I sucked on my paper cut.

Holy macaroni. The balance was…wait a minute. Let me count the zeros…seven million three thousand six hundred dollars and forty five cents.

It had to be a big fat computer error in my favor. They had probably discovered it by now. But it was a nice big figure to gaze at. I stuffed it back in my suitcase and zipped it shut.

* * *

At 8:00 P.M. the Cocoa Beach Chapter of the Global Order of Scribes shuffled into the business car for our evening workshop. Maybe Tony O'Rourke somehow managed to hop aboard in Pittsburgh or something since we didn't stop for him in D.C. A girl

66

could dream. I tried not to get my hopes up because that wasn't too plausible but of course my tummy had butterflies as my adrenaline trickled through my veins.

Rosemary stood at the head of the table and asked us to join hands and close our eyes. We did. I heard a door at the other end of the car close. A moment later *Tabloid Tilly* released my hand and the late arrival clasped it. Matilda Irwin's hand was cold and bony. This hand was warm and muscular. Large fingers.

"Please Jesus, carry our dear sister Norah to heaven and bestow upon her your everlasting peace and love. Amen," prayed Rosemary.

We ran "Amen" around the table then let go of hands and opened our eyes. I heard a deep cough next to me and turned to see that it was Lieutenant Hottie who had joined us. Great. Was he going to arrest me so I couldn't participate in Tony's workshop? I was still hoping he had found the train.

"I am so thrilled to present to you our keynote speaker, Tony O'Rourke, author of seventeen bestsellers including *The Naked Detective*. Please give a round of applause for him." Rosemary gestured to my end of the table.

I didn't see anybody. He wasn't there. Yet the ladies were applauding wildly. What, did we have the ghost of Tony O'Rourke on the train? Why couldn't I see him? No fair.

Lieutenant Hottie ambled across to Rosemary and smiled. "It's an honor to be here. I really don't have a speech prepared because I thought I'd entertain your questions."

Arms shot up.

I thought I was going to puke then become deaf and blind and paraplegic and infertile and incontinent.

My literary idol Tony O'Rourke was the pseudonym of my Lieutenant Hottie!

Chapter Eight

"Mr. O'Rourke, where do you get the inspiration for your plots?" *Weepy Wendy* asked as she twisted a tuft of white hair around her finger.

"From my closed cases. I change the sexes, body-types, names and small details of the crimes. This is very important in fiction. You need to protect yourself from liability. And if you model a character on someone you know be double sure you do a sex, age and body-type change. But just between us most people don't see themselves as others do and your own mother probably wouldn't recognize herself if you characterized her dead on."

I wondered who Mr. a.k.a. Tony O'Rourke's mother was. A mistress of disguise? A pathological liar? Lois Lane after her fling with Clark Kent? How could Lieutenant Hottie have kept his true identity from me? Well, okay, so technically his true identity was Lieutenant William Hernandez, Homicide. So he didn't lie about that. But he did lie by omission by not telling me he was a bestselling police procedural writer. Tony O'Rourke. Darn it. No wonder I never got over my thing for him. It wasn't just the pheromones between us. I was head over heels in love with his imagination. I had thought we had absolutely nothing in common. Maybe he wanted it that way. But why?

Oh, yeah. Hurricane Alfredo. I was a married woman. But how did he find out? Because he was the great detective extraordinaire. Lieutenant Hottie Hernandez-O'Rourke. No case was too complicated for him to crack wide open. Except for mine. Maybe he didn't exactly know everything about me. Perhaps I had a big mind blowing secret of my own that he would someday discover. At the time and place of my choosing.

"What is the most gruesome crime you've ever come upon?" asked *Hack 'em Up Hazel*.

"A car was pushed over a cliff. The driver's penis was impaled on the accelerator pedal," said Tony O'Rourke.

She smiled and made a note.

"Why did you arrest Al Dente?" I asked.

He looked at me with that you've disappointed me again

attitude. "RICO violations."

"Oh, I know that that means. Organized crime. His Uncle Santy Claus Dente is in the mob," said Dina.

"That's a lie. Al Dente would never do anything illegal." I couldn't believe Dina would turn on our best pal. Her own step-cousin. "Well, yeah, he has done a few slightly illegal things like eat Jell-O underage. But we didn't drink anything. And he was in the United States Navy. Not a mobster. His uncle was a biggie Italian guy. Scary."

I started wondering about the red limousine and *Mini Mary Agnes's* marbles and her overhearing *We'll get Donaldson*. Was Al Dente after the Reverend? Nah. How about his uncle's heavies? Could they be out to get Rosemary's hubby? Maybe. There was money to be had in tithing to the church. Maybe the mob was strong-arming the reverend for protection money. Maybe they had something on Eugene Donaldson. Some sordid thing from his past he didn't want uncovered. Nah. Reverend Donaldson was squeaky clean. As nice a guy as anyone would ever want to meet. And he wouldn't have a girlfriend because his wife dressed trashy for him. He needn't wander into livelier pastures.

Unless he had a thing for dwarfs…and did *Mini Mary Agnes* take her life because she was full of sin after one night with the reverend? *Or did he hang her?*

The dog tags were involved. Al's. And Mom's yarn. My yarn. Hey, what ever happened to my two wooden knitting needles? And *Mini Mary Agnes'* marbles? Very curious. Very curious indeed.

I tuned the questions and answers out. I was mad. Bent out of shape because my bubble had been popped. My idol was Hottie in sheep's clothing. We did have something in common after all. Why couldn't he have told me?

* * *

After the guest speaker concluded, I stepped up to Lieutenant Hottie. He gave me that awful, disapproving look. I couldn't muster up a coherent sentence. I had so many questions, but really now I just wanted to cry.

I squeezed in front of him and plodded to the parlor car. Good. No church ladies were waiting to threaten me. I had the place to myself. I curled up hugging the round center of the sofa. I covered myself completely with a white synthetic blanket. I was cold and it was scratchy. This was so not how I wanted to spend my vacation. My life.

The outside door slammed shut. "Who is under there?" asked *Tabloid Tilly*. She yanked the blanket off of me. I scowled and yanked it back. We had a tug of war until I tumbled onto the floor.

"Please just leave me be. Why can't you leave me alone?" I asked, genuinely wanting to know why she was so rude. My body was turning into one big pulled muscle, bruise and abrasion.

She narrowed her Cleopatra eyes. "I know what you did."

My pulse raced. *No. How could she? I knew I should have been more careful...Wait! I haven't done anything! Why am I feeling guilty? Oh...the potty business.*

"No you don't. I haven't done anything. Other than be stupid enough to board this train of ghouls."

She wiggled her retroussé nose and strutted out to the observation deck. To smoke another cigar probably. How disgusting and unladylike.

Bicep Betty shuffled in with a boom box under her arm. She set it on the credenza, sweeping aside some used napkins. Grunting, she reached the electrical outlet then turned it on. Vintage Bee Gees sang in the night. *I've Just Got to Get a Message to You.*

Did *Bicep Betty* know my secret, too? What the heck was my secret?

My mind raced with fear and guilt. Over what? This song was a guilty man about to be put to death who desperately wants to get a message to the girl he killed for. And a preacher wants to take one last walk with him before his life is through.

Is there a message for me in this song? Did some guy kill for me? No, no guy would kill for me. I don't think one would, anyhow. So what girl did he kill for? Are the cops closing in on him? Does he expect suicide by cop? Or whatever they called it when people baited cops to kill them because they had a death wish.

And how is Pastor Donaldson all mixed up in this? Is he in cahoots with the murderer? Or is he trying to help his soul prepare for the afterlife? *Sandra, seize into yourself. You're thinking way too much. Careful or you'll end up in the sanitarium. Oh, right. I'm already there. I'm on the GOOS Express. Riding the rails to insanity. Hey, how about naming a town Insanity? That would be a great place to set a story.*

I slept until Friday morning when Dina traipsed in toting a bag of white cheddar popcorn and two grape sodas. I looked at her for a brief moment trying to stay mad at her for turning on Al Dente. Maybe she knew something about her step-cousin that I wasn't privy to.

"Be careful now when you open the soda. It might explode," she said as she handed me one.

"Did you bring all of this delicious food with you or do you know about a secret pantry?" I was so happy we were snacking friends.

"I found it in the baggage car. It showed up when we picked up the Special Investigator."

We carefully opened the cans over the credenza. They didn't explode. Plopping down in two chairs with a table between us, I opened the popcorn and we commenced gobbling.

I didn't care for warm soda. "I'll go and get us some ice. See if you can find some glasses to pour it in," I said.

"Okey dokey, pal."

I left the parlor car and made my way down the corridor of the sleeper.

Andy and Jimmy Tamales carried the late *Napping Norah's* soiled mattress out of Compartment H. "I've got it," said Jimmy as he propped it on his shoulders and headed down the hallway.

I inhaled a big whiff of death and scrunched up my face.

My brother smiled at me. "Cheer up, Sis. She passed away in her sleep. We should all be so lucky when it's our time."

I shielded my eyes with my hand. I didn't want to look in the room.

"It's all cleaned out. I'm making the bed up. Are you sure you don't want to keep this compartment?" The room smelled heavily of a citrus scented Febreze.

"The toilet's backed up. Did you plunge it?"

"These are very sensitive computer operated mechanisms. They can't be plunged in the normal way. North American Passenger Railway employs highly trained computer waste engineers with special tools."

"I know! Do you think Jimmy would take this room and I can bunk in with you? Is your toilet stopped up?"

"I don't have a private toilet. The crew gets roomettes. Nothing but two bunks, a wall and a door."

"That's okay. Will you ask him to switch?"

"Against regulations. The crew cannot sleep in the same quarters as the passengers. Besides, one of the people in the crusades car has been on a waiting list to move in with you book people."

"Really?" I asked, intrigued.

"Mom." My brother laughed.

Part of me wanted my mommy. With all that had happened to me and around me I yearned for her security and unconditional love. Even with all of her disapproval. And I would feel a lot better if she were nearby. I worried for her safety. And for Andy's and Dina's and Al Dente's and even old Benedict Arnold Lieutenant Hottie's. Even though he and Andy were armed and trained to take care of themselves.

"No! Mom can't ride up here. She thinks this is a book club. She thinks we read books. She'll have a cow and a bull and a mule if she finds out I'm a writer. You have to keep her back there. Tell her the toilet is backed up and it stinks something awful. Tell her it's creepy. Tell her..."

"Why would Mom care if you wrote books or not? What is it you write? Those porno romance novels?"

"Romance novels are not porno! Sheesh. I'm getting so tired of defending—"

"I know. Dina explained all about the modern romance novel to me. Then she gave me a look at her Kindle. Hot stuff!" Andy sniggered.

"Well, I write cozy mysteries. No blood, no guts and certainly no erotica."

"Then what are you worried about? Mom would be proud of her daughter the published author." Andy smoothed fresh linens on the bottom bunk.

I thought about that. She would love bragging to her Mah Jong friends and the ladies at the knitting cottage and to her kick boxing class and to the ladies police auxiliary and to the gardening club and to her house cleaning club. Oh, and to the girls at the country club she played tennis with. Mom loved joining clubs.

"But I'm not a published author yet. No. She can't know until I have a book in print. Then I'll take her to the bookstore and pull it off the shelf and present it to her. That will be a wonderful day in the neighborhood."

"Sandra, no offense intended but when are you going to take a shower?"

"Well, I'm not taking one in compartment A or H."

"You may use my room," said Lieutenant Hottie. "But you'll need fresh towels."

I turned to see he had snuck up on us. I wondered how much he had heard. And so what if he did hear that I'm a cozy mystery writer. Perhaps it was time I owned up to it. Made my plans public. Then I'd have to finish one of my books. All of my books.

"Go and get your suitcase," said Andy. "I left it by the potted plants in the parlor car. I'll fetch you some fresh towels and meet you in Compartment G."

"Thanks, guys." The thought of a nice hot shower with cleansing suds pounding down on my battered body was euphoric. "Lieutenant, why are you still on the train? You gave your keynote speech. Is there more to the investigation?"

"We'll get into that later," He checked his cell phone and left.

* * *

I retrieved my duffle bag and met my brother in Compartment G. As Andy explained how to turn the water off and on I dug through my suitcase yanking out my toiletry kit and a change of clothes.

"Don't touch the lieutenant's laptop or mess with his stuff. I mean it."

"Me mess with stuff?" I batted my eyes at him.

"Have a nice shower, stinky." He left.

Boy I hoped he was kidding. Did I stink? How mortifying.

I locked the door and stepped into the bathroom. Hot water rushed through the pipes the instant I turned it on. This was much different than taking a shower in my apartment where I sometimes didn't get any hot water if I was a late riser because the other tenants would have used it all up.

As the water pounded down on my head I fretted over Mom possibly coming to room with the writers. My secret jig would kaboom. *Oh, so what, Sandra. It's not like it was the worst thing you've ever done. It's not like you robbed a bank or murdered someone.*

I thought Mom would be so much happier if she stayed put. She enjoyed the company of old geezers. She liked playing cards and knitting and, well, she didn't like Christian rock music or sermons…hmm… I guess she's had her fill of being born again. Poor Mom. I pictured her wedged on a sofa shoulder to shoulder with the reverend on one side and Andres-the-lush-lifeguard on the other.

Andres! He was a computer whiz! I would bet he could go online and hack into the North American Passenger Railway site and find instructions on how to unclog the toilets. I could pay him to fix the potties and return the dog tags and bleach bottle to me. And then instead of being the disturbing girl of death, I could become everyone's heroine. Or he'll be the hero and I wouldn't have to dread explaining the dog tags and bleach bottle when we arrived in Chicago.

As I shampooed for the third time I schemed.

How could I get a message to Andres? He was riding back with the crusaders and I think he was also volunteering as a sous-chef or dishwasher or waiter or something.

I could open up Lieutenant Hottie's computer and sneak a little email time. I had Andres' email addy in my webmail account. Wait, no. Stupid! I could not use the lieutenant's laptop to hire a hit man. I giggled. Okay, so I was not hiring Andres to rub any wise guys out. I supposed I was hiring him to tamper with evidence…

No. Now, Sandra, you don't know for a fact that it is evidence. Al Dente probably just stuffed his dog tags into your yarn to surprise you. Plausible. Al Dente-like. But what about the brown paper package all tied up with string—these are a few of my favorite things—bleach?

Could be Al Dente again. He loved Broadway musicals. Yeah, but if you didn't think it wasn't evidence you wouldn't have freaked out and tried to hide it.

Think, think, think, think, think, Sandra.

I know! I'll help out in the kitchen. That way I'll be able to talk to Andres face-to-face. That way we'll be on the same page and if he's hesitant I'll charm him into it. I'll introduce him to Tabloid Tilly or Weepy Wendy or Contest Carly or something. I'm sure he's tired of the septuagenarian good girls in his part of the train.

* * *

I dressed in a short blue chambray skirt, a crisp white button down shirt and Navy polka dotted ballet flats. It took me fifteen minutes to blow dry my hair and another fifteen minutes applying smoothing balm. I ended up just pulling it back into a ponytail. A few sweeps of mineral powder foundation, mascara and peach lip-gloss and I was ready for jewelry. I chose a yellow gold and diamond cross necklace, fake diamond stud earrings and an authentic circulated Italian lire coin bracelet. In total they cost less than $300. Mom bought them for me from the *Have I Got a Deal for You* home shopping channel. She was addicted.

I strapped on Tinker Bell. She said it was 11:07 a.m. I sprinkled her pixie dust.

I'd better hurry if I wanted to help prepare and/or serve lunch.

I peeked out into the hallway. *Hack 'em Up Hazel* was kibitzing with one of the new Global Order of Scribes speakers.

No time to kiss-up to the agent now. Every writer aboard the train would no doubt fawn over her.

I trotted across the hall. My brother was emptying the trash in Hazel's room. I tried to peek to see what she threw away. Some balled up papers, a broken shoelace and cellophane wrappers.

"Hi, Andy."

"Well, nice to see you, lady. You smell so much better."

I rolled my eyes.

"Hey, Andy, I was thinking."

He groaned. "Oh, no, now what are you up to?"

I could trust him so I just blurted it out. Most of it. "Isn't Andres, the lifeguard, working in the kitchen?"

"Yeppers."

"I want to help out down there because I need to talk to him."

"Why?" His voice was full of suspicion. He knew me well.

"Why?" I tightened my ponytail. "Some of the girls want to meet him and if he's game I'll arrange a hook up."

"He's pretty busy you know."

"Well, he must have an hour or two off sometime for good behavior."

"You really want to work in the kitchen? With that wing-nut chef?"

"Sure. It might be good character research." I'd heard the chef was rude and extremely intolerant of humans.

75

"Come along."

I followed Andy along the empty hallway. He carried the garbage bag to the lower level of the train and stowed it in a closet.

After he washed his hands in a restroom we headed across the hall and stepped into the kitchen.

The chef was a very short and round bald man with wire glasses dressed in black and white checkered pants, a white chef's coat, a dirty white apron and chef's torque.

Andy said, "This is my sister, Sandra. She is here to help out on the extra board. Be nice to her. She is a volunteer."

"Chop Vidalia onions. Down there," huffed The chef. He vaguely gestured toward the end of the kitchen.

I squeezed past him and was delighted to find Andres, slicing cherry tomatoes in half.

"Hi!" I said.

"Hello, Sandra. What are you doing in the kitchen? Serving time? I heard you've been up to suspicious activities." He spoke in his sing-songy German accent.

"No, nothing like that. I just decided that since the Donaldson's are so nice to let our writing group travel with them, the least I can do is volunteer a little time. If we were at a standard conference at a hotel we would all be expected to pitch in with things like giving out name badges and introducing the speakers and such."

"Well, it's good to see you," he said. "I've been a little lonely in the crowd if that makes sense."

"Totally."

The chef squeezed past us. He grabbed my wrist and led me behind Andres to the end of the car. Stopping in front of a paneled door, he yanked it open and tossed an apron and a ball cap at me. "Wear these."

I pulled the apron over my head and wrapped the belt around and around and around me. The little black and white checkered cap was cute. I threaded my ponytail through the back strap adjustment thingy.

He grabbed my coin bracelet arm again. "Déménager. Déménager!" The chef tried to slide the bracelet off with Tinker Bell. That hurt. I struggled with the thief. He cursed me in French, I think.

Andres called out, "He wants you to wash your hands. Put your

76

jewelry in the cupboard over the sink. You don't want it to get dredged through onion juice, believe me."

I nodded and complied. I soaped my arms up to the elbows and rinsed them. He threw a small brown paper towel at me. I soaked it good trying to dry myself.

* * *

It was nearly 1:00 P.M. by the time Andres and I were finally left alone in the kitchen. He turned on the dishwasher. I turned off the lights.

"Oh, Sandra, I thought that's why you wanted to *work* with me. Come here you little gidget you…"

I fumbled the lights back on and shoved him away. He pulled me close. "Sandra, you are such a lovely fräulein. I would love to share my wiener schnitzel with you—" he whispered and gradually lapsed into German.

I whispered back," I need a big strong man with big strong brains and computer skills to unclog the toilets for me."

"Yes, fräulein, whatever you wish." He cuddled me closer.

I was having a hard time not laughing. I'd wondered if he had been hitting the sacrament wine a little too hard.

"Do you have a computer you can access?" I asked, kitten-like.

"Why for, my little pineapple streusel?" Andres kissed my finger tips and started kissing a path up my arm.

"To crack…er…to hack into the North American Passenger Railway manuals and find out what tools you need to unclog the toilets in the last two cars."

"I do not need a computer for that, love."

"Why not?"

"I've already unclogged the ones in the Donaldson's suite."

"Oh, you big strong man you. Come with me and set the sewage free." I took him by the hand and led him out.

We walked through the lower levels of the train where the crew quarters and storage space and refrigerated cars were.

"Up these stairs, Brutus." I batted my eyelashes. They still stung with onion juice. My mascara must've been positively raccoonish.

"Wait. He opened a panel on the wall and flipped a circuit breaker. "Now let us go forth to raise and lower and raise and lower and raise and lower the toilet seat to send the scheiße swimming."

"What is scheiße?" I asked.

"Poop."

We went through the train and he raised and lowered the toilet seats until the poop swam.

I made him go into Compartment H by himself because that room freaked me out.

Tabloid Tilly snapped our picture as Andres and I emerged together from the potty in the parlor car.

Chapter Nine

Caught in the act. Of unclogging a toilet.

What could I do?

I smiled, turned to Andres, grabbed his golden whiskery face and gave him a big kiss. He responded very well. I was shocked at how good of a kisser he was. Or maybe it was just the simple primal fact that he was a man and I was a woman...who hadn't been kissed in over five years.

I pulled away, gazed into his glassy eyes and said, "Andres Pröell, I'd like you to meet Matilda Irwin." I smiled at her and said, "Matilda Irwin, this is the great Andres Pröell. A big strong man capable of completing any challenge with verve."

* * *

I rapped on the corridor window of Compartment A. Dina peeked between the gold drapes and waved me in. I waved her out. She waved me in. I waved her out. She finally slid the door open.

"Well, where is the ice?" she asked.

"Ice?"

"You went for ice for our grape sodas. I finally gave up and came in here to write. Hey. What time is it anyhow?"

I checked with Tinker Bell. "Nearly 4:30." I wiggled my wrist and enjoyed watching the pixie dust shimmer.

"Wow! I've been writing all day. Hey. I missed lunch. Where have you been?"

"At Lieutenant Hottie's boudoir for a shower and then crying in the kitchen and finally unclogging the commodes with a German gigolo."

"Aw. No fair. You have all the fun. Next time, I'm going for the ice."

"Check your toilet," I said proudly.

"It's working, I already know. A tremendous flushing noise thundered through. Three flushes and a whoosh. It was as though a ghost plumber visited us..." Dina said as she saved her document on her portable word processor.

"Have you had any other visiting poltergeist?" I asked.

"Nah. But I'm writing a vampire ménage. It's going pretty good now. Just can't decide where they should spend their happily ever after. The Greek Riviera or Boca."

"Neither location moves me. Can't you think of something more otherworldly? Some place you wouldn't expect a couple to choose. Not paradise. Some place different…like Rio de Janeiro or the Bermuda Triangle?" I suggested.

"Nah…maybe Alaska where it has those two weeks of solid night time or something like that. Wendy told me she used to live in Alaska when her father was stationed there. She said there are so many more men than women in Alaska and the running joke is that if a lady visits Alaska, 'Odds are she'll get the goods but too bad the goods are odd,'" Dina said.

"*Weepy Wendy* actually told a joke?" It wasn't that funny but I was so tired and relieved that I had solved one dilemma.

"Yes. She seems to have perked up." She slipped her word processor into a tote bag bearing the image of *Fully Involved Firefighter*, her critically acclaimed hunky firefighter novel. It was her only book in print. The rest were all electronic editions for e-Book readers.

"So you want to sleep in here with me tonight?" Dina asked.

"No! Sorry…Mini Mary Agnes. I need to let her rest in peace."

"Suit yourself." Dina shrugged her shoulders. "So you'll be in Compartment H then?"

I cringed. "No. I need to let *Napping Norah* rest in peace, too."

"So you're sleeping in the parlor car? But what if poor old *Missing Big Marc* needs to rest in peace?" Dina asked.

"Shoot! I forgot. Oh, my goodness what if he is dead too? I can't sleep in there. I'll just have to go back to Lieutenant Hottie's, change into my nighties and sleep on the conference room table."

"Suit yourself. Sweet dreams, Sandy."

"You too, Dina."

* * *

The light was on inside Compartment G. I tried to peek in between the gold silk panels but the Velcro held them snug together.

I smoothed my skirt down, flipped my pointed collar up, let my hair down and slipped the elastic band over my wrist near Tinker Bell. I took in a deep breath and shook some pixie dust.

I knocked on the door.

One dark eye and a nose peeked out at me through the drapes.

The pocket door slipped open and Lieutenant Hottie's strong arm with a silver-tone Timex on his wrist grabbed mine and yanked me through the drapes over the threshold.

He shut the door and adjusted the silk.

Oh, did he smell good. He must've just showered, his perfect hair was damp.

His laptop was open on the lower bunk. This time the upper bunk was also unfolded from the wall and made up. Tight light blue sheets and navy blue blanket looked so appealing. After all there were no tormented spirits in this room. *Please God. Let's keep it that way.*

My suitcase was stowed under the bottom bunk and my dirty clothes were neatly folded on the top bunk. I squeezed my eyes shut. I had left my dirty worn for two days uniform and unmentionables on his bathroom floor. I envisioned him using my mechanical snatcher device to pick them up at arm's length.

"I'm so sorry you had to pick up after me."

"It was a distraction. But while I was tidying, my subconscious came up with some good conclusions."

I really wanted to sleep in a bed tonight. "Do you mind if I take your top bunk? I promise not to snore or be any trouble at all."

"That's why it's made up. Your mother talked me into it," he said flatly.

"Mom? Why would she want me bunking in with an unrelated, unattached hunk of a man?" This can't be right. He has to be joking…but Lieutenant Hottie does not joke.

"She wants you bodyguarded and I presumed it was easier to mollify the commissioner's wife rather than put up with his rage when she complained to him about my incompetence."

It was clear from William's voice that bodyguarding me was business and an unpleasant task at that. No big surprise there. And I knew the police commissioner very well. This little girl had been on the business end of his temper and grounded for the terrible crime of trying to explain. I'd hate to work for him.

"I don't know how you guys work under my dad. His temper is volcanic," I sympathized. I wasn't scared of him anymore but at the same time I had learned just how far to push him and not step over the invisible line of lava.

William sat on his bunk and picked up his laptop.

"Where is Al Dente?"

No response from Hottie.

"What is happening with the dead sailor investigation? Is it all completed now?"

Obviously, whatever file Hottie was perusing was more interesting to him than answering my burning questions.

"Well, I'll just brush my teeth and change and be out of your way then." I rummaged through my duffle bag, extracted the necessary items, trotted into the bathroom did what needed doing, and emerged, all inside three minutes.

Hottie had undressed and was underneath the covers on the bottom bunk lying on his side with his little black notebook and a stubby pencil in his hand. He was naked. Well at least from the chest up. My mind drifted to what might or what might not be underneath those covers.

"Leave your clothes on the chair. I'll give them to Chico in the morning," he said.

"Why are you giving my clothes to Chico? I like my clothes. He can wear Rosemary's."

Hottie laughed. His left dimple showed. He only had one and it was a rare event to see it. This was a special occasion.

"Chico will wash them. He laundered your uniform and leopard print panties and bra…"

I grabbed them off the top bunk. My shirt was even pressed. "Again, I'm so sorry to have left a pile of dirty clothes—"

"Dirty indeed. I had no idea what you wore under that uniform of yours."

Okay. Blood was rushing to places it shouldn't. I'd better climb the ladder before I ripped the covers off of my guardian. I climbed as fast as I could and crawled under the covers. "This feels heavenly…"

"Mrs. Donaldson had featherbeds installed on our bunks. Special for the speakers," he said.

"Why didn't you ever tell me you were an author?" I asked.

"Why didn't you ever tell me you were a reader?" he retorted.

"I didn't know it was relevant," I snapped.

"Same here."

"Why aren't you mad at me anymore?" I asked.

"Because I deposed your husband. Why the hell does he talk like an alien idiot?"

"That's not nice. Al's mother died when he was little. His father remarried and they sent him to a summer camp for the performing arts in Europe, so they could have a honeymoon. He came back miming, juggling and speaking creatively. He outgrew the miming and juggling, but his speech pattern stuck."

Hottie shook his head.

"What did he tell you?" I asked.

"Enough to know it was a marriage of convenience and as soon as his trial is over you can get it annulled."

"Annulled? So that means we didn't—"

"*No*. You did not. According to Dente."

I was so relieved. And I thought I detected another smile in his *No*. "What trial? And why do I have to wait until the trial is over?"

"A wife cannot testify against her husband and vice versa."

"Testify about what?"

"Money laundering. That huge deposit in your joint checking account."

"But Al Dente is a harmless guitar picker. He would never—"

"But his uncle would. That's what the Special Investigator from the President was all about." The lieutenant lowered his voice.

"From the President?"

"Yes, a clandestine meeting aboard this train of fools between the President's man and Dominic *Santy Claus* Dente. Pastor Eugene Donaldson moderated," he whispered.

"Why or how is the President mixed up in all this?" I whispered back…incredulous.

"I am not privy to the details. Suffice it to say this is how it is all being hushed up. Your husband of convenience, Alfredo Dente, will take the fall, serve a year of his sentence and then quietly be pardoned on the last day the President is in office. He'll be given a new identity and relocated to Iceland."

"Iceland? It's so cold there." I pulled the covers up to my chin.

"That's where the kid picked."

"But what about the business with the dead sailor?"

"Dente didn't kill him."

"Sweet dreams, Lieutenant Hernandez."

"Good night, Mrs. Dente."

I lay there in a wave of relief. My dirty little secret was out. Well, at least to the police. Shoot. Did Dad know? Never mind, I didn't want to know if Dad knew. My tummy did flip flops. So what if Dad knew. It was a stupid thing I did years ago and I would soon be erasing it from my record anyhow. It could be annulled. And besides Dad liked Al Dente. So on some level I think he'll understand. But Mom…well, that's another problem entirely. I wouldn't mind it so much if she would just yell at me and tell me how stupid and inappropriate and immature it was. But she'll bring it up again and again until I'm a grandmother.

Why did Al Dente ditch me and enlist? Was he trying to disappear? Were some of his uncle's enemies after him?

Did he know David Starr? Mini Mary Agnes? Focus, Sandra.

Why am I being bodyguarded? Because Mom is disturbed at the coincidence of David's and Mary Agnes' deaths and their common denominator, me.

I guess I can explain away the dog tags—Al Dente. But what about the bleach bottle? Is that a clue or a prank?

I remembered the laundry detergent and bleach waiting to be loaded onto the train. I guess they belong to Chico since he's doing laundry. Could he be the murderer? Was he ever in the Navy?

Back the locomotive up. *Big Marc*, now missing, is a retired sailor. He was telling me about a top secret operation in Brazil after World War II ended—when his terrible accident occurred. Now he's missing. This all has to tie in somehow. He said he was in Australia. Should I put the squeeze on *Tabloid Tilly* to see if she's mixed up in all of this?

No wonder I'm not getting anywhere with my novel. I'm trying to write a nice simple cozy mystery, *by the book*. There is nothing *by the book* in real life. No easy formula. Truth really is much stranger than fiction. Well, truth as I tangle up in it anyhow.

The train slowed and stopped. The air circulating system shut off. I could hear Lieutenant Hottie's steady breathing. I leaned over the side of the bed. He looked absolutely angelic when he slept. What a guy.

I heard whooping noises so I hoisted myself back up on my bunk and peeked out the gold silk drapes on the window. A helicopter jumped up into the darkness. I guessed the Special Investigator was now leaving.

I was pretty impressed that Rosemary's hubby Eugene brokered a deal between the President's man and one of the leaders of the mob. Talk about a powerful man of the cloth. Wow.

The train whistle tooted twice. The air circulating system kicked on and we lurched forward. I curled up on my side, facing the wall. I slipped a hand under my pillow. It was so nice to have a pillow. And sheets and a long soft bed. And best of all, my own personal bodyguard. Lieutenant Hottie. Oh, and I was glad Al Dente was all right. Well, yeah, he's in the hoosegow but he'll be released and live happily ever after. Did I regret getting hitched? Yes. But hey, it's all part of my kooky life and it makes me who I am. Someday this will come out in my voice in my books and add richness and a unique flavor. Nobody else in the world has walked in my sneakers.

I closed my eyes and pictured myself perched upon a tall ladder gingerly positioning a bright shiny blue star on top of a Christmas tree in the White House. Volunteers did that every year. It was not so much of a stretch that I could be selected someday. If only I had an in at the White House. I could go online and see if I could meet somebody to introduce me to the White House florist. I think she's the one that is in charge of decorations at Christmastime. Nah. Bad idea. I shouldn't stalk anybody at the White House. With my luck I'd become Al's cellmate.

Poor Al Dente. Such a sweet guy. Talented songwriter, too. Well, at least he'll have a long time to write new material. He'll need a guitar though. Maybe I can get Dad to talk the prison into letting him have his guitar.

I drifted off to sleep.

* * *

I dreamed I was at the White House. Decorating a tiny Christmas tree. In front of a fountain. It had a Greek God statue in the middle and water was bubbling from the front of it from an urn. The kind like my grandpa was in on the mantle at my parent's house. It smelled funny. Like chlorine bleach. I heard my name and a lot of curse words. I began to run. Somebody was chasing me. But who? Every time I stopped to catch my breath, I'd turn around and look into heavy fog. Maybe I had run into London. My cell phone wasn't working. I kept dialing 9-1-1 but the dispatcher couldn't understand me.

* * *

Saturday morning the Cocoa Beach Chapter of the Global Order of Scribes assembled in the conference room of the *GOOS Express* for an uplifting prayer breakfast. His Highness, Pastor Eugene Donaldson, led the service.

"We're all living in a world of fools trying to break our spirits down. But no one can demean anyone without that person's permission. So do not give these fools your permission to belittle your efforts. For you, every one of you, are a direct descendent of the highest all mighty God. Royal blood is running through your veins. He knows your potential. Yes, you have had setbacks but he did not abandon you. He is carrying you to a higher place…"

I kind of got caught up in his feel good sermon and my sausage gravy and eggs got cold. I caught Andres' eye and asked him to warm my plate up. He took it and mumbled something about frankfurters.

"Now remember, ladies," Reverend Donaldson continued, "Do not let those rejection letters lessen your drive to succeed. They are validation that you are a competent writer. You have written a book. So many people mean to write a book someday but you actually have. It is all subjective and there is a higher power looking out for you. So what if a world class editor sends you a form rejection letter. You book did not belong in her stable. Your book belongs in the stable where Mary gave birth…"

"In closing," continued Pastor Donaldson, I would like to take this opportunity for each and every one to welcome Jesus Christ into their lives. All you have to do is simply invite him. Say 'Lord Jesus, I repent of my sins. Come into my life. Amen.' Ladies, if you say that simple prayer I believe you are born again and all of God's great blessings are bestowed upon you. Get into a good Bible based church and watch good things come to you. Reap what you so richly deserve. And write the next great American novel. In Jesus' name, Amen."

He waved with one hand and floated out of the car, back to his people. He was followed by two ushers.

As Jimmy Tamales cleared everyone else's plates, Andres delivered mine. He hadn't heated it up. He'd cooked me a whole new breakfast. A frankfurter with two small boiled Irish potatoes cuckolded up to one end of it.

Tabloid Tilly raised her eyebrows and shot looks between Andres and me. I could care less. I winked at him and licked one of the potatoes.

86

Bicep Betty offered *Weepy Wendy* a piece of black
and whispered in her ear. I watched the rumor spread a.
table until it got back to me. Dina had sense enough not to bothei
letting me in on it.

Rosemary cleared her throat. "Now I want you all to take the
pad and pencils in the tote bags hanging on the backs of each chair.
When I say *begin*, I want you to just write. Wherever you left off in
your story. Just write what pours out. Don't think. Don't worry about
spelling or chapter breaks. Just write until I say stop."

Fine. I can write. But I don't like my story anymore. I'll write
something fresh.

*...Once upon a time it was a dark and stormy night. The clerk in
the gift shop at the hotel asked me, "Why is it considered such a bad
way to start a story, It was a dark and stormy night?"*

*I told her it's all in the execution, gave her a mint, told her my
first book was in print and I was signing it at the literacy event the
next day.*

*Hotel security followed me through the lobby and onto the
elevator. A tall good looking black guy said, "Charles sure would
like a mint." So I smiled and gave him one. When the elevator doors
opened we saw a woman strangling another woman. Charles and I
wrestled to get them apart. The strangler broke free and I watched
her run down the corridor. I looked and Charles was making out
with the stranglee. So I shrugged my shoulders, kicked off my pumps
and ran after the strangler. She disappeared into a stairwell. So I
entered after her. I stopped to listen. The footsteps seemed to be
running up so I did, too. I chased the bad girl to the roof. We got
into a struggle on a couple of planks running between us and the
hotel next—*

"Pens down!"

We proceeded around the table reading aloud what we'd
written.

"Sandra, please read us your prose," said Rosemary.

I cleared my throat and proudly read, using all of the inflection
and cartoon voices I could muster.

I waited for applause and great enthusiasm. I got silence then
suddenly everyone was talking at once picking it apart. They didn't

like my characterization. I was stereotyping black men as security guards and lovers. I was stereotyping the hotel gift shop lady as being dumb. And nobody was dumber than my heroine. Hannibal Lechter was more sympathetic than my heroine. Apparently.

A North American Passenger Railway cop walked through the car. I swiveled my chair around and raised my wrists. I was ready to be arrested for impersonating a writer. I felt that bad.

Dina spun me around and grabbed my wrists. "Stop. Stop being so melodramatic. You are just feeding into their belittlement. Nobody can make you feel inferior unless you allow them to. They just don't understand your voice. You are writing a very original story. That's what all the editors say they want. Something fresh. Not the same old formula fiction."

I heard her and she made sense, but I wanted to feel sorry for myself so I gathered my belongings and ran back to Lieutenant Hottie's room.

As I closed the door I heard Jimmy Tamales in the hallway telling my brother, "No. Don't enter Compartment D. The dame doesn't want anyone disturbing her. We're not to ever empty the trash or change the sheets or anything."

Who was in compartment D? And who hadn't been attending group events?

Very strange.

Well I could rule out *Weepy Wendy* and *Tabloid Tilly*. Who had been missing? *Pat-the-Pirate? Hack 'em Up Hazel? Contest Carly? Who am I forgetting?*

What the heck was going on?

The lieutenant's room had been converted back for daytime use. I dove onto the red velvet couch and buried my head into my arms. I needed to cry or get mad or pout but nothing came. My mind was completely blank.

The chug-a-chug of the train lulled me to sleep.

* * *

I woke up to darkness. Just a faint light peeked from the crack in the drapes to the corridor. It was quiet. Well, the whir from the air circulating system and the sound of the locomotive, but I mean there was no loud talking or walking or laughing or crying from the other riders.

I rolled over on my back and didn't have any more ambition

other than to go to the potty. I stood up, stretched and walked over to the bathroom door. I hesitated. *Oh, Sandra, you are being silly.*

I yanked it open and screamed.

So did the guy flossing his teeth.

Chapter Ten

I slammed the door shut, ran and closed the peep hole in the corridor drapes and made good and sure the lock was locked.

Alfredo Dente walked out of Lieutenant Hottie's potty, tugging at a short piece of green floss broken off in his two front teeth. Very large and crooked two front teeth.

"What in the fettuccini are you doing aboard the train still, and in the lieutenant's bathroom?" I asked, incredulous.

"It gladdens me to my very core to know you are intrigued by my life form, lovely marionette of mystery. I will be honored to debrief you on my current status."

"Cut to the chase, Al Dente."

I shoved him into the chair, slapped his forehead up against the wall and yanked the shredded floss out. I scrunched up my face and washed it down the sink with a lot of lather. As I dried my hands, I whispered, "I thought they arrested and deported you or whatever. No not deported. Well, I don't know. The lieutenant said something about sending you to Iceland after your trial."

"The large muscled police pontificator has no jurisdiction aboard a transcontinental train traveling outside of Florida. Cocoa Beach even."

"But my brother cuffed you."

"Brave brother of the marionette of mystery is similarly impotent." Al Dente sniggered.

"How about the North American Passenger Railway cops?"

"Them, I'm hiding from."

"In a cop's compartment? That's crazy! Why? What is it you've done now?"

"'Tis but a wee matter of semantics. Alfredo Dente frequently toiled at the family Laundromat. The authorities twisted it into money laundering. But rest assured, the whole matter has been washed away and a deal has been negotiated. But I have chosen not to abide."

"You fool! Did you know David and *Mini Mary Agnes* Starr? *Napping Norah*? *Big Marc*?"

"Not I, fair lovely."

"Are you telling me the truth?"

"Cross my heart and hope to perish, oh, fascinating marionette of mystery." He crossed his heart.

I'd known the kid since kindergarten. He didn't fib to me. I believed him.

"You can't stay here." I furrowed my brow and tried to look like I meant business. I didn't want Lieutenant Hottie to return and catch me harboring my fugitive husband of convenience.

"I shall soon be on my merry way. Uncle Santy Claus is making preparations for my hasty recoil."

"Why don't you just turn yourself in and get it over with?"

"Where would the fun lie therein? Life is but a battle of wits with fools and foes. I will never give up, give in or give out. I do want to wish you able-bodied in all you endeavor, my lovely marionette of mystery. May you soar in all you venture. May the laundry be with you." Al Dente peeked out the corridor curtains. He quietly slid the door.

"Where will you go?" I whispered.

"Antarctica and the Galapagos Islands."

You can't live in either place. It's not allowed," I scolded.

"Precisely why I'm up for the dare."

"Wait. Where are you going right now?" I asked.

"To kind cousin Dina's." With that, he slipped out the door and hopefully out of my life.

I shut the door and curtains and freshened up. Lieutenant Hottie would be returning any moment to escort me to the diner.

Just as I settled back down to sprawling on the red velvet sofa, feeling sorry for myself, trying to conjure up a new premise for my next great novel. Well, first great novel, next great novel to start. There was a rap on the door.

"It's me. Let me in," called out Lieutenant Hottie. Well, it sounded like him anyhow, that deep testosterone that I so swooned over. Just to be sure I peeked out the drapes. Yep, Hottie. Hottie with his arms loaded down.

I unlocked the latch and slid the door open.

He leapt inside and told me, "Shut it and lock it, quick."

I did as told. I was so glad Al had left. I hoped he'd gotten to Dina's room before Hottie or anybody else saw him.

Hottie tossed two red cardboard boxes on the little table and then stowed his laptop computer in the little closet.

"Where is he?"

"He who?" I knew very well of whom he referred.

"Dente."

"He was here but he left."

"Here where?"

"In your potty."

"What?" Lieutenant Hottie was extremely agitated.

"He had floss stuck in his teeth. I yanked it out and yadda yadda he said he wasn't abiding by the deal and was on his way to Antarctica or the Galapagos Islands."

"What?"

"He's weird. I don't know. But he's gone."

"When did he leave?"

"He got off at that last stop." My fingers were crossed behind my back. I was in a conundrum. My allegiance to my lifelong pal versus my yearning for a hot lifelong pal. For all I knew, Al did get off the train. It could have happened. "Are you ready to go?" I asked, my tummy rumbling.

"Go where?"

"To lunch." I smiled, dreaming of some piping hot broccoli cheddar soup with a roasted red pepper garnish, a turkey assagio panini with asparagus and—

"I brought lunch." He opened one of the boxes and plopped down on the sofa as he unwrapped what looked like a peanut butter and jelly sandwich on white bread.

I grimaced and plopped down opposite him in the red velvet chair.

Hottie flipped his phone open and stepped into the hall. He returned quickly. "Dig in," he said, swallowing a big wad of sandwich. He cracked open a bottle of water.

I reluctantly spread the contents of my box on the table and took a loud bite of a crisp red delicious apple.

"So, who is it you are protecting me from and why are you bodyguarding me in Ohio or wherever we are when you have no jurisdiction?" I crunched and waited for his clever answer. I just loved listening to him speak.

"From yourself. And I'm unofficially bodyguarding you to keep the commissioner's wife content. It's a great excuse to have a week

92

off to write."

"Is that what you've been doing? Where did you go? Why didn't you stay in here and write with me?"

"No offense, but I thought you needed some time to get over that rejection out there. Did you?"

"Who said I was rejected? They were only offering helpful critique. And mean spirited put downs and taking advantage of the climate to knock me down as some have been wanting to do the whole trip."

"Why is that?" He took a swig of water.

"They think I'm white trash, that I cavort with the underworld, and they are very suspicious of why I keep discovering dead bodies."

"Well, white you are, trash you pick up from the sand, you are married to the mob and you've stumbled over more cadavers than I have in my seventeen years on the force."

I scrunched my eyebrows together and glared as evilly at him as I could. I gobbled the apple and dropped the core back in the red box and unwrapped the sandwich. I took a big bite. It was quite tasty. Comfort food. Something I really needed.

I realized I was making yum noises. How embarrassing. I got my enthusiastic taste buds under control, drank half a bottle of water and came to the point.

"If you don't have jurisdiction aboard this train then neither does my brother, but he's just here to play on the train anyhow. So it reasons to me that there is no suspected murderer aboard the train. That's not why either of you are here." I looked at him as I cocked my head to one side and played with a strand of my pale hair.

"I'm here as an unofficial observer. So is young Officer Faire."

"How many murders are tied together?"

"One murder. David Starr."

"So *Mini Mary Agnes* committed suicide?" I asked, hopeful.

"Yep. The note was in her purse. She climbed up on a stepladder and kicked off of it once she got the makeshift noose aligned," he said, all lieutenant-like.

"And *Napping Norah*?"

"Massive stroke. She'd been having a series of TIA's... transient ischemic attacks. Mini strokes."

And *Big Marc*?" I asked, cringing. I hoped he had turned up.

"That is not of interest to me. He was a volunteer. Perhaps he'd

93

gh of the shenanigans aboard and when you stopped the
_____ ⸴ok the opportunity to unvolunteer. That is how the rest of
the staff is categorizing Clinger's departure. Said he was a cranky
old guy prone to do as he pleased."

"But you keep me locked up in here and you made me lock the
door as soon as you stepped in with lunch."

"So?" He drained the rest of his water from the bottle. "I did not
want any of those corn fed writers pawing at our food."

"So I don't need the bodyguard then," I said.

"Suit yourself, but if I am relieved of your detail then where will
you sleep?" he asked.

"You do have a point. I think I'll lie back down. Do you mind?"

I pulled a blanket and pillow from the closet, plopped the pillow
at one end of the sofa, shook out the blanket and stretched out with
my feet in Lieutenant Hottie's lap. I closed my eyes with a big grin.
It morphed into something else when he began massaging the center
of the bottom of my right foot.

* * *

A literary agent presented a writing exercise in the afternoon. "I
have saved my son's spelling words since pre-school…"

Her son had spelling tests in preschool? What kind of
overachieving nerd school was the poor kid enrolled in? My only
memory of preschool was of making a hand-shaped wreath with
candy glued to it. I ate all of the M & M's off of mine and the
teacher got upset and made me sit in the naughty seat. Well, I think
the story goes I ate all the M & M's off of every kid's wreath and the
whole class cried. I wondered if I got sick from the paste.

"All of you should have a word source," continued the agent.
"Spelling words, the newspaper word of the day or an ongoing
journal of words you come across which have a nice ring to them.
Keep your words, cut them up into individual slips of paper, place
them inside a hat… This part is important. If you are writing a
mystery, use a deerstalker hat. Writing an historical adventure, use a
pirate hat."

Everyone looked toward Pat.

"If you're writing a love story, use a French Beret," said the
agent. "Draw five words form the hat and use them in your next
scene. You will never be stuck again. It really works." She passed
hats down the table. I pulled five words from a magician's top hat.

Normal
Expensive
Percentage
Lodge
Voyage

"Now, everyone use these words in your next scene. Come on now, you can do it. Be creative."

I wrote:

...I was tired of my normal mundane life. I needed something exciting to spice it up. Perhaps an expensive voyage to a secluded island. I'd lodge on top of a volcanic mountain and give a percentage of my income to help the natives buy mosquito netting. I saw on television that 3,000 children die every day of malaria. I thought for sure they meant every year but perhaps it is every day. Those poor little darlings...

Wait a minute. I was just rambling. I should try for real to write a scene for my mystery. Maybe I'll do better if I don't write in first person. I seem to keep running off on tangents when I'm writing *I did this* and *I did that* and it soon morphs into fact instead of fiction.

I started over:

...Judy slid the letter opener through the envelope with the skill of a surgeon. In one swift movement the contents had been excised.

It was a poorly printed invitation to her ten year college reunion. She shuddered, remembering all of the small town skeletons back in Percentage, Connecticut...

Okay so that was probably cheating making percentage a town but I had to admit it was a pretty good opening.

I glanced around the table. Everyone seemed hard at work except Rosemary. Oh, right. She was not in a hurry to finish her book.

I looked around and noticed Lieutenant Hottie had rolled his chair into a corner and was typing away on his laptop. I didn't think he was participating in the drill. Well, I mean he certainly didn't need to learn how to write. I wondered what his current work-in-progress was about. And if someday I might show up as a love

Ɪꞏne of his police procedurals.

, I have the best news!" enthused Rosemary. "We are Ɪꞏ the windy city, Chicago, soon. Right on schedule. So, this little layover is perfect for a scavenger hunt writing exercise, and also it will give us some much needed physical exercise."

I scanned the room. Nobody was smiling. Nobody looked interested. Everybody looked like they were suppressing groans and formulating excuses.

"Now since we are women," Rosemary continued, "Safety first in the big city. So I have prepared a list of partners to head out into the city lights with. I've paired you up with people you might not otherwise spend much time with, a little how do you do, what do you write, get to know you better bonding."

I could see everyone shrinking into their chairs.

"Carly you and I are team Rose…" said Rosemary.

"Wendy and Betty, you are the Iris team."

I looked down the table for their startled expressions.

"Matilda and Sandra are the Tiger Lily team."

I could care less. I'll be on Lieutenant Hottie's arm the entire time. Tabloid Tilly can give me the cold shoulder as much as she wants.

Rosemary completed her pairings. "Now as far as the scavenger hunt goes each team needs to find the following:

A building to set your story in

A house or apartment where your hero grew up

A favorite restaurant for your characters

A hospital or doctor's office for your sick heroine

A night spot for your couple to dance the night away

A seedy location where a crime is committed

A romantic spot for a proposal"

Dina raised her hand.

"Yes?" asked Rosemary.

"You took our cell phones. How are we going to take pictures of these places?"

"You are writers. You use your pen and paper. Describe them vividly."

Well, that makes sense. Actually this could be a very helpful exercise. I suck at description.

"May I have your attention please?" asked Jimmy Tamales via

the public address system. "We will be arriving in Chicago, Illinois in approximately twenty minutes. We will be servicing the train and request and require all passengers to detrain. Make sure to take valuables and your ticket stubs with you, as well as picture I.D. You may board the train when the announcement is made in the main station approximately at 10:00 P.M."

I looked at Tinker Bell and inhaled. What was I going to do, wandering around a strange city for seven hours with Tabloid Tilly as I try to warm up Lieutenant Hottie? Oh, no, what if she puts the moves on him? This could be a disaster. I'd better go slip into my best flirting outfit. Best flirting outfit? I don't own one. Well, surely I have something.

As the writers began filing out and chattering, I made my way over to Lieutenant Hottie a.k.a. Tony O'Rourke. He was typing intently. I hated to interrupt him but he was the reason I needed to hurry back to his room to get all dolled up for him, of course.

"Excuse me," I said.

"Yes?"

"I need to go freshen up now and get ready."

"Sure." He closed his laptop and accompanied me down the aisle.

* * *

I dug through my suitcase, pulled out my only other skirt: a calf length eyelet skirt in white. And a white tank top. I grabbed my toiletry kit and rushed into the bathroom. I flung open the door.

Good. No one screamed.

When I finished, I stepped back into the compartment and set my toiletry kit on the table and kicked my sneakers under the sofa. I plopped in the chair and pulled on my little polka dot flats.

"You need to pack up everything. Make sure you don't leave anything. They're cleaning the room for the next speaker."

"What?"

"This is the speaker's room. They pick new ones up at every large hub stop. Tony O'Rourke is done."

"Well, you are not leaving. You are my bodyguard."

"I'll be moving into *Big Marc*'s bunk since he's AWOL."

"I'll take his top bunk then."

"The chef has the top bunk."

"So I'm woman without a country again. No bed for the weary."

97

"No. That's all been sorted out. You'll procure your mother's room up with the crusaders and she's switching to Compartment H in this car."

"Fine." I packed up my worldly possessions. "Do I have to haul it all the way?"

"The crew will handle the exchange," said Lieutenant Hottie. "Have a fun time in the city."

"Aren't you coming?"

"Nope. I'm here as an unofficial observer, so I will make a sweep of the train. And I'd better not find your husband."

"But my mom wants you to bodyguard me. You can't…"

There was a knock. I peeked through the curtains, sighed and opened the door. "Hello, Mom."

"Hello, baby dumpling. Are you ready? I hear we're off on a treasure hunt. Do you have the list?"

Oh, no. She just called me baby dumpling in front of Lieutenant Hottie. I cringed. "Matilda is my partner." I was looking forward to getting to know the aloof Aussie. I looked at her like a challenge, like one of the Buckingham Palace guards. I'd try to get her to crack a smile. Perhaps I could even get her to laugh. If I could only figure out what they found humorous down under…

"Oh, Matilda told me she has some errands to run. I asked if she didn't mind if I switched with her. She was agreeable. We'll have so much fun! Your father and I came here to Chicago in 2007 to the International Association of Police Chief's conference. We had so much fun. I went on the spouse's tours. You know. The Sears Tower, the Oprah Winfrey studio, the green river and the deep dish pizza place. It was on the Food Channel. What the heck was it called? Oh, well, that's not important; I'm not hungry right now are you? I have my pad and pen, do you have yours?"

"But I need a bodyguard…" I looked longingly at Lieutenant Hottie's caboose as he was bent over his suitcase.

"Sandra Marie Faire. I have been through the citizen's police academy. I'm the best kick boxer in my class and your father has been telling me about all of his calls for years. I am perfectly capable of protecting my little baby dumpling."

"Goodbye, ladies. Have a safe and exciting time now," said Hottie, politely getting rid of us.

"Toodle-loo, Lieutenant. Thanks so much for keeping my little

Sandra safe."

"It's my job."

Of course it is. Was. Nothing personal.

"Honey, make sure you have your driver's license and all your valuables and your ticket stub."

"They're in my purse."

"Let me see them. Show me yours and I'll show you mine. We can't be too careful now. We want to be sure to get back on this train of fun."

I dug my three things out, Mom flashed hers and we replaced them.

"Put your arm through your purse strap across your chest. We can't be too careful now," said my new bodyguard, dressed in a long navy skirt with Kelly green whales around the hem and a matching tee appliquéd with a huge whale spouting green sequins. She was wearing Kelly green clog style sneakers and her headband was a green bandanna. She'd be a great undercover agent. No one in a million years would suspect Terry Faire of being dangerous. Or capable. Or anything other than being my Mom.

I wasn't really scared anyhow. If Lieutenant Hottie was convinced there wasn't a killer after me I should take his experience and gut instinct and give myself peace.

As we walked down the aisle, there was a minor ruckus at *Bicep Betty's* doorway. It seems her partner was ready to go and she refused to leave.

"I'll handle this. I'm a great arbitrator." I had brokered deals between my four warring brothers my entire life.

"Sandra's really good at helping people see that compromise can be a win-win situation for both parties," said my mother.

I slid Betty's door into the wall, ripped open the drapes, stepped inside her room and gasped.

Big Marc was tucked into her bed, handcuffed to the drink holder.

Chapter Eleven

Before I could process the situation my mother lunged inside the room, hiked up her skirt, kicked Betty to the floor and plopped on her.

Lieutenant Hottie swaggered in.

"This is *Big Marc*! The missing conductor. Betty has kept him here kidnapped and probably done horrible things to him. You should see what she writes about. Or look at the drawings," I said.

I stepped over Mom and Betty and checked *Big Marc*'s pulse. He was alive. "*Big Marc*! *Big Marc*! It's Sandra Faire. Andy's sister. Are you all right?" I asked. It's okay. We're here to save you now. I turned toward the gaggle of ladies at the door. "Go get Wendy! Call an ambulance!"

* * *

Mom and I walked out of Chicago's Union Station arm in arm. "I'm so proud of you, Mom. The way you took charge. I was frozen."

"You think of me as Terry homemaker. But there are sides of me you don't know about."

Yeah, me too…and I guess you'll probably find out sooner or later. I'm hoping for later.

As we waited for the walk light to turn, we stood on the corner and watched *Tabloid Tilly* jaywalk through traffic and run into the *Daily Planet* Newspaper building.

"What's her hurry?" Mom asked.

"Maybe she has a juicy story from the train to turn in. Did she take any pictures of poor *Big Marc*?" I asked.

"I don't remember any flashes."

"She probably has a special lens that doesn't need a flash. Boy I'll bet she wrote a juicy story to go along with the photo," I said.

The walk sign beckoned us so we crossed and headed toward the hot dog vendor. I was so hungry.

Mom ordered two hot dogs with mustard and relish and two bottles of water. We strolled over to a bench and plopped down, enjoying the greasy hot dogs with the soft fresh buns. We talked loudly over the noises of the city. The traffic. The steam from underground. The jackhammer breaking up the pavement. The ambulance siren wailing by.

"So. Sandra. What do you write?" Mom asked.

I coughed and drank some water. My secret was out. I inhaled and rattled out, "Mystery. Cozy mystery. Clean. No romance, nothing dirty. G rated Disney kind of stuff. From the era when Walt Disney was head of the studio…"

"Well, no wonder you aren't published yet. Sex sells. You ought to get Dina to teach you how to write erotic romance. She has such a flair for it," Mom said proudly, as if Dina was one of her own baby dumplings.

"That's fine for her but I really like a good puzzle. I love mystery."

"All righty then. Sandra Marie Faire, mystery writer extraordinaire. Let's look at the list and get you started. First we need to find you a building. Something intriguing." Mom took my wrapper and napkin. She dabbed a spot of mustard off my nose then threw away the trash as we strode down the avenue.

I felt like I was dreaming. Here I was. In Chicago with my mother helping me find inspiration for my book. She wasn't judging me harshly at all but actually supporting me. Shazam.

Tabloid Tilly rushed past us. "Hello…" My mother tried to greet her.

A tall man dashed after her. Matilda looked over her shoulder and ran out into traffic. I opened my mouth and tried to call out to her to be careful.

Mom had pounced on the guy chasing *Tabloid Tilly*. They were rolling around on the sidewalk until he broke free and rolled under a car and slipped out the other side. He got away.

I helped my mother up. Incredulous. "Mom, you are not a super hero. When did you suddenly morph into one of Charlie's Angels?"

She dug out her cell phone.

"Who are you calling?"

"I'm not sure."

I dusted the back of her off. "Are you all right?" I could feel her trembling.

"I just need to sit down for a moment."

Of course there was no bench in site. I wrapped my arm around her and hobbled her over to the window ledge on the *Daily Planet*

101

Newspaper building. I leaned her against it.

"Do you need some water?"

"In my bag."

"I dug a bottle of water out of her Maxx New York black patent leather tote bag. I cracked the lid off and pressed it to her lips. She took a small sip.

I checked her pulse. I have no idea what a normal pulse rate is for a middle-aged woman but hers seemed to be galloping. She looked pale.

I flipped my cell phone out and dialed Andy's number.

"We're across the street from the station. I have Mom propped up against the Newspaper building. She needs to lie down, her pulse is racing and her color is gone."

"What? Mom's sick? Is she having a heart attack?"

My eyes grew big. I looked at my mother. "Mom, do you have any pain in your left arm or chest?"

"No. I'll be fine, baby dumpling. No need to fuss over me." She dropped the bottle. The water ran down the concrete and into the gutter.

I cradled my mother in my arms, sheltering her from the city noise and gawkers-by.

Andy and Reverend Donaldson rushed to her aid.

"Mom, are you all right?"

"I'm fine. Don't fuss over me. I'm just a little shaky that's all."

"What happened?" Andy asked.

"Matilda Irwin, one of the writers, was being chased into the street by some thug. Mom tackled him and they had a go of it, rolling around. He rolled under a car and got away. This is the second person Mom's tackled in the last hour. Between the excitement and the unusual physical exertion her body is screaming for a break."

Reverend Donaldson scooped my mother into his arms and carried her across the street. Andy ran interference in front, stopping traffic. I was right behind the reverend, carrying both of our purses.

He took her into the stationmaster's office and they let her rest on a black leather couch. Their company nurse checked her blood pressure and pulse.

While the nurse examined Mom, I huddled with my brother and the pastor.

"Please check on Matilda Irwin. I'm very worried about her. She didn't want to participate in the scavenger hunt with us—she told Mom she had 'pressing business.' She hurried into that building and then was chased outside. She could have been struck by a car. I hope the guy chasing her didn't catch back up. Please try to find her."

"Andy, you go on and alert the station police. What did the suspect look like?" Eugene Donaldson asked me.

"White guy. Forty. Tall. Bald. Not shaven headed—he had hair on the sides. Brown. He was wearing a black suit. Looked like a businessman...*or mob enforcer*."

"What was Miss Irwin wearing?" the reverend asked.

As I tried to conjure it up, Andy said, "Form fitting black pants, white sweater and her black hair was long and loose."

Once the nurse assured us Mom was going to be all right, Andy left to get a posse up to search for Matilda and her assailant.

The nurse gave Mom Benadryl to calm her down. She dozed off in about forty minutes. She really needed the sleep.

The reverend and I stayed with Mom. He had dinner sent in for us.

"Sandra dear, how are you holding up?" Reverend Donaldson asked me.

All of the adrenaline from the past three days spewed out. "I'm so worried about Mom. She is not acting like herself. I don't know why she insisted on moving back with the writers. It doesn't make sense because she is giving me her room up with you all."

"Perhaps she was uncomfortable with someone up there. But I don't remember anyone being disrespectful to your mother. I'll have to think on that."

"Then she finds out I'm a writer...um...she thought I was here with a book readers club. Anyhow, she was very supportive of me writing mysteries. I wouldn't have kept if from her all these years had I known."

"Why would you think your mother would disapprove of you writing mysteries? My Rosemary writes Muslim romance and I'm very supportive of her endeavors. She so enjoys learning about new cultures and religions."

"Yes, but you have an open heart and mind. My mother is very disapproving of everything I do."

"Really, how so, Sandra?"

"Well, for one, she didn't want me climbing aboard this 'train of fools.' She thought your followers were a cult." I wished I hadn't said that. I squinched up my face. "I mean—"

"Rosemary told me she stopped by the house and volunteered to come along and teach the crusaders to knit. Perhaps she might talk tough. Your loving mother found a way to come along and make sure we were not a cult so you would be safe. She could protect you."

"Wow. I never thought of it that way. I just figured she was being pushy and wanted to tag along because…I don't know what I thought. To irritate me? Mom is also acting weird about protecting me. I entered *Bicep Betty*'s room on the train and found she had our missing conductor, *Big Marc*, shackled to her bunk. I screamed. Mom busted in and kicked Betty to the floor."

"Again, this does not surprise me. It's mother's instinct. Her baby screamed. She reacted and removed the danger. The threat to her child. Very natural."

"Okay, then explain why she tackled the guy chasing an unrelated Australian woman."

"Was she one of the writers?"

"Yes."

"Had your mother met her before?"

"Probably. We held our monthly meetings in a bookstore. At least once Mom came in browsing during that time. She might have struck up a conversation with Matilda. I think I do remember them chatting. Mom is an easy person to talk to. She has a way of making everyone feel special…except her kids."

I rubbed my eyes. "No, that didn't come out right."

"Sandra, your mother does a dozen little things for you every day. Now you know that. Just think for a moment."

Tears flowed down my cheeks. "You're right. Why is it I focus on the criticism and not all of the good and the sacrifice she does for me?"

"Why indeed?"

Reverend Donaldson wiped my tears and held my hands. "I believe we have the answers to all of your questions right here. God put your mother on this train for you. All of the seemingly bizarre things she did, even the collapse, was to bring you two closer together. And He has succeeded."

We were quiet for a few minutes.

"Reverend, why is it I am so judgmental and petty with people, prejudging and jumping to conclusions that they don't like me? And then when something puts them in danger, a switch clicks and I'm full of worry and compassion for them desperately wanting to help?"

I looked over at my mother. "She looks like an angel when she sleeps."

"Terry is an angel. Wrought from the finest royal blood of Almighty God. And so is her daughter." He squeezed my hands. "I could tell you why you've acted the way you have: defensive and judgmental and petty..."

Hey, who's he calling petty?

"And I could tell you how to stop that step and just skip to the compassion and caring and the instant need to help people. But I'm going to let you figure it out. It will be a much more powerful change if it comes from within your heart, Sandra. Peace be with you, my dear."

* * *

We showed our identification and ticket stubs and walked down the platform to board the *GOOS Express*. They had hooked a North American Passenger Railway car onto the back of the train. As we boarded, Andy told us all to assemble in the conference room. I stuck by Mom's side. I had decided I'd sleep on the floor in her room. That was where I wanted to be. I was so glad she'd horned her way in on my special secret trip of a lifetime.

I squatted next to Mom's chair.

Rosemary took her place at the head of the table and the ladies quieted.

"I trust everyone had a joyous time in Chicago. We'll get to your treasure hunt finds in the morning. Right now I'm sure you all want to shower and sleep so without further delay..." She cleared her throat. "I'll give you your new room assignments. I apologize in advance for the modern accommodations but out of respect for Mary Agnes and Norah, the reverend and I thought it best to retire that car where they passed through to the Pearly Gates. The good news is everything in the North American Passenger Railway car is clean, fresh and in working order.

"Terry, you and your daughter are in Compartment A..."

105

That was all I needed to hear. I helped Mom up and we headed for our room.

The pocket door was open, the blue wool drapes pulled back and tied with matching fabric. The set up was the exact same as in the opulent car belonging to the Donaldson's, but the fabrics and accoutrements were modern, modest and durable. Instead of paneled walls they were some kind of hard plastic manmade material. Mom's things were wedged under the bed which had been pulled into two bunks. My stuff seemed to be missing.

"I'll have to ask Andy where he hid my things."

Mom sat on the end of the bunk and looked into the mirror over the sink. "Sandra, why didn't you tell me my face was a mess? Look at my lipstick all smeared under my bottom lip. And oy vey with the raccoon eyes."

I soaked a washcloth in warm water and handed it to her.

"Thanks. Now fish out my toiletry kit and hand me my make-up remover."

I got down on the floor and shuffled things around under the bed. "Mom, it's not here. It must have gotten lost in the shuffle. I'll give you mine...as soon as I find my luggage. I need to go to the potty."

I opened the bathroom door and screamed.

So did the man sitting on the toilet. Dad.

Chapter Twelve

Dad greeted us.

"Wally! What are you doing here? I'm so glad to see you. Do you remember the FOPC conference in '07?"

He grinned at my mother. "What a ride, Bubbles, what a ride."

"Well, I guess I'll see if someone needs a roommate…"

"Try Dina," said Mom.

"That's right. She lost her roommate through attrition. I guess we both did."

I started to open the door. Dad said, "Hold on, I'll go with you."

"Why?"

"That was my excuse for coming on the trip overnight. Business. I need to notify the next of kin."

"Who's next of kin?"

"Beverly Dente. Dina's Aunt. She passed away."

My stomach sank. Poor Aunt Beverly. Dina will be devastated. Poor Al Dente. She was his step-mother. My step-mother-in-law of convenience.

Oh, was this getting complicated.

* * *

Dad made me leave Dina's room before he made the next-of-kin notification. He informed me he would be taking Mom home with him. It figured. Just when I wanted her with me. I was feeling sorry for myself again as I walked down to the parlor car. Rosemary sat sipping ginger ale, staring absently out the window onto the station platform.

"Hi, Rosemary." She didn't seem to hear me. I walked closer. "Hi, Rosemary."

She blinked and turned toward me. "Pardon?"

"Hi."

"Oh, hi," she said, sadly.

"What's wrong?" This was the first time in my memory that she wasn't bubbly.

"I had to throw Betty off the train."

"Wow." I was stunned. *Picturing Betty rolling down the hill into the car junkyard like Al Dente and I did.*

"I did not permit her to board the train tonight. I know this is America and all men are presumed innocent until proven guilty, but come on. She had kidnapped a dear old man. A dear old comatose man. How do I know she didn't induce the coma? Or what unspeakable things she might have done to him while he was unconscious?"

I shuddered, thinking of some of her story chapters she'd read at our critique sessions.

"Rosemary, this is your train. You are holding a private party and you have the right to revoke the invitation of any guest for any reason. And you have a good reason."

I saw a tear slipping down her cheek. I hugged her. We fake kissed the stale air by both cheeks.

"Thank you for your support, Sandra. You don't know how much that means to me."

"I'm honored to be a part of this historical conference."

"Historical indeed..." She seemed to fade off into her own world.

"Did Matilda get back on the train all right?"

"What?" she asked.

"Matilda Irwin. Did she board the train?"

Rosemary consulted her clipboard. "Oh, yes. Matilda is in Compartment C. We've lost so many among us that we all get rooms to ourselves. Except you and your Mom."

"Nope. Mom got off the train. She's flying back home with Dad."

"Oh. I'm so sorry. I guess all of this death was just too much for her. Well, I can't say as I blame her. I hope everyone doesn't leave now..."

"Well, Dina left but that's because her aunt died."

"No! Not another one." Rosemary collapsed into a chair and held her face in her hands.

I rubbed her back. "It was probably a staph infection from her recent surgery." I just blurted that out. I had no idea how she died. I hoped it was from natural causes.

"Sandra, treasure every moment. None of us knows how much longer we have here. We must make the best of each day. Be the best we can be to others, to the Lord and to our own hearts. We must follow our dreams."

"Amen to that," I said.

I sat with Rosemary and offered her bananas. That was the only food left on the credenza. She accepted. So we sat there in silent friendship slowly chewing under ripe bananas. Between the two of us we ate the whole bunch.

There weren't any teabags left and the coffee pot was empty so I made us instant hot chocolate. It didn't have the little crunchy marshmallows that I like so much.

I missed Dina. She and her Aunt Beverly Dente had some issues but they loved each other dearly. Beverly was the big sister of Dina's mother. After Dina graduated from high school her parents bought a fifth wheel, a recreational vehicle that they tow around on the back of a pickup truck. They travel the continent. She sees them at Easter and Christmas. Aunt Beverly was kind enough to offer a home to Dina. Her husband, Al's father, Vinnie Dente, was incarcerated. She divorced him when he was convicted of the usual things Italian mobsters get caught doing. Gambling, receiving stolen merchandise and filing serial numbers off of guns.

I never did know what happened to Al's biological mother. He never talked about her. Beverly was the only mother figure I can remember.

"Rosemary?"

"Huh?"

"What are you thinking about?" I slurped some very hot chocolate.

"About honor and loyalty."

"Very noble."

"You'd think."

"Huh?" I asked.

"At what point is blind loyalty the foe of honor?"

I slurped more hot chocolate and thought about that. "Well, personally, I've been blindly loyal to a dear friend for over five years while I had no idea what this person was up to. And now that I know it was possibly illegal, I'll still stick by them, to help them out and when I'm sure they are safe, I will shake hands and part ways."

"And how much of your life did you sacrifice for him?"

"I didn't say it was *a him*."

"You didn't have to. It had to be *a him* for you to do such a noble thing."

109

I shrugged my shoulders and blew on my chocolate.

I started to wonder if Rosemary was privy to the details of the meeting between the Special Investigator and Santy Claus. Of course I couldn't ask because I wasn't supposed to know, and no way would I get Lieutenant Hottie in trouble for telling me. And no way would I do anything to get Al Dente in trouble. He always was a rather wounded puppy dog. Maybe because of losing his mother so young. And his dad wasn't exactly the sweetheart play ball in the yard kind of dad. Well, neither was mine. But that's okay. He did the best he could with me and my brothers.

I glanced at Tinker Bell. It was after midnight. I finally had a private room to myself and I couldn't excuse myself to go and climb under the covers and sleep a full night.

Rosemary's cell phone rang to the tune of *How Deep is Your Love*. She said, "Hello? ...in the parlor car with a friend...Yes...Yes...I'm on my way...I love you, too...God bless you...bub-bye." She flipped it closed and stood. "I have to get back to my quarters now. Thank you for sitting with me. You helped me a great deal."

What was she talking about? I helped to replenish her potassium and serotonin levels with the bananas and chocolate? Well, any compliment, I'll take. I smiled and rose. "Go on ahead. I'll clean up this mess."

She grabbed me and hugged me tighter than anyone ever had. And then she left with a stride of purpose I had never seen.

As I threw the cups and banana peels in the trashcan under the credenza I thought of poor *Big Marc*. His last conscious moments were spent cleaning up my mess right here. Kind of dejavu-ish. I hoped he'd be all right. When he regained consciousness, I hoped he had a full recovery and many happy days ahead. And if it was his time to pass on may he have a peaceful voyage.

I walked through the dark sleeper car illuminated only by the letters marking the doors and a strip of lights on the floor along the corridor wall. I opened the door to Compartment A, flipped on the lights and stepped inside. My duffle bag had arrived. Good old Andy. I shut the door and pulled the drapes closed. I changed into my polka-dotted jammies and brushed my teeth at the sink. I stood in front of the bathroom door and lightly knocked. Good, no answer. I squinted my eyes shut and opened it. Nobody screamed. Good. I opened one eye and didn't see anybody *or any body.* I opened the other eye, stepped inside, closed the door and did what I needed to.

I stepped out of the bathroom and gasped. So did the guy on my bottom bunk. Hurricane Alfredo revisited.

Chapter Thirteen

"Superb salutations, lovely marionette of mystery."

I ran to the door and locked it. I wished I had done that before I went to the potty. Note to self: Always lock door upon entering room. Any room.

"What in the fettuccini are you doing still on the train?"

I loved saying what in the fettuccini to my friend Alfredo Dente. I think that started in seventh grade. Boy was seventh grade hard for us. Middle school kids can be so cruel.

"I am traveling north to Alaska."

"But this train is going west to California."

"By way of Arizona. I will tuck and roll when we get there."

"They know you escaped. How have you been alluding them on the train? You aren't invisible."

"Don't worry, lovely lady of my longing."

"I don't want to be arrested for harboring a fugitive."

"Don't worry my sweet bride. Alfredo Dente would never put you in a precarious predicament."

I was so tired. I didn't want to argue with him. I just wanted to sleep. I could argue extreme exhaustion if we got caught. Or something. Oh I didn't care. I just wanted to sleep. "Do you know your step-mom passed away?" I squatted at his bedside.

"Sadly I have received the sorrowful news. Uncle Santy Claus told me. We should pray for her spirit."

"Sure."

He rolled onto the floor and knelt near the bunk. I knelt next to him. We interlocked arms and folded our hands in silent prayer.

I finished and opened my eyes. His lips were moving. My arm was getting numb so I fidgeted a little. His lips were still moving. Finally he said, "Amen."

We stood and I gave him a big hug. He hugged me back even tighter than Rosemary had. I was getting sore from this bear hugging.

I kissed his forehead and climbed the ladder.

"Sugary dreams, marionette of mystery."

"Melodic dreams, minstrel of melody." I turned off the light.

I woke up Sunday morning and saw light peeking in from between the crack in the drapes. I wondered what time it was. Tinker Bell wasn't on the sink. I was positive I had left her there. I rolled over and peeked over the side of the bunk. It was empty and made. Just like no one had ever slept there. Just like the empty hotel room in Vegas. He was gone. Did he even sleep there at all? Al Dente stole Tinker Bell!

No, that's silly. He wouldn't. I got up and searched, looking all through the covers on both bunks, on the floor and in the bathroom. Alas, Tinker Bell had gone to Neverland without me. I was so sad. Maybe she'd turn up. She had to. I must have left her somewhere and I'll remember. Soon.

I heard singing in the corridor. One of Al's songs. But it wasn't his sweet voice. It had a Mexican accent. Or something Latino. I crawled down to the end of the bunk and peered out the top of the corridor drapes. Chico was delivering laundry to Lieutenant Hottie's room. Well, where his room would have been if we weren't in a new car and if he hadn't moved in with the crew.

I decided to climb back under the covers and go back to sleep. While I could. Who knew when the next disturbing thing would pop back into my life. I needed to be well rested and fortified to think on my feet and react accordingly. Just like Mom did. What a gal. My mom, one of the original Charlie's Angels. Who knew.

I drifted off into dreamland. I was in the enchanted forest again near the circle of witches conferring over something known only to them. The ugly one with the green face and wart on her nose with two black hairs in it pointed to me. All the other witches turned and pointed. The green one said, "Nicer."

I wondered what that meant. Was I nicer than most? Did I need to be nicer?

I felt like I was rolling downhill. Then I felt my ribs compress. I opened my eyes and realized I was being folded up into the wall. I screamed. Jimmy Tamales yanked the bunk back down.

"Jeeze! Say something before I fold you up. I thought you were at lunch with the rest of them."

"Lunch? What time is it?" I slept through breakfast?

"It's about 1:00 P.M. I'll come back later."

"Thanks. Sorry for the trouble."

113

"You're the guest. No trouble at all." He tipped his hat and closed the door when he left.

I plumped up my pillow and snuggled back in. I'd missed lunch, too. They would be clearing the plates by now. I missed the morning speaker, darn it. Who did they have scheduled? I tried to remember. I think it was some guy speaking about how to write screen plays. Not my cup of tea, though it could be more satisfying because screen plays are so short compared to novels. I just don't think I have nearly enough drama in me to come up with clever dialogue, scene description and to keep the audience on the edge of their seats. What was it Alfred Hitchcock said, "The suspense is in the anticipation? There is no bang in the boo..." or something like that.

I can't watch too many Alfred Hitchcock, or Stephen King movies, either, they scare me. I can't read his books. Well, I have seen edited versions of Carrie and Misery... Oh gosh, poor *Big Marc. Bicep Betty* played misery with him... No, Sandra. You don't know that. Perhaps she was taking care of him. And she handcuffed him to the bed so he wouldn't fall out since he was comatose... I wondered what would happen with all of that...

It occurred to me I didn't check to see if Al Dente was in my bottom bunk.

I leaned over. Nope. Perfectly made. He'd be back though. I was sure.

Well, I hoped he'd be back anyhow. I couldn't be tried for harboring my husband after all. At least I hoped not. And I'd do it anyway. Al Dente had saved my life twice and I would always help him. God bless Alfredo Dente, my minstrel of melody. And help him succeed. And forgive him for his sins and crimes since I'm not sure they are automatically all inclusive. With extenuating circumstances and all. And God rest his stepmother's soul and bring peace to Dina and her Mom. Amen.

* * *

I was lying there thinking inappropriate thoughts about Johnny Depp hoping to conjure him in my dreams when the P.A. system so rudely interrupted.

"Attention all members of the Cocoa Beach Chapter of the Global Order of Scribes," said my brother's disembodied voice. "Please pack up all of your belongings and be ready to detrain in approximately thirty minutes when we arrive in Kansas City,

Missouri. Thank you."

Wait a minute. We aren't scheduled to stop in Kansas City. That isn't a big hub stop. Why do we have to take everything off with us this time? Did somebody stop up the potties again? It wasn't me...I don't think. And it wasn't Dad last night. I thought about the plunger he keeps in the powder room. It gets frequent use. I giggled. Perhaps dear old Dad flushed evidence, too. Wouldn't that be an ironic hoot? A Faire family dirty little secret.

I kicked off the covers and climbed down the ladder. I took a fast shower and once I was dressed I opened the compartment door hoping to overhear some sort of explanation. No time to ask. I had too much to pack. I didn't want to leave anything. I got down on my hands and knees and checked under the bottom bunk. Nope. Didn't leave anything there. I pivoted and looked under the chair. I pulled out a gum wrapper. Juicy Fruit. My mind flashed back to the beach. I had picked a Juicy Fruit wrapper off of the beach in front of the Copacbana, while waiting for the authorities to show up...Lieutenant Hottie. He looked so good all of the time...

I shook my head. Focus Sandra. I pulled the gum wrapper out and spied a slip of paper behind it. I grabbed it. Just a little sliver of paper ripped off of a bigger sheet. It was a list:

D
MA
N
M
B
S
A
F
J
T

Dina loved puzzles. I wished she was here. I missed her so much.

"Attention please, Global Order of Scribes," said my brother on the P.A. system. "We have arrived in Kansas City, Missouri. Please take your valuables and step off the train. The crew will handle your luggage. You may leave that in your rooms."

115

I stuffed the trash in my pocket and followed Pat-the-Pirate off the train.

We were herded into the station and told to wait for Rosemary.

We trudged in. I counted us off. Me, Pat, Weepy Wendy, Tabloid Tilly, Contest Carly, and Hack-'em-Up Hazel. When Rosemary returned there would be seven. Seven little Indians left. We started with nine. *Bicep Betty* and Dina were gone. I really missed her. Maybe I should just take a flight home.

I looked around the fairly empty train station. There were rows of hard plastic blue seats all joined together. I counted fourteen. It was similar to seating at the gates at airports. I plopped down under a TV. CNN was being broadcast but the volume was muted. It was closed caption. A story on the dismal housing market. My parents' house had dropped nearly $100,000 in value in the last four years. But they had lived there long enough that if they had to sell, they had enough equity in it to make a profit.

Pat-the-Pirate sat in the chair next to mine. I shuffled my purse between my feet to give her room for her knapsack in pink and taupe fatigue print and her matching laptop case.

"Thanks," she said.

"It's such a shame about the mortgage crisis." I gestured to the TV.

"I think some people are just in denial, they want a house so bad." I thought about the kind of house I wanted when I began my new life. That reminded me. I pulled my resignation letter out of my purse. I looked around and spied a stamp machine by the pamphlet stand. "Excuse me. I need to mail a letter."

"Sure. I'll hold your seat," said Pat.

"Thanks." I dug some change out of my purse as I made a beeline over to the machine. I was never so happy to affix a stamp. I looked around but didn't see a mailbox. So I walked up to the ticket counter and stood in line.

I asked the man to please mail my letter.

I skipped back over to my chapter mates and took my place by Pat. She was reading a newspaper.

"Did you get it mailed?" she asked.

"Yes. It was my resignation letter."

"Oh, is everything all right?" She seemed concerned. She folded her newspaper up.

"Everything is just fine. It's time for me to move on to my next goal."

Pat smiled.

Hazel was sitting across from us. She said, "Hey look, there's Rosemary's husband. On TV. And Rosemary."

We all watched. And read the closed captioning. Something about Pastor Donaldson confessing to an inappropriate relationship involving one of his parishioners.

My stomach sank. Poor Rosemary. He seemed like such a wonderful man. I remembered her being upset last night. I guessed this was why. She was preparing herself to be the stoic wife standing by her man.

Pastor Donaldson stepped away from the podium and Rosemary pulled away from him. She stepped up to the microphone. Apparently she was not standing by her man.

"Good for her!" said *Hack 'em Up Hazel.*

CNN cut to a related story. *A photograph of Eugene Donaldson and oh my God! Mini Mary Agnes!* It was grainy and looked very lurid.

Rosemary walked up to the TV and turned it off. "I see you all know what has happened. I'm very sorry you have had to bear witness to this private trauma. But since I'm married to a celebrity I have no privacy." Rosemary screeched on and on and we nodded and tried to support her. Her anger was at a high level.

"The bus has arrived," interrupted Andy. "We've loaded your luggage."

"Thank you," said Rosemary. "I cannot, will not continue on that crusade of concubines. I have chartered a bus to take us home. I'm very sorry and I hope you all understand." She finally wept.

I wrapped my arms around her. She buried her head on my shoulder and sobbed and sobbed and sobbed.

* * *

We all sat separately, spread out throughout the bus. Except for Rosemary. She boo-hooed all night in Chico's arms.

I had slept so much that day that I was having a hard time turning my mind off to let the sleep come. I wished I had my cell phone so I could call Mom. I wondered if the box full of our cell phones was stowed in the luggage compartment under the bus. If only I could get to it. I wished Mom would call me. Boy was that a strange urge. I hoped she and Dad had made it home safely.

I leaned my head against the window and counted the headlights on the highway. They weren't like sheep. They gave me a headache from the glare. I wished I had some Aspirin or Extra Strength Tylenol. Or happy pills. But not blue Jello-O shooters. Once I throw something up I'll never eat it again. Like Shepherd's pie. I won't eat that or cracked pepper ever again.

I looked past the headlights and saw a train chuffing alongside the road.

Rosemary must've been dehydrated because she ran out of tears and appeared to be sleeping it off. This must be so humiliating and odd for her, riding on a bus. She was used to a chauffeured Bentley. I saw Chico's head resting against the window. His mouth was gaped open. Rosemary was reclined in her seat.

The driver had the radio on soft and low. He or she hadn't been on the bus when we boarded and I was seated way in the back so I don't know if it was a man or a woman or how old of a person. I hoped for someone around fifty with plenty of driving experience under the belt.

I squirmed in my seat. I tried sprawling across two. I just couldn't get comfortable. Oh, well sooner or later probably sometime tomorrow after dawn, I'd finally doze off from it all. Just as the others were coming to life. I wondered how long of a trip it was from Kansas City to Orlando. I guessed we'd be dropped off at the Orlando North American Passenger Railway station since that's where most of us had our cars parked. I had a gently used Kia, in blue. It got me where I wanted to go.

I wondered how much I could fit in it for my move. Not much more than my limited wardrobe and maybe my blue African violet.

Should I sell my furniture and TV? Nope. I'm not selling my TV. It took me a year and a half to save up for the little high definition flat screen. I never want to have to go back to one of my parents' old archaic twenty-five inch diagonals that don't have the right ports to plug my video games into.

I thought I heard the *Look at me I'm Sandra* Dee song on the radio. From the movie *Grease*. Mom loved that movie and I hated it when she sang that song. Thank goodness my middle name was Marie not Dee. I decided to take a walk up front and see if the driver was friendly.

When I got two seats away I deduced it was a woman. With a blonde ponytail. Average sized. I plopped down in the seat behind her and said, "Hi."

She looked up at me in her rear view mirror. "Oh. Hello there, baby dumpling. Can't sleep? I've told you time and again that napping goofs you up. If you'd cut down on your carbohydrates…"

Chapter Fourteen

"Mom! Pull over. You can't drive a bus." I admonished in the quietest screech I could muster. I looked around. *Tabloid Tilly* shifted in her seat but didn't open her eyes. Rosemary and Chico were still lost in slumber land. I really didn't want to wake the poor woman up. Everyone else seemed to be peaceful in the dark.

"Mom. Never mind about my sleeping and eating habits. Pull the bus over! What do you think you're doing? You can't drive a bus."

"Of course I can drive a bus. I have a commercial driver's license. I used to drive a school bus."

"No you did not."

"Yes I did. Before you and Matt and Andy were born."

"What are you talking about? You were a substitute teacher."

"But before that I went through the city school bus driver's training, received my license and was employed as a driver."

"Are you sure you didn't dream this?"

"Well, I only worked one day as a school bus driver. Well, more like one bus stop but it was not my fault about the flat tires. How was I supposed to know you couldn't back up over the spikes in a gated community?"

"I don't believe you passed your test at the Department of Motor Vehicles. Who did you pay off?" *Oh please tell me I didn't say that out loud.*

"I have never bribed a public official in my life, Sandra Marie Faire," she said with just the right bite in her voice to let me know I was grounded. "My instructor fell asleep while I was parallel parking. I had two minutes to get the bus within two inches of the curb. I woke her up when I was done, about thirty-five minutes after she started snoring. But I can drive. Going forward. So who cares if I can't back up or park? Sheesh. Rosemary was in such a bad way I thought it was the least I could do. You should volunteer to help out too, little lady."

She had a point. I should do something to help out. Several of the other ladies had held little workshops when we were on the train. But what could I teach them? How to pick up garbage off the beach?

How to drive a golf cart on sand? What it's like to be born into a family with so many cops, you have congenital flat feet? How to discover dead bodies? Oh, I was really an expert at that one. I'm surprised I wasn't the one to turn up Aunt Beverly's corpse on the conference room table or stuffed inside Mom's green steamer trunk.

"Why aren't you home with Dad?"

"I changed my mind. I wanted to continue on the adventure with you, baby dumpling."

I was glad Mom was back. But I couldn't bring myself to say it to her. I gazed out the window and noticed we were still pacing the train. And I was pretty sure that was the train formerly known as the *GOOS Express*. Wait a minute. They were continuing on with the crusade. So that meant we were heading northwest as well.

"Mom! Aren't we supposed to be returning to Florida?"

"That's what Rosemary told me."

"But Florida is southeast of Missouri. We are paralleling the train, heading northwest."

"Uh huh."

"Mom, are you taking happy pills?"

"No and stop bringing that up. My abscessed tooth really was excruciating and I did need the relief. I am purposely continuing on with the *GOOS Express* itinerary. I know Rosemary will thank me in the morning."

"Come again?" She wasn't making any sense.

"Things aren't always as they seem and I feel certain if she'll just give her wonderful husband a chance to explain his side of the story, they can clear up this whole misunderstanding."

I peeked over her shoulder to check the speedometer. We were going forty miles per hour. The speed limit was seventy. No wonder everyone was whizzing by. It's a good thing there wasn't heavy traffic in the middle of this night. I looked straight ahead and saw the moon. It looked pitiful, barely an eighth showing. *I feel like I'm barely an eighth of my potential sometimes.*

There just had to be something spectacular I was placed on this earth to do. I was not an ordinary human female. I always have known I was special. I just needed some sort of sign, some heavenly or otherworldly indication when it was time for me to act.

My eyes were getting achy. Finally. It was time for me to sleep. It figured. I should stay awake and keep Mom company to make sure she was awake and didn't drive us into a corn field like she did when her tooth was abscessed and I had insisted I had to meet Dina and the gang at the movies. What a trip that was. I hadn't even known anyone farmed corn in the city of Cocoa Beach, Florida. I hope nobody ever prescribed her happy pills again.

I was so sleepy. I blinked and blinked and blinked and then just closed my eyes a moment and rested my head back on the cold window. I pressed the button and reclined the seat. Snuggling in good, I was off to sweet dreams of Johnny Depp chewing on a pencil while running from an alligator.

* * *

I woke up to see the bus had stopped in a corn field.

"Mom. Wake up, Mom."

She was seated next to me. "Shh…baby dumpling. Get some sleep now. It's too early to watch cartoons, they aren't on yet."

I looked around and everyone seemed to be sleeping peacefully. Boy could this gang snore. Wait a minute, how can everyone sleep through everything? Something hinky was going on. I got that shiver of a premonition. The women's intuition thingy.

I was so sleepy yet adrenaline surged. Either we've all been drugged or else…it's carbon monoxide poisoning. I climbed over Mom, yanked the handle to open the door and stumbled down the stairs into the corn field. I got my footing and picked my way around to the rear of the bus. I found the tailpipe. With a green tennis ball shoved into it! Oh my god!

I pried it out and dropped it on the ground, climbed back on board the bus, switched the motor off and screamed.

"Wake up! Everybody wake up! Get off the bus!"

Nobody moved. Other than Tabloid Tilly, scratching her neck with her eyes closed. I opened windows and then ran back to Mom and dug her cell phone out of the heart shaped pocket on her fuchsia charmeuse jacket.

I had no idea where we were. I looked around and could not find a mile marker sign. I punched in 9-1-1.

It rang and rang and rang. How could no one be picking up for 9-1-1? What the heck is the highway patrol number? Pound seventy seven? I tried that. It was busy. I hadn't heard a busy signal in years. Everyone had call waiting or went to message now.

I grabbed my mother under the arms and dragged her off the

bus. I dumped her in between rows of corn. I checked her pulse. Good, she had one and she was breathing.

I ran back on the bus and yanked Tabloid Tilly off, too. I deposited her near mom. She too was breathing.

I leapt back onto the bus, dizzy. I felt everyone's carotid artery and breathed a sigh of relief. I dragged Rosemary off next then tried 9-1-1 again on the cell phone. Nothing.

I punched in the speed dial for Andy.

After the fourth ring, he picked up.

"Morning, Mom."

"It's Sandra. We're parked in a corn field. Everyone has carbon monoxide poisoning. I can't get through to 9-1-1. I don't know where we are but we were pacing the train. Help, Andy, you have to help us. Everyone is unconscious but me and I feel woozy. Track me on GPS or something. You've got to save us, Andy!"

I lost the signal. The call dropped. Crap!

* * *

I managed to get everyone off the bus except my friend *Hack 'em Up Hazel*. She was so heavy. I just couldn't get her down the stairs. I did get her upside down with her head out in the fresh air before my world went dark.

* * *

I woke up in the arms of a really handsome firefighter. He was carrying me somewhere. Not the firefighter's carry that Lieutenant Hottie did. The honeymoon carry. He plopped me down on the cold straw floor of what seemed to be a barn. I turned my head to the left and saw my chapter mates and Mom over on the other side. They were being fussed over by a motley crew of country folk. It seemed like they were getting some makeshift medical attention. I saw I.V.s and stethoscopes and syringes.

The hunky country firefighter placed an oxygen mask over my face and told me to breathe quietly.

Breathe quietly? Sounds like something Mom would fuss at me about, how my breathing was disruptive and inappropriate.

I laid back and breathed, wishing I had a nice warm bed and lots of covers.

A very portly gentleman in a very large and bursting at the seams turquoise suit coat with a shiny gold star on the lapel towered over me. "What is your name?"

123

"Dixie London." I grinned. *I am Dixie London the New York Times Bestselling Author. Or I will be as soon as I finish writing a book.*

Why did you shove a tennis ball up the tailpipe of that thar rental bus, Miss London?"

"What? I did no such thing. I…"

"Your fingerprints are on the murder weapon."

I yanked the oxygen mask off and sprung up. "Murder weapon? What are you talking about, *Bubba Boy*?" Oh, shoot, did I really call this small town sheriff *Bubba Boy*?"

"You will address me as Sheriff Oliveri or not at all. Do you understand me?"

"Sorry, sir—"

"I said, you will address me as—"

"Sorry, Sheriff Oliver—"

"Sheriff Oliveri!"

"Sheriff Oliveri." I felt like I needed to throw up. "What do you mean murder weapon? Who died and by what method?"

"You are under arrest for the suspicion of murder by tennis ball of one Chico de Playa Encherito. You have the right to remain silent—"

"Murder by tennis ball? I awoke to find everyone on the bus passed out cold. I investigated and found the tennis ball stuffed up the tailpipe. I yanked it out. That's how my fingerprints got on it. And how did you fingerprint the ball and my fingers so quick?" I looked at my French manicure with the little butterflies airbrushed on. No ink stains. He had not fingerprinted me…

"You have the right to an attorney—"

"But I didn't kill anybody. I saved them." Oh, poor Chico. Rosemary must be doubly devastated. I stood up and staggered toward the others. Sheriff Oliveri took hold of my arm and yanked me back.

"I'm adding fleeing from arrest to the charges." He cuffed me.

I remembered Lieutenant Hottie's handcuffs, upside down. Where was Lieutenant Hottie now? Washing dishes on the *GOOS Express*. Shoot. Where was Andy? Where was Dad? I wanted my Daddy really bad.

* * *

The Sheriff shoved my head down as I clumsily climbed into the

124

back seat of his brown Crown Victoria with a big gold star on the hood. The door read "Nester County Sheriff's Department."

He slammed the door and took a seat up front. As he drawled into the microphone it occurred to me that despite being the daughter and sister and niece and granddaughter of cops I had never been inside a police car before. I'd never handled a gun either.

He turned the siren on and we zoomed over those back roads lickety split.

It seemed like a really long ride, but since Tinker Bell was lost in Neverland, I really had no exact knowledge of how long we took. Sheriff Oliveri talked into his ear phone mumbling something about smothered pork chops and bass fishing.

I hoped Mom would be all right. She'd been through so much health wise in the past couple days. But she was young and otherwise healthy. Perhaps this might spur her to do a few more pushups from the table.

Murder by tennis ball. Well, this one certainly has a different M.O. than the others. A possible drowning with chlorine bleach involved but a happy corpse. A suicide by hanging. A death by sleep. Natural causes. Now death by tennis ball.

Hmm…could they all be related if *Mini Mary Agnes* and *Napping Norah* didn't die of natural or self-inflicted causes? Did anyone smell bleach on them? I didn't remember it, but then again the air on the train was heavy with rose fragrance. Shoot. I should have sniffed the bodies. Eww…

I looked out the window at the bucolic scene of cows in the meadow.

We arrived at the Nester County Court House. Sheriff Oliveri screeched to a stop in front of the flag pole, hollered over the seat, "Keep still," and slammed the door as he squeezed his portly frame out.

I watched him hike up his britches, check his boys and mosey on in through the front door.

For a county courthouse, there wasn't any activity. Only one other vehicle in sight, a small foreign pickup truck light blue and dirty.

I turned my head as I heard a jalopy of an old farm flatbed truck circa 1950 something. A man jumped off the back and the vehicle sped away. The man ducked down low and crab walked behind the cruiser.

Very suspicious indeed. My womanly radar was on overdrive. Or was it my arms going numb from being strangled behind my back for so long?

The rear car door inched open but nobody was there.

My heart pounded in my throat. Great. I'm being abducted by aliens.

"Greetings, marionette of mystery. Your loveliness exceeds the sparkle of the universe," said Alfredo Dente.

The door squeaked and we both flinched. He looked around, grabbed my arm and yanked me out of the car.

We landed in a heap on the broken asphalt of the parking lot. I was straddling his chest.

"We've got to stop meeting like this. What in the fettuccini are you doing?"

"I am whisking the wrongfully accused lovely away to her happily ever after."

"How?"

"Get off of me."

I managed to raise my knee high enough for Al Dente to roll out and spring to his knees. He took me by the arm and we ran on our knees around the back of the squad car. He helped me to my feet and we dashed behind the courthouse of all places. We kept going until we were in the cover of some scrub pines. Alongside the road we ran. Husband and wife. Suddenly he pulled my arm and stopped me. He removed a vibrating cellular phone from his pocket and answered.

"It is I, Alfredo Dente, Minstrel of— In the trees to the west...affirmative." He closed the phone. He shoved me out of the trees. I tried to back up into him as a red limousine screeched to a stop. The door opened and Al Dente shoved me inside.

Chapter Fifteen

I rolled onto the floor of the limo which was carpeted with crumbs. Cookies.

"Oh, Sandy. Stop! You're crushing all my cookies to smithereens!" said Dina.

I couldn't get up because the vehicle was zooming too fast. Must have been way over the speed limit for this winding country road. I finally stopped writhing and gave up, settling in on my side with my face near her unpedicured jagged toenails. Gross. At least they didn't smell too bad.

I rolled over to the other side and saw Al's nose. My, wasn't it a magnificent honker. Huge. I pulled back a bit.

"Well, I can't very well lie face down and I can't lie on my back because of the handcuffs. Anybody got a key?"

Nobody came forward.

"Why are you here, Dina, and what the heck is going on?"

The driver slammed on the breaks, skidded into a ditch and just as quickly recovered and resumed driving in the other direction. "Please tell me my mother isn't driving,"

Nobody was talking but me. I just wanted to know what the heck was going on. "Are we being chased by any chance?" I asked.

"Lovely marionette of mystery, we are making a hasty retreat from your false imprisonment."

"Thanks for busting me out of the squad car. How did you know I was in there?"

"That is quite an elementary explanation, dear lovely one. We had been following the bus since it left the train station."

"Why didn't you help me drag everyone off the bus then? I didn't see the red limo anywhere. I was in the back of the bus yanking the tennis ball murder weapon out of the tailpipe. Who put it there?"

"A nefarious naughty no-gooder, whom I have yet to unmask."

He tossed a tennis ball at me. It hit me in the nose.

"Hey," I whined.

"Sorry, lovely lady of lusciousness. My aim is off in all things athletic. Rest assured herein lies the alleged evidence without which the local yokel sheriff of Nottingham cannot press charges against your high above the fray-ness."

"You stole evidence?" Dina asked.

"Cool," I said. "I'm not the one who tried to kill everyone on the bus. Who did?"

"We shall deduce that momentarily," answered Al Dente.

Dina yanked the bag of cookies out from under my butt. "Thanks," I said.

"Well, they're not all broken." She dropped an inch of a frosted lemon cookie in my mouth. I chewed and kept rolling it around on my tongue until it was just paste and I finally had to swallow. "Dina, I'm very sorry about your aunt...and what are you doing back so soon?"

"She wanted to be cremated. No service. My mom will go through her things some other time."

"What was the cause of her passing? I asked.

"A raging staph infection which she chose to ignore hoping it would go away. She died alone. Then there was a fire, but the sprinklers put it out."

"A fire? Where was her friend who was taking care of her?"

"She drove him crazy and he went to a Harley rally," explained Dina.

"Well, then who found her?" I asked.

"The firefighters. Marvin had left a pot of chili on the stove. The smoke detector blared and the sprinkler system popped on and sounded the alarm and anyhow they showed up and found her," said Dina.

"What a sad way to die. Alone and helpless. She must have suffered," I said.

"Probably not. The police found a gallon of vodka with a long bendy straw next to the bed."

"Step-mother dearest did enjoy her Russian sustenance," said Al Dente.

Al Dente was eating what appeared to be a peanut butter cookie he pulled from under his armpit.

"Are my mom and all the people on the bus all right?" I asked.

"I don't know what is going on with them. It seemed like they were at a makeshift morgue/triage hospital in that barn," said Dina.

"Don't call it a morgue. My mom and all of my other friends

were in there. Well except for Igor and Eagle but I'm not that chummy with them. I really do miss my mundane job back on the beach. There is just too much excitement since I left on this writing retreat."

"I just love every little twist and turn," enthused Dina.

"Where are we headed? Do you have a safe house lined up?" I looked hopefully between Dina, who was now devouring a ham sandwich, and Al Dente, who had climbed into a seat and strapped in.

"We are returning to the train of travesty, my dear marionette of mystery."

"Why?"

"To get your brother or Lieutenant Hernandez to remove your handcuffs," said Dina.

"Why them?"

"Because they will do it. They'll ask plenty of questions but ultimately they'll turn the key," said Dina.

"Good point. I'll tell them the truth on a need to know basis, of course. Maybe between the five of us we can make sense and stop the murders," I said.

"Undoubtedly and you, our fair maiden, Sandra Faire Dente, will ferret out the dirty dog and the world will live in peace forever and ever more."

"We just have to stay focused," enthused Dina. "Keep chanting who, what, where, when and how."

"Who is driving this car?" I asked.

"It is the beach patrolman known as Eagle. He works part-time for my Uncle Santy Claus. This is his vehicle."

"He's an odd one, that Eagle," said Dina. "All he does is frown and grunt. I couldn't make any time with him at all."

"He's married," I said.

"Oh. Never mind."

"The bird known as Eagle is married to my cousin, Judy. Uncle Santy Claus's only child," said Al Dente.

I envisioned a female version of Al's nose. Hopefully he got that from his mother's side of the family...well, yeah. Because both Al and Santy Claus have the same last name, Dente. His father in prison must be Santy Claus's brother.

Boy would I love to see my brother sooner than later. I hoped

Andy brought his handcuff keys along for the train excursion. Well, at least I know Lieutenant Hottie has his. I guess. He has the cuffs. "Is Lieutenant Hernandez still on the train?" I asked.

"I dunno," said Dina.

I was worried about Mom and the others. "Can I use your phone, Al Dente?"

"Certainly. I shall hold it to your lovely ear. To whom should I place the call?"

"Mom. Her cell phone number is— Oh nuts. I have her cell phone. Well I did. I don't know what might still be in my pocket.

"I really want to use my hands again!"

* * *

I drifted off to sleep. This time Johnny Depp was making me walk the plank of a pirate ship. He was wielding a sharp pencil and licking the tip.

I hurried as fast as I could down the plank but I was dragging a ball and chain around my ankle and inched along slowly.

I woke up to hear Al Dente softly singing. I just loved his tenor singing voice. He was singing Pirates of Pinzance. Well, that explained my dream but what was my ball and chain? What was holding me back?

Well, my marriage to Al Dente was holding me back from pursuing a meaningful relationship with Lieutenant Hottie. My inability to finish what I start was holding me back from being a published author. I just have so many great ideas swirling around in my head. And these darned handcuffs were holding me back from everything I wanted to do. Literally.

The car stopped abruptly. Eagle flung open the door. "Out!"

Al Dente stepped out and then helped me. Dina tripped on her skirt but Eagle caught her. I was worried she'd swoon. Thank goodness she heard the train whistle toot twice. We made a run for it.

It better not take off because I couldn't jump on with my hands bound behind my back. Eagle scooped me up and lit out running. Al Dente jumped on the back at the observation car. Eagle stuffed me up over the rail and I fell into a heap on Al Dente. Dina flew through the air and landed on top.

The rear door flung open.

"Oh. I should have known," said Lieutenant Hottie. He helped

Dina up.

"Thanks, officer." She adjusted her clothes.

He pulled me up next and into the train. "Who handcuffed you?" he demanded.

"Long story but could you please unlock me?" I asked.

He grabbed Al Dente by the collar and asked, "What do you think you're doing back on this train?"

"I am assisting my lovely wife, to solve a most unfortunate series of misadventures in the mist."

Lieutenant Hottie threw Al to the floor and shoved a knee in the small of his back. "Shut the Hell up! Don't you ever say that again!"

"Lieutenant, the handcuff key? Please unlock me."

Hottie pulled the keys from the lanyard inside his pocket. I squatted and he unlocked me. He then cuffed Al, yanked him to his feet then threw him in a chair.

"Thank you!" I rubbed my wrists and longed for Tinker Bell.

"Who is going to explain what's going on?" asked Lieutenant Hottie, face red, eyes bulging.

"I, Alfredo Dente, would be more than ecstatic to go over the details of our misadventure. Firstly—"

Hottie pulled Al out of the chair by his collar. "You shut the fuck up. No more talking gibberish!" He dropped him back down then looked at me and Dina.

There wasn't a thing I could think of to say that wouldn't get me arrested. Dina smiled and walked out of the car.

As the explicatives flew, I cringed and headed for my room. I was relieved Al was finally back in custody. He needed to stand trial. As his wife, I wouldn't have to testify against him. Afterwards, our marriage could finally be annulled. And I could get on with my life.

I didn't even turn the light on. I dove for a bunk and slipped under the covers. I didn't even care about the itchy synthetic blanket. I just wanted to sleep in peace. Looking out the window, I could see we must have been on a bridge because there was a car bridge directly across from us. I looked at the headlights and taillights whizzing by. I hated the bright blue-white halogen headlights standard on some of the cars. They always distracted me when I drove after dark. I liked driving at night with all the windows rolled down. Dina and I would crank up the radio and cruise around at a low rate of speed, hopped up on sweet tea from McDonald's every

Friday and Saturday night. Boy did I miss the simple things. How did my life get so crazy?

I yearned for a nice boring docile existence. But since this recent hullaballoo happened in Missouri, I decided the Midwest wasn't my dream location anymore.

How about California? I had never seen the Pacific Ocean. Hopefully I will if we ever arrive at our destination.

Poor Chico. He had been Rosemary's pool boy, hairdresser and paid companion for as long as I had known her. A quiet fellow except for his humming and singing. He was pleasant to have around. Really great at getting clothes clean, crisp and wrinkle free too. Could he have had something to do with David Starr? I'll never forget that pungent aroma of chlorine bleach pierced with death and fishy ocean when I discovered the sailor's body.

Was Chico ever in the Navy? Was the Navy conducting an investigation? Was David Starr really enlisted or had he ever been?

Big Marc was a retired sailor. Every ship he was assigned to sunk. He liked working in Australia. Was there an Australian connection to David Starr? If so, was Tabloid Tilly involved? Was there even a Clinger – Starr connection? How did secret submarine refueling in Brazil play into all of this? Could Chico have been Brazilian? I love Brazil nuts. They are pretty easy to crack but then I had to dig out the meat with a pick. Is there a nut from Brazil behind the death or deaths? Can I crack this case and pick out the clues?

Maybe I should go down to the crew quarters later and visit Lieutenant Hottie. I could tell him about the bus sabotage. Or I could tell him other things with body language. Lips in particular. Damn. He was the world's best kisser. Not that I've had all that much experience but ooh la la. He's electrifying. If I were ever stranded on an arctic desert island and could only bring three things with me, I'd bring Hottie, macaroni and cheese and some sort of keyboard or note pad that we could write books on and live happily ever after in our ice palace. Well, yeah, the igloo would have to be prebuilt. And some nice native servants would be good to have around. You know, to chop the firewood, melt ice for water and to take care of any plumbing emergencies because I demand hot and cold running water and a proper bathroom. Oh, would it be nice to linger in a bubble filled bathtub with Lieutenant Hottie by candle light. Not too many bubbles though. Just enough to mask my figure flaws. His broad shoulders and chest and abs and etc. must just have suds slipping around them erotically. I threw off the covers. It seemed to have warmed up for some reason.

I wished I had my summer pajamas to change into. Little cotton knit shorts, chambray blue with dobby polka dots. The top has soft white crocheted work around the neck, collar and hem.

Boy, I hoped Mom was all right. I can't believe she drove the rental bus for Rosemary! I thought they usually came with drivers unless you were the A Team. That was Andy's favorite 80's TV show on DVD. On Sunday afternoons we all gathered at Mom and Dad's house for lunch and a DVD.

Well, I'm not sleeping again tonight. I rolled onto my side and looked out the window. Nothing whirring by. Only blackness...

* * *

I freshened up as well I could without a toothbrush or change of clothes. The train seemed to have picked up speed and it was hard keeping my footing as I navigated down the hallway back into the parlor car. I crossed the vestibule and fumbled for a light switch. Darn it. There was no coffee or tea or cookies or fruit on the credenza.

I switched the light back off and retraced my steps. All of the rooms in the sleeper were quiet. I guessed they were empty except for Dina.

When I reached the other end of the car I saw the light on in the business car. Good. Maybe there were some refreshments in there. I kicked the toe release and opened both doors. Stepping inside, I saw Lieutenant Hottie seated at the conference table typing away on his laptop. No, wait. He wasn't Lieutenant Hottie at the moment. He was bestselling author Tony O'Rourke. I always envisioned him as an Irish recluse. Well, I still can. Hmm....if he's an Irish recluse holed up in his dank castle basement typing away on deadline, I could be his chamber wench. I slipped over to the sideboard and prepared a cup of coffee for him. It occurred to me that we'd never had coffee together. All we'd done was kiss and grope. Never a proper date.

I pondered things for a moment and sized him up. Sandra, focus. Not that size. What kind of coffee drinker would he be? Definitely not decaf. Cream maybe but no sugar. I'd go ahead and try. I carefully spilled cream all over the sideboard as the train rocked and rolled. I looked over my shoulder. Good. He hadn't noticed. I grabbed a napkin to wipe it up with and patted down the sideboard front all the way to the floor. On my hands and knees. I saw something glinting underneath. I lowered my head and raised my rear end to investigate.

I felt him sidling up to me and his hot breath on my neck. He ran his hand down my arm and I tingled from my nose down to my toes. I grabbed the object and pulled out salad tongs.

The next thing I knew, I was flat on my back and his tongue was taking my palate to Neverland. He softly moved his body against mine with the sway of the train.

I heard the doors open from the other end of the car.

"Sandra Marie Faire, what are you doing up so late and where on earth have you been? I've been worried sick about you. You could at least have contacted me to let me know you were all right."

Chapter Sixteen

Needless to say, the making out stopped and we both stood up and tried to act casual like it was the most natural thing in the world. Well, it was. If only I weren't married to another man. Mom didn't seem to react to my dalliance. She was just mad at me for disappearing. Well, it was high time we compared notes.

I pulled out a chair and gestured to her. "Come here, Mom. Sit." She did.

"William, you sit, too. Please," I said. *Good. I didn't call him Lieutenant Hottie.*

He sat next to her and I scurried around the table and parked myself across from them.

The train was really racing down the tracks. Chairs rolled to and fro piling up at the west end of the car.

William wrapped his leg around the wooden table leg. I threw my hands up in the air and enjoyed the ride. Mom did too. We giggled.

When the train slowed a bit, I said, "First of all, how are you feeling?" I looked at Mom.

"Fine. Why shouldn't I feel fine?"

"You were rendered unconscious from carbon monoxide poisoning," I countered.

"Oh, that. Forgotten."

"But how is everyone else doing?" I asked.

"*Carbon monoxide poisoning?*" asked Lieutenant Hottie.

"Somebody stuffed a tennis ball in the exhaust pipe of the bus. Everybody on it but me passed out. Rosemary's personal assistant, Chico, succumbed to it…"

His dark brown eyes narrowed as he rubbed his stubbled chin. "Did they get the suspect?"

"Umm…well…" I stuttered.

"Umm well what, Sandra?" Mom asked.

"They thought it was me, but I didn't do it! I mean I would never do such a thing and I don't have a grudge against anyone on the whole planet and besides I don't play tennis or own a dog, therefore I don't have any tennis balls."

"There must have been some basis for the local authorities...who are they?" he asked.

"Nester County Missouri Sheriff's Department. *Sheriff Bubba Boy Oliveri.*"

"Bubba Boy?" Mom asked.

"He didn't like me calling him that." I cleared my throat.

"Sandra Marie Faire, you know you shouldn't give everyone inappropriate nicknames. Yes, they are entertaining sometimes but when you slip up and..." Mom began her lecture. I smiled. This meant she was back to normal.

"In what manner do you feel you were a suspect?" Lieutenant Hottie unwrapped his leg from the table and reseated himself in the chair.

"The cop said they had my fingerprints on the tennis ball. Of course they did. I pulled it out and saved everyone," I said.

"Bravo for my courageous baby dumpling." Mom beamed.

I slumped down in my chair. Why did she have to call me that in front of everybody? Sheesh. I was so embarrassed. Well, it hadn't been the first time she'd called me that in front of Hottie so I inhaled and tried to focus.

"I came-to in the arms of a firefighter. He put me on oxygen. The sheriff told me my fingerprints matched the ones on the murder weapon. Murder by tennis ball. Hey, I should use that as a book title!"

"You can't lift fingerprints from the fuzzy surface of a tennis ball. Unless they have some very advanced CSI team. Highly unlikely. Which hospital did the firefighter take you to?" asked Lieutenant Hottie.

"No hospital. A big barn set up somewhere in the country. They laid everyone out there," I said.

"It was completely unsanitary. I'll be surprised if some of the victims don't come down with mad cow disease or the bird flu or swine flu. And I'm trying not to think about what insects and parasites might have latched onto us, sucking the..." Mom shuddered and rubbed her arms. She stood up and brushed herself off from head to toe.

"Maybe you should take a shower and change your clothes," I said.

"I already did." She sat back down. She was dressed in washed red denim crop pants, a red polka dotted tee shirt, a white soutach three quarter length sleeved big shirt open on top of it and white tennis shoes.

Lieutenant Hottie pushed back from the table and rolled across the train. When his chair stopped midway down the car, he stood and turned to us. "If the sheriff suspected you of the murder how are you released so quickly? What, did you hire a guy from lawyer-in-a-box to get you released?"

"Well, not exactly. I had a friend in a limo."

"Come again?" He stared into my eyes.

I stared back. He had the cutest little crow's feet hinting around his big brown eyes.

"Who got you released? Are you out on bail?"

"Technically I'm a hypothetical escaped prisoner...but not really—"

Mom gasped. "Sandra Marie Faire. Your daddy taught you better than that. You should have cooperated with the authorities, called him and he'd get you a lawyer and have this matter cleared up. Why, I'll bet he has a couple of friends working in the department."

I sincerely doubted Daddy had friends the likes of *Sherriff Bubba Boy Oliveri* but then there is no accounting for taste. Maybe he had some political pull at the state level.

"Who is your friend with the limo?" Lieutenant Hottie asked.

I cleared my throat. "Al Dente."

Mom's eyes looked like ping pong balls, bouncing between the lieutenant and me and back again. She took me by the arm and shoved me to the rear of the car. I struggled with her but as the lieutenant's expletives escalated I turned and ran back to my room. Mom followed.

I walked into my compartment and stood at the window. I heard her slide the door closed behind us. I scrunched up my face, closed my eyes and braced myself for the worst lecture of my life.

"Well, Sandra. He's come back. So now what are you going to do? It's time to choose."

"Choose what?" I asked.

"Are you going to grow up and become a wife or are you going to stay in denial?"

"Huh?"

"Beverly Dente told me all about you and Al at the beauty parlor. To say I was shocked is not accurate. It did not surprise me one bit. I just was hurt that you did not even bother to tell your family you were married…"

Mom continued her rant. It all poured out about how this was the most inappropriate thing I had ever done and now was the time to make things right and how I needed to read some of Dina's steamy romance books to get some ideas for the bedroom. At this point my ears shut down. I did not, would not discuss sex with my mother. After all, I was hatched on a big hot rock in the dessert. Parents didn't make love. Parents were above all of that.

I plopped down in the chair. She paced the car, gesturing like an Italian symphony conductor.

So my dirty little secret which I had guarded so dearly for over five years was no secret at all. The whole town knew, especially the people I wanted to hide it from the most. Mom and Lieutenant Hottie.

Hey, Lieutenant Hottie was enraged to see Al Dente. Was he jealous? That had to be personal. It just couldn't have been because he's a fugitive. After all, he'd told me Al was just the scape goat, more or less. Money laundering wasn't that big of a deal. Laundering…laundry. Chico…bleach. Millions in my joint checking account.

"Mom…Mom…Mom!" I interrupted and she finally stopped talking. She had a bizarre look in her eyes and turned to the sink. She splashed water on her face. She pressed a towel to it, dabbing it dry.

"Mom, who gave you that package?"

"What package?"

"The brown paper package tied up with string. You know, at the car junkyard."

"Oh, that." She picked some sleep out of her eye. "That hotshot young beach patrolman. The one they call the Eagle. He's an odd one. Never says boo… Why?"

I might as well bounce things off of her. There was no sense in keeping anything from her. She would just find out at the beauty parlor, anyhow.

"Eagle was the getaway driver," I whispered.

"What? What did you say?"

"Eagle drove the red limo that Dina and Al were in. They

138

followed the bus and then followed the sheriff's car and Al yanked me out and stuffed me in the limo and brought me back to the train."

"Sandra, you are a fugitive. You need to turn yourself in." She sifted through her pockets. "I can't find my phone."

I had taken her phone and used it to try to call for help in the corn field but my calls didn't get through. I wondered why nobody was manning the 9-1-1 and the state police phones. I searched through my pockets and I didn't have it either. I must've lost it in the field.

"I am not a fugitive. I am not guilty," I reiterated. I was glad she didn't have a phone because she would have called Dad for sure and we certainly didn't need her bringing the Cocoa Beach Florida Police Commissioner in on a crime in Missouri. Besides, we were probably in Kansas or Iowa or somewhere by now anyhow.

"Was Eagle on the train before?" I asked.

"Yes."

"When? The whole way? Did he board in Cocoa Beach?"

"I'm not sure...I only remember seeing him tending bar in the evangelists' lounge

"Say, what was in the package anyhow? Who sent you a gift? One of your admirers? *Was it your husband or your lover?*"

"I don't have a husband. Not really. Just technically. It was a marriage of convenience and we'll annul it after Al's trial."

"Al's trial? What kind of trouble is that sweet boy in?"

"Money laundering...allegedly...technically...for the family."

"What? So Lieutenant Hernandez sent you a gift then. *Your lover.*"

"He is not my lover. Well, yes we have feelings but, oh, never mind, it's too confusing and doesn't matter anyhow."

"It doesn't matter anyhow? Sandra Marie Faire. The love of a good man is the most important thing in the world. Without that, a woman is only half of her potential. You have no idea how a man can complete you."

Here we go again. Mom launched another lecture.

I tuned her out and got back to sleuthing. Eagle or someone he was working for sent me the empty bottle of bleach. Why? Two possible reasons: Either they want to scare me because I'm the next target or else they want me to uncover the crime. Hmm...

So far there are four—no, five—deaths in which I'm connected.

I discovered the bodies of David Starr, Mini Mary Agnes Starr and Napping Norah. I was arrested for Chico's death. My best bud in the whole world's Aunt Beverly also died suspiciously if you ask me. Though I did not discover her. But perhaps the murderer or the person who knows who the murderer is—wanted to get Dina off the train and away from me. If so, why?

What else do all of these deaths have in common? The first one was homicide but I need to ask Lieutenant Hottie what the method of murder was. Drowning? Asphyxiation by mixing chlorine bleach with ammonia? *Something else?*

Mini Mary Agnes died of strangulation…*or did she?*

Napping Norah died in her sleep. Of a stroke. Was it a natural death or *did someone do something to cause it?*

Chico died from carbon monoxide poisoning. Death by tennis ball. Allegedly.

Aunt Beverly died of a staph infection after routine surgery. Did the staph infection really do her in *or did someone do something else to hasten her demise?*

What did these four people have in common? Mary Agnes and Norah were part of Eugene Donaldson's congregation. Was David? How about Beverly? I could ask Mom about Beverly. No, wait. I'll ask Rosemary…But where is Rosemary? Surely she didn't get back on the train. I know! I can go right to the horse's mouth and ask Reverend Donaldson.

I waited until Mom wound down and took a breath and I blurted, "Mom, you're absolutely right." Not that I had any real idea what advice she'd just given me but it seemed like the polite daughterly thing to say, plus I needed to end this lecture and get to Reverend Donaldson lickety split. "I need to go and speak to Reverend Donaldson right away…"

"That's a wonderful idea, baby dumpling. Christian counseling will do you a world of good."

Yeah, whatever. I split.

* * *

I took a deep breath before I opened the vestibule doors and entered the business car. I dreaded the fallout from the collision between Lieutenant Hottie and Al Dente. I hoped Dina hadn't taken the brunt of the collateral damage.

The car was devoid of voices, the air circulating system and the clickety-clack of the train were surreally ominous.

I peeked around the corner and saw Dina seated at the table noshing pickles. I didn't see anyone else so I walked on in. Oops. Poor handcuffed Al Dente was seated in a chair in the corner with his nose to the wall. Like the old jokes about school teachers drawing a circle on the blackboard and then making the naughty student stand with his or her nose pressed in it.

Lieutenant Hottie hovered over him.

"What happened?" I asked.

"The strong armed lawman strong armed me into the corner and threatened to turn the minstrel of melody into a mythic eunuch if I did not remain in this seat until the proper authorities arrive and ferret me away," lamented Al.

"Speak again and I'll duct tape your weasley lips to your Dumbo ears."

I tried to catch Lieutenant Hottie's eye but he refused to look at me. I shook my head, shrugged my shoulders and sat with Dina.

"Lieutenant Hernandez won't let him sneak away again," said Dina. She slipped a pickle between her lips and gestured toward the jar. "Want one? They're bread and butter. Sweet. Yummy."

"Thanks." I plucked out three thick slices and chewed them one at a time.

I sat on the table and stared out the window. We were whizzing through some town. Medium sized.

Dina chewed like a goat. Whenever she was really nervous she ate nonstop. "Dina, what's wrong? What have you gotten yourself into?"

"Nothing. Nothing at all. I'm fine." She grabbed the pickle jar as I screwed the lid on. We played tug of war with it until the train pitched hard to the right and we both lost our grips on it. The bottle flew off the table and rolled over to Al Dente. Lieutenant Hottie kicked it back down to us. I set it on the center of the table.

"I might be next," whispered Dina.

"Next to do what?" I asked.

"Die!"

I leaned down and hugged Dina hard. I rubbed her back and ran my fingers along her curls. "I'm scared for you to. And for Al Dente and my mother and brother and Rosemary and all the girls in the Global Order of Scribes. And for Reverend Donaldson, his followers, the train crew and, oh, my goodness for Lieutenant Ho— Hernandez as well."

Dina pushed away from the table and stood. "You know, touring the United States and Canada in a fifth wheel with my parents isn't such an unseemly option anymore. At least they are safe. Except for bears and rattlesnakes and scorpions," she said.

I cleared my throat. "Dina, how did you come to be in the red limousine?"

"Uncle Santy Claus sent it for me. He's such a sweet old man except for the mob business which everyone always seems to bring up. He's the sweet rich uncle everyone would be lucky to have." She smiled weakly.

"But is he really your uncle?" I asked, trying to figure out the blood and marriage connections, six degrees of whatever.

"Well, it's convoluted but the first time I met Uncle Santy Claus, he took me around with him at the flea market. He introduced me to some of the vendors and his friends as his beautiful niece," she said.

"That's really sweet. I think I'd like to meet your uncle someday. He has friends who are flea market vendors?" I asked.

"He purchases guns from them—on the side. He took me home to his trailer and showed me the closet where he kept a purple hatbox. It was full of guns. He taught me how to file the serial numbers off."

I giggled. "Oh, I wish I were in your family," I said.

"But you are, lovely marionette of mystery. You are the wife of Alfredo Dente, nephew by blood of the Godfather Santy Claus."

Lieutenant Hottie ranted as he yanked Al Dente out of the chair and dragged him through the vestibule into another car. I'd never heard some of the word choices Hottie was using but I was sure Al would not be talking any more on this train.

"Was Beverly Dente a member of Reverend Donaldson's congregation?" I asked. Surely Dina would know this.

"She didn't attend church very often but she always watched it on T.V. And the repeats. It's broadcast four times every weekend. The same episode," explained Dina.

"Did you ever attend any of the services?" I asked.

She shook her head.

"Did you know David Starr, the dead sailor I found on the

beach?"

Dina shrugged her shoulders.

Al Dente burst back into the car.

"What's going on?" I said.

"I made bail."

"But you were never processed, were you?" I asked.

"Uncle Santy Claus has some pull." Al softly sung *The Impossible Dream as he sat down and opened the pickles.*

I spun his chair so he faced me. He clutched the open pickle jar tight. The lid fell on the floor. I picked it up, took the pickle jar from him, no easy task as he was clutching it like candy. Not much juice slopped out. I replaced the lid and set it on the conference table. "Did you slip away from the lieutenant again?" I demanded.

"No. The imbecile made bail. Now keep him away from me before I become his judge, jury and executioner," shouted Lieutenant Hottie as he stomped in through the length of the car and out the other end.

"Al, was David Starr in the Navy with you?" I asked.

He sang louder.

"Al, were you or are you really in the Navy?"

He smiled and said, "Yes."

"Why did you enlist?"

"Uncle Santy Claus thought it would build me up. Make a stronger man out of the minstrel of melody."

"Come on. Tell me the real reason," I said.

He sang "Car Wash" and I couldn't get any further information out of him.

"The Impossible Dream" and "Car Wash." I'm sure those were clues he fed to me. I'd let my subconscious mull them over.

I was going to have to question Reverend Donaldson or Rosemary if she was aboard. "Do you know if Rosemary got back on the train? Have you seen her?" I asked.

Dina stood up and smoothed her red skirt. "She's my new roommate."

"Which compartment are you in?" I asked.

"D."

"Are the rest of the ladies back on the train?" I asked.

"I don't know. I think so. I heard Pat and Hazel talking up in the crusader car. Perhaps they are taking a little religion this time," she

143

said.

"Al, do you have a room on the train?" I asked.

"But of course. I will be sharing my beautiful wife's abode," he said.

"Mom is in with me."

"Well, that creates a cramp in our honeymoon. How deeply does the mother of the bride sleep?" he asked.

I shook my head incredulously. "I'll see you guys later. Dina, stop eating. You won't be able to fit into your skirts," I said.

I left the business car and nervously stepped through the vestibule into the first crusader sleeper. The curtains were drawn in the bedrooms. There was nobody at the end of the car in the little sitting area. I stopped at the credenza and made a cup of English breakfast tea and grabbed a handful of Ritz crackers. I plunked down in a leather arm chair by the window and looked out the opposite side. The tea was hot. I could only take little sips. But I had plunked in four sugar cubes so it was good and sweet. I should be looking for Rosemary, but I didn't really want to find her. I just wanted to arrive in California, swim in the mighty Pacific and finish writing my book. I was so tired of this state of mystery I was living in.

The door banged open and shut. *Big Marc* shuffled in dressed in his blue conductor's uniform. He walked to the credenza, bent down and looked over the food and beverages. He took a rag from his back pocket and wiped crumbs into his hand then shook them into the trash can. He rearranged the fruit and straightened the crackers.

How déjà vu-ish.

"Hello," I said.

He whirled around. "Who's there?"

"It's me, Sandra Faire. Andy's sister."

"What are you doing up so late making messes?"

I walked across the car and touched his arm. I looked through his Coke bottle thick cataract glasses and said, "How are you feeling? You gave me such a scare."

"What? I'm fit as a horse. Ready for combat. Just tell me my position, skipper."

"You're a conductor on a train now, Marc. You aren't in the Navy anymore."

"The troop trains will carry us to the port, ma'am. I'll be ready with my ditty bag when you sound the alarm."

Big Marc had transported himself back to the war. Which one? Korea? World War II?

"Seaman Clinger, do you know a sailor named David Starr?"

"Why of course. He's in the Negro division. Crackerjack with the machine gun. Makes a pretty fine stew, too."

Well, *Big Marc* certainly has gone crackerjacks. However, it's obvious he must know David Starr or know of him since he mentioned his race and the Navy...

My brother ran through the car with his railroad radio to his ear. He actually shoved me out of the way and I landed on the sofa.

I jumped up and lit off after him. Where was the fire?

I ran through all of the crusade cars trying to catch up with Andy. When I reached the one next to the engine, the North American Passenger Railway crew chief grabbed my shoulders and stopped me. "Get back. Get out of here!" she growled.

"Why? I'm Sandra Faire, my brother is a conductor. Andy Faire. He ran through here—"

"Get back to your seat right now or I'll put you off this train!" she ordered.

The roar in her voice was all I needed to coerce me to comply.

I turned around and took long fast steps through the train back to the conference car. *Big Marc*, Al Dente and Dina were playing cards.

I breathlessly said, "Something bad happened."

Dina tucked her cards in her cleavage and rolled her chair closer to me. "Who, what, where, when, and how? Do tell."

"My brother ran through the train with the railroad radio to his ear. He actually knocked me off my feet and I sailed across the car. I followed him up to the engine and the crew chief she-manhandled me and ordered me back to my seat lest she throw me from the train."

"Wow. That's spectacular. You should use it in your story. Here, let me get you some paper." She hopped up and trotted to the credenza and returned with a yellow legal pad and sharpened pencil.

"Write down everything you can remember and especially what you are feeling. And what did it smell like up there? And the temperature. What did you hear? Was she cute?"

Al Dente stood, straightened his fly and strode past us toward the head of the train.

145

"Where do you think you're going?" I asked.

"I, Alfredo Dente, husband of the lovely marionette of mystery, am off to slay the dragon who so wrongly accosted my wondrous wife," he said with stoic conviction and wild fear in his eyes.

"Sit down, Al. You won't get any further than I did," I said. "And the lieutenant warned you to stay right here."

"Gin," said *Big Marc*. He threw down his cards and stood, removing the earphone from his ear. He cursed as he yanked out the radio from his inside vest pocket. "This damn thing always tangles up on me. Shit on it all."

I grabbed Al's shirt collar and pulled him back.

"*Big Marc*, congratulations for winning the gin hand. Do you know what is wrong on the train?"

"I was the gin rummy champ back on the USS Wasp. We have been hijacked." *Big Marc* marched down the aisle to the men's room and stepped inside.

Chapter Seventeen

"Oh, boy! The cowboys will be sauntering through any minute. With their black hats and red bandanas covering their faces. They'll have shiny silver pistols and tell the passengers to give them all their jewels and money…" said Dina.

"It is my greatest hope your dream of being carried away by a cowboy on a white horse will someday come to fruition, country cousin of Alfredo Dente. However, let me conjecture that the hijacker is more likely of the pirate variety. Corporate pirate, that is," said Al Dente.

"Do you guys really think the train has been hijacked? I mean, do we take the word of…" I dropped my voice down to a whisper. "Of a man who's been having memory problems? He's living back in World War Two! Who would hijack a train full of crusaders? I mean we aren't carrying North American Passenger Railway passengers anymore or valuables or freight. It's just evangelists and writers and all the crap they brought with them. Nothing valuable. Well, I don't know. Rosemary and her friends might have some valuable jewelry. Gold is trading for over $1,500 an ounce. Some jewelry stores can't afford to stock it anymore."

"Treasure! Pat-the-Pirate has a trunk full of treasure," said Dina.

"Mom was the one with the trunk. Full of yarn and knitting needles…" I hesitated because I didn't remember telling anyone about the dog tags. "And dog tags. Al, why did you stuff your dog tags inside my skein of yarn?"

Jimmy Tamales waddled in breathlessly. "Go back to your rooms and stay there."

"What is the cause of such a stern commandment, historical railroad one?" asked Al Dente.

"Go back to your rooms. The train has been hijacked. Come on. Move it. Let's go," Jimmy Tamales reiterated.

Dina and I pushed the chairs out of our way and started hurrying back to the sleeper. *Big Marc* emerged from the bathroom.

"*Big Marc*, keep this car empty. Don't let the passengers through," said Jimmy Tamales.

"Ay Ay, Skipper." He removed a small antique looking revolver

147

from his ankle holster. "The Japs won't get through here alive."

Dina squealed in delight.

I turned to see Al Dente walking north toward the front of the train.

"Where are you going, Al?" I called out.

"With the men to defend the empire," he answered.

Jimmy Tamales shoved me and Sandra through the vestibule.

"Go to your compartment, latch the doors and close the curtains, both inner and outer. Do not open the door for anyone except a uniformed crew member. Do you understand?"

"Yes. Absolutely. Can you give me anymore information? Who hijacked the train? How many are there?"

"Just do as I told you to." He pulled my door closed and watched through the window as I locked it and pulled the drapes.

"What's going on?" asked Mom. She rolled over in the top bunk.

"Nothing. Something about the train being hijacked."

"Hijacked?"

"That's what they said." I sat in the chair on my knees, peeking outside through a small little slit between the drapes.

"Hijacking is unacceptable," said Mom. "I won't stand for it."

My mind was working overtime trying to figure out what the hijackers wanted.

Actually I wasn't scared, not for myself. I felt as if I were channeling Dina because this was like living on the edge. I was a character in one of my novels. The heroine of course. So that meant I was the one who had to thwart the terrorists. Or bandits. Or pirates. I wondered how *Pat-the-Pirate* was feeling after her carbon monoxide ordeal. Poor thing. It was a good thing her bird wasn't on board the bus but then again if he had been, he would have given us advanced warning there was a problem with the air quality. That's what the coal miners of yore used as an early warning system. They'd take a parakeet in to the mine and if the parakeet died they scrambled out-- quick. I wasn't sure what kind of poisonous gas the mines had.

Wait a minute. Where was *Peetie-the-Parrot*? Did he get left behind on the restored vintage train car when we all boarded this modern one? Surely Pat would have missed him and thrown a fit. I know they wouldn't have stowed him under the bus in the awful closed in luggage compartment, would they? So the most likely

148

scenario was that *Peetie-the-Parrot* was not aboard the bus and that was fine with Pat. Had she arranged for him to continue on the train? If so, why? Or did she deliberately leave him on the train because she was the murderess? Could she have stuffed the tennis ball in the tailpipe?

I tried to replay the bus boarding in my mind but it was a blur. I got on first and dibbed a middle seat. I know Pat was on the bus because I pulled her out in the corn field.

"I can't stand the suspense. I have to do something productive. I'm going to take a shower. You don't think we'll be stopping soon, do you?"

"With a hijacked train? I don't know. Go ahead. I'll come and get you if something exciting happens," I assured her.

Mom stepped into the bathroom. I walked over and peeked out the interior window. Nobody was out there. I tiptoed over and peeked through the exterior window. We were passing through a town. I wondered how far they let good old Alfredo Dente advance on the train. He could be useful as a hostage negotiator. Listening to Al Dente talk for a few minutes and anyone would surrender in exchange for a couple of Aspirins. I was one of the few—perhaps only person who found his choice of words adorable. It made him sound smart. I hoped to be smart someday.

I settled back in the chair and propped my feet up on the bunk.

I tapped my fingers on the armrests. What was that noise? The train clickety clacking along, the air system and the shower running were soothing. But I could pick out some sort of rhythm every so often. I stood up and realized somebody was knocking on the wall next to me. Oh, the door in-between compartments.

"Who's there?" I asked.

I heard knock-knock.

"Who's there?"

Again with the knock-knock.

"Knock-knock who's there already?"

More knocking.

I made sure the little hook chain was secured and then unlocked the door. I opened it a smidge and peeked through.

"Who's there?"

"Who's there?" asked the knocker.

"I asked first. Who's there?" I demanded, pushing the door

149

nearly closed.

"It's Hazel. Who is over there?" she asked.

I peeked through. Yep, it sure looked like her. I undid the chain and opened the door ready to pounce on the bad guy if he were hiding around the wall out of my site.

Hack 'em Up Hazel said, "Come here."

I did, on high alert. I peeked around the corner. Nobody was there. Her drapes were all drawn.

I whispered and gestured toward her bathroom.

"What?"

"Is the hijacker in your bathroom?" I asked.

"No. Why do you ask?"

"Just making conversation."

She opened the bathroom door to show me and then quickly closed the door between the rooms.

"We need to stop this train and capture the terrorist," said *Hack 'em Up Hazel.*

"Are they terrorists and are they plural?" I asked, my heart pumping. At last someone with information and she is willing to share.

"No. Just one lone terrorist. My man is high up in the investigation. He just texted me confirmation. There has been credible chatter."

I heard a ruckus in the hallway. *Hack 'em Up Hazel* peeked out the drapes. She wielded her black iron fireplace poker and ran out the door.

I followed her into the hall and tried to open my door but it was locked. Shoot. I ran back around into her room as I glimpsed *Contest Carly* and *Tabloid Tilly* poking their heads out of their compartments.

I opened the adjoining door into my room, pounded on the bathroom door and screamed, "Come on, Mom! Now!"

The bathroom door burst open and out popped my mother, wrapped in a white terry cloth towel that barely covered her. Lather ran from her hair down her arms.

"Let's roll!" I struggled to unlock the corridor door. We zipped down the hall in the direction *Hack 'em Up Hazel* had run. We followed *Weepy Wendy*, hot on her footsteps. So close, I was worried a bat or something might fly out of her hair. We crossed the

150

vestibule into the parlor car where I couldn't believe my eyes.

Rosemary Donaldson was holding a gun to my brother's throat.

Mom screamed and her towel fell to the floor. Reverend Donaldson, Al Dente and Lieutenant Hottie's jaws dropped as they ogled my mother. *Big Marc* let out a lascivious wolf whistle.

With one hand I ripped a panel of drapes from the window. With the other I pulled the emergency brake. Again.

Chapter Eighteen

With a hellacious squeal, the train abruptly halted. I kept my eye on Mom and dove for her, covering her with the gold silk.

Rosemary, Andy, Lieutenant Hottie and Reverend Donaldson were a big tangled heap rolling and grunting on the floor. Alfredo Dente wiggled his way from under the pile. He had a gun in his hand. I hoped it was Rosemary's.

Hack 'em Up Hazel made a beeline for the back door. She ran outside.

I waited for *Peetie-the-Parrot* to screech by but he was noticeably missing this time. Pretty much confirming my suspicions that he was no longer aboard the train or else he had been bird-napped.

Lieutenant Hottie handcuffed Rosemary. "No! Please don't do that," pleaded Eugene Donaldson. "Don't do that to my Rosemary. She is just upset about our boy, Joel. She didn't mean it."

Andy yanked his assailant to her feet.

Mom wrapped the drapes around herself and tucked the ends into her cleavage.

Andy shoved Rosemary in front of him, his arm gripping tight around her upper arm. As they disappeared down the corridor with Lieutenant Hottie, Mom called out, "Rosemary Donaldson. With God and these people as my witness, you will be punished for harming my baby boy. So help me God. Cross my heart and hope to die. May lightning strike you dead."

Eugene Donaldson was on his knees, trembling. I walked over to him and touched his shoulder. "Why did Rosemary have a gun on my brother?"

He didn't respond.

I caught Al's eye. "What happened?" I asked him.

He strode over to me. "Alas, I was called to duty to save my brother-in-law from the tawdry appareled holy one's wife."

"Why?"

"It is not for me to understand."

"Stay with the reverend." I took Al's hand and patted Eugene's head with it.

I peeked out the back window. *Hack 'em Up Hazel* was gone. No one in easy sight.

Eugene was weeping. I hated when men cried. I hated when anyone cried. I especially didn't like to cry.

"There, there, holy husband. Pray to the Holy Spirit to show you the light. He will guide you through this most unfortunate spin of events," Al Dente said.

I stared at the vestibule near the sleeper and looked up at the ceiling, down the walls and across the floor. I methodically swept the car looking for clues. This was surreal. What were the hijackers doing? I didn't know if *Hack 'em Up Hazel's* info was true about just one lone guy. There had to be more than one person. Where were they?

Mom walked by me. "I'm off to finish my shower," she announced, hiking up her drapes.

"Have fun with that," I answered.

"Adieu, mother-in-law dearest. May your beauty shine even brighter with the soap washed off," called out Al Dente.

Eugene blubbered louder.

"Where is *Weepy Wendy*?" *Shoot. I wished I hadn't called her that out loud. But it was only Al Dente, and the reverend was in his own world.*

"The nurse with the bat nest tresses seems to have sprinted through and vanished," said Al Dente.

"Is she the one Hazel chased?" I asked.

Eugene wailed. Al Dente looked at me and threw his hands up and cradled his head.

I walked over to them. "I'll go and check on Rosemary," I said. Just to finish my sweep before I left the parlor car, I walked around the back of the sofa. I looked behind the potted plants. A marble was tucked into the corner. I rushed over to the credenza and picked up a small drink napkin. I gingerly picked up the olive green Cat's eye marble with the napkin, wrapped it up and stuffed it in my pocket. This was one clue I vowed not to flush. I would take it directly to Lieutenant Hottie and my brother.

As I stepped through the vestibule the train tooted twice and chuffed forward. *Contest Carly* and *Pat-the-Pirate* were standing at their doors peeking at each other. They were chatting.

Carly opened her door further and stuck her hand out to stop me.

"Is it safe now? What happened? Why was Rosemary in handcuffs?"

"Umm…She wasn't feeling well," I brushed them off and continued past to my compartment. I stepped inside and heard the water running in the bathroom. I opened it a crack. "Mom, are you okay?"

"Just peachy, baby dumpling. I'll be out soon and you can have it. Don't forget to scrub behind your ears. I noticed a little dirt and old skin had built up behind your left ear yesterday. It's really noticeable when you wear a ponytail. You really should coordinate some jewelry more often. Don't leave home without earrings and lipstick at the very minimum," she said. As if she just hadn't witnessed her youngest son being held at gunpoint. And flashed a room full of men.

The train was picking up speed at a fast clip. I left my compartment and headed into the business car and then down the stairs. I could hear Lieutenant Hottie yelling at Rosemary. I didn't think this was the time to give him the evidence but then again, maybe it was important.

I peeked into the next room and watched Andy washing his face. I slid the door open and asked, "Are you all right?"

He dried his face with a white towel.

"Yeppers."

"Mom's finishing her shower," I said.

"So?"

"Oh never mind. I guess you didn't see."

"See what?" he asked.

Maybe we could just keep Mom's exhibition a secret. Well, except from everyone that was in the parlor car.

"I found a marble."

"You found a what?" he asked.

"A marble. In the corner of the parlor car behind the potted plants." I took it out of my pocket and carefully unwrapped it. The train pitched hard to my left and the marble flew out from my hand. It ran down the floor and into the door track and disappeared into the wall. "Oh, shoot!"

"It was only a marble, Sandra."

"But was it? It might have been an important clue."

"Clue to what?" he asked.

"I don't know. But *Mini Mary Agnes* said she spilled the

154

marbles out of her purse in the parking lot near a red limousine. Bad guys said, "We'll get Donaldson."

"When? How do you know?"

"Before she boarded the train. She told me when we met. She was really scared. Said there was a big muscle-headed guy. And he threatened her."

"Why didn't you or she come to me with this earlier?"

"I forgot."

"You forgot?"

"Well, so much happened so quickly. Dina wanted to tell you about the red limousine but I was really hungry."

"Dina?" he asked.

"Yes. She saw it, too."

"When and where?"

"Back in Orlando before we left. And it could possibly be the same red limo that was my getaway car. Driven by Eagle. But he's not what I'd describe as muscle headed, so he must have an accomplice or it was a totally different red limousine. Apparently he drives for Al's uncle." I grabbed onto the doorframe. The train was really rocking and rolling. "Hey, Andy? That hijacker business. Has it been neutralized yet?"

"No."

"Well, why you didn't guys swarm the engine when I pulled the emergency brake?"

"That was you? Again?"

"Yes," I said, confused. "So Rosemary was not the hijacker?"

"No."

"Why did she have a gun on you?"

"I don't know. I walked in on her yelling at her husband and the next thing I knew she had me in a headlock. It's embarrassing and I don't want to talk about it. All right?"

"Well, what are we doing about the hijacker or is it a terrorist?"

Lieutenant Hottie placed his hands on my waist and gently moved me out of the doorway and into the hall. I tingled at his touch.

"Faire, do you want to press charges?"

Andy shook his head. His cheeks were red.

"All right. She's in there balling her eyes out. I couldn't stand to stay any longer," said Lieutenant Hottie.

"I found a marble," I blurted.

Lieutenant Hottie gave me one of those *very nice for you* looks and said to Andy, "Go back upstairs and make sure the passengers are still secure in their compartments."

Hottie moved me aside again. For a brief moment in time, our eyes locked. I felt a rush from my toes to my nose.

He said, "Pardon me. I need to squeeze by."

"What are you doing about the hijacker?" I asked.

"Nothing," he said in that deep testosterone voice that never failed to move me.

"Nothing?" I asked, confused.

"The authorities know. We estimate the train will run out of fuel near Albuquerque. They are monitoring the defect detectors and will respond when it stops."

"Why didn't you do something when I stopped the train?"

"I was a little distracted between wrestling the gun from Mrs. Donaldson and then seeing your mother…"

"Why would seeing my mother preoccupy you?"

Lieutenant Hottie trotted up the stairs.

"Go back to your room. Come on," said Andy.

"Maybe I should talk to Rosemary," I said.

"Why?" Andy asked incredulously.

"Good point. I'm really mad at her for what she did to you. I guess you'd better not leave us alone."

I walked in front of Andy.

The train was speeding so fast that we kept getting knocked into the walls on both sides. He grabbed the microphone in the sleeper car. "Ladies, may I have your attention please? Return to your compartments, lock the doors, pull the drapes and shelter in place until a member of the crew or the police tell you it's safe to move about the train. Do not open your doors for any reason unless instructed to do so by a crew member or the police. If you have any emergency needs, press the call button in your room and wait for help. Again, return to your rooms immediately."

"What about Al Dente?" I asked.

"What about him?"

"Does he have a room?"

Al Dente walked down the hallway toward us. "Get in a room." My brother shoved him into Dina's compartment.

Mom opened the door for me and I slipped in, locking it behind

156

me and pulling the drapes shut.

It was good to see Mom dressed again. She was wearing a crisp white tee shirt, a white eyelet skirt, a lime green belt and her lime green sandals.

"Are you all right?" I asked.

"Just fine. Where's the outlet for the blow dryer?"

We searched until we found it next to the closet. She plugged it in and commenced drying her hair. I plopped down in the chair near the window. My mind went blank. I peeked out the window at the driving rain. We were whizzing through a town of old industrial buildings and beyond them some high rises. I guessed we must be pretty close to Albuquerque. I might have dozed off.

* * *

"Is your brother hurt?" Mom asked. "He sounded fine on the P.A. system."

"He's fine. Just his pride is a bit tarnished. He won't press charges," I answered.

"Well, then I will. How dare that woman do what she did to my son. No, I won't press charges. I'll take justice into my own hands…"

Mom was off on a rant again. But this time she was really worked up. I could see the vein bulging on her temple. If she and Rosemary did tangle, I would bet *Tabloid Tilly* could get a lot of money for selling that photo. I could see the caption now. *Pastors wife and Police Commissioner's wife catfight aboard the train of terror.*

The locomotive was going so fast that it tossed Mom onto the couch. That shut her up.

"It seems like whoever has commandeered this train knows what he or she is doing. They are still blowing the horn through the grade crossings," said Mom.

"I just wish they'd slow down and keep the train on the tracks." I was envisioning a derailment.

"The faster it goes the more fuel it burns up. And the quicker it burns up the diesel fuel, the sooner the train stops, the authorities do their swarm thing and then we can get refueled and back on the road to California," said Mom.

I felt warm all over. I had gotten my adventure gene from my mother. Through all of the wild things that have happened to her and

157

that she has witnessed, she is still looking forward to the destination.

"Have you ever been to California, Mom?"

"Once. My grandfather took me when I was five. Well, I guess my mother and sisters went too. But I vividly remember holding Papaw's hand as we walked down the boardwalk and he bought me cotton candy. Purple cotton candy. And then I buried him in the sand. His feet."

"Your papaw sounds so Norman Rockwellian. How come mine is such a stick in the mud?"

"Now come on, Sandra Marie Faire. My father loves you very much."

"Not as much as he loves his toy trains. That's all he's interested in doing. It would be different if he'd let me run them but he's too selfish with them."

"Selfish? He's probably afraid you'll push the wrong button and the cars will uncouple…"

Mom kept talking as my mind ratcheted into overdrive. "That's it!"

"What's it?"

"All we need to do is to uncouple the first car from the locomotive."

"And you'll derail us all. You just erase that idea right out of your head, little lady…" Mom started another lecture.

I wondered if *Hack 'em Up Hazel* knew how to stop a train. Did she ever get back on, anyhow? I got up and staggered over to the door between the compartments. I smashed my ear against it but couldn't hear anything over the loud rumble of the train. The engines were so noisy.

I knocked on the door. And knocked and knocked.

"Sandra, what on earth are you doing? Don't disturb the lady next door."

"It's *Hack 'em Up Hazel*. She's the one who went chasing after…" Hey, just who did she chase? Rosemary? No, if she was trying to stop Rosemary then why did she get off the train before Rosemary was in custody?

I tried turning the handle to see if the connecting door was unlocked. It did and it was. As I pulled the door open, Mom grabbed my hand and tried to shove it closed.

"Sandra, stop. What are you doing? That is very rude,

opening—"

I managed to yank the door open. I screamed. So did Mom. So did *Hack 'em Up Hazel*. And so did the cowboy she was riding, Jimmy Tamales.

Chapter Nineteen

Mom smashed me between the door and herself. We were both shoving on it so hard it's a wonder we didn't split the car in half.

After an interminable moment of silence, she let go of the door, staggered over to her suitcase and removed her mint green knitting. Mom plopped herself in the chair and commenced weaving her thoughts away. She sometimes used knitting as an escape.

Escape by knitting…knitting to escape…the victim knitted an escape rope…the victim stabbed the perpetrator with a knitting needle. The victim followed "Robert's Rules of Order" and outwitted the terrorist…Terrorist? Oh my God. Terrorists are suicidal. They want to die for their cause so they can get fourteen virgins in Heaven or something like that. They aren't going to run out of fuel. They are going to crash this train into the fires of Hell.

I thought I was going to faint. My blood coursed through my veins faster than the locomotive was chuffing down the tracks. Somebody had to stop this train and soon. This could be the one great thing I did for the world. *Sandra, you could make up for twenty-three years of slacking by saving most of the innocent passengers…*

My mind flashed on *Hack 'em Up Hazel* riding Jimmy Tamales…strike innocent…passengers.

I was pretty sure that I couldn't just walk through the train and into the engine. I could probably walk through to the last car before the engine or engines then out the side door then climb onto the catwalk of the engine or engines then slink my way down to the door and inside. Yeah right. I would ring the doorbell and the terrorist would open up and let me in. Who was I kidding? Not even me.

My eyelids were getting heavy. The train had slowed down and the clickety-clack on the rails and the clickety-clack of Mom's knitting needles lulled me to sleep. I didn't fight it. At least sleep would pass the time.

* * *

"Ladies, may I have your attention please? May I have your attention please…?" Boomed my brother's voice on the public address system. I opened my eyes to Monday morning. My mother had packed everything up and changed into a little pink crop pants suit embroidered with cherries. Her shoes were red Keds sneakers and she had a red and pink bandana tied in a bow as a headband holding her freshly washed hair out of her face. Little eighteen carat gold cherry earrings pulled the outfit together.

"Breakfast will be served in the dining car momentarily," said Andy.

"Well, fix yourself up. I'm starving," said Mom.

"But what happened to the terrorist?" I asked.

"He just told us. Not five minutes ago. It was handled. We'll get the whole story out of your brother later. Now go on in and take a bachelorette shower or something. Oh, wait...I forgot. You aren't a bachelorette anymore..."

I didn't like the way she let that hang in the air. I felt another lecture coming. I interrupted her. "Mom, you go on ahead. I'm going to take a shower and shampoo and blow dry and moisturize and paint and pluck."

"For Heaven's sake, don't pluck. If you over-pluck you'll ruin your brows for life. You need to come down to the beauty parlor with me and see Mercedes. She is the genius of waxing brows..."

"Thanks," I said as I closed the bathroom door behind me and turned the hot water on.

* * *

That afternoon in the conference car somewhere near Colorado, *Hack 'em Up Hazel* introduced our next speaker, a petite twenty-one-year-old editor from a small ePublisher. She was Dina's editor.

"Good afternoon, ladies. It's so exciting to be the guest speaker on a moving train. This is a first for me. I'm here to spill the secrets to writing short stories. They are very sacred so listen up..."

Sacred secrets. There sure seemed to be a lot of those floating around this train of fools. All the men on the train know what a woman who's had two sets of twins plus one singleton looks like naked. Health insurance companies should start paying for tummy tucks to remove the extra skin those instances.

"The first secret is to take your hopelessly stuck novel and hack away at it. Surely there is one scene, one paragraph, one line or maybe even just the title that is spectacular. Delete the rest. Throw it away, burn it. Now you've got the start to your story..." the editor continued.

Poor Rosemary was a sniffling mess at the head of the table. Her hair hung in limp tangles around her garish white facade. Chico, rest his soul, apparently took her face to the grave with him.

I had volunteered to help prepare dinner again this evening. Not because I'm a helpful person. Well, yeah. I need to work on that. But right now, I needed to speak to Andres again. And I wanted to get a better take on the chef. Everyone was a suspect on this train.

"When you are faced with a sagging middle, burn the house down. That always perks up the plot. You heard me. Burn the house down," said *Dina's editor.*

Poor Mom's sagging middle. Burn the house down? Well, at least we can be thankful no wildfires have broken out...yet. Everything else that could happen on this trip had.

I glanced at Tinker Bell. She wasn't there. I looked at my wrist again and stared at Tinker Bell's shadow. The white skin that didn't get tanned because she was protecting me. I tried to shake some pixie dust but it wouldn't sparkle. I stood up and shuffled through the handouts then crawled under the table. She just was nowhere to be found. How did I lose her?

"Excuse me. You there. What are you looking for?" asked the editor, all huffy as if I'd interrupted her big presentation or something.

"Tinker Bell is missing!" I said and retraced my footsteps back to the dining car.

Dina tagged along. I could hear groans and tisks behind us. I didn't care. They just did not understand how much Tinker Bell meant to me. She was my guardian fairy. Without her, who knew what monstrous messes I'd get myself into.

We stepped into the empty dining car.

"I'm so sorry, Sandy. Don't worry, we'll find Tink. Good old Tink," said Dina. A true pal.

"Go on back. Don't you want to hear about secret shorts?" I asked.

"She's my editor. She publishes my short stories. But if they are talking about *secret shorts* then that might keep me awake," said Dina.

We climbed under the booth I had sat in during lunch. We found nothing. Not even a crumb or an ant. "This place is too clean. I'm suspicious," I said.

162

"What does your mystery alarm system suggest is awry?" asked Dina, all enthusiastic.

We sat in the booth. The train chuffed through a forest. Pine trees as far as I could see.

"How was the terrorist situation 'handled'?" I asked.

"Money probably," Dina said.

"Money?"

"What else? Hush money. Whoever had commandeered this train obviously wasn't in it as a terrorist in the traditional sense," she explained.

"Since when did terrorists become traditional?" I asked.

"I mean they aren't like the 9-1-1 guys. This was somebody who wanted something. Like in the 70's when that guy demanded money and hijacked a plane and parachuted out and was never seen again. He got what he wanted."

"How do you know all of this? Who told you about it?"

"No one. Just deducing." She glanced at her plain silver tone watch. "It's almost four o'clock."

"I've got to get to the kitchen. I'm helping out again. If you find Tinker Bell, please take good care of her. I'm afraid she's broken."

* * *

"Nobody handles the fish but me. You! Go chop parsley. Now," barked the chef.

Sheesh. All I was doing was moving the tray a little farther down the counter so that it wouldn't fall off onto the floor. The train was going at a pretty steady clip now and I could easily see everything flying onto the floor with one little sideways jolt. It amazed me how we didn't have a dozen broken plates yet. I'd caught four, piled with lemon slices.

I checked inside the cabinet over the hand-washing sink in the kitchen. Nope, no Tinker Bell. So, okay, I had removed her once because the chef made me. But I know I strapped her back on. I was positive. I think. Pretty positive. I probably strapped her back on…Well, okay so just supposing I forgot to put her back on. Then she should be right here where I left her. And she isn't.

"Somebody stole Tink," I said.

"Somebody stinks?" asked Andres. He had been softly singing while peeling potatoes. He sniffed his armpits.

"No, you don't stink. You usually smell pretty good. What kind

163

of sunscreen do you use at work?"

"Seilerbodden SPF 90. I get it in my country."

"Your country? Aren't you an American now?"

"I am a resident alien. My mother would have a stroke if I renounced my citizenship," he said, scraping a huge pile of potato peels into a trash can lined with a black plastic bag. Just like the ones I used at work.

I wondered if Igor had received my letter of resignation yet. "I quit," I said. My stomach sank a little. I was scared of my decision.

"Well, hold on. I'll do the parsley, my little apple streusel."

"What? No. I like parsley. I peeked down the line and saw the chef gobbling fish. I snuck a little sprig of parsley. Yum.

"I mean I quit my job at the Department of Public Works. I sent Igor my resignation letter," I whispered.

"Why? You have a very fun job. Zipping around on the beach in the little golf cart. You don't want to be stuck inside an office all day and live like a vampire, do you?"

"You know, Andres, I didn't think that hard into it. But then again perhaps an office job may be intellectually stimulating for a change."

"Why, my little schnitzel, I will stimulate your intellect any time you'd like. Let us slip into the refrigerator after we clean the kitchen tonight."

"No. That's not what I intended." I started remembering our potty kiss and comparing it to kissing Lieutenant Hottie on the floor of the business car. I decided Andres probably could keep me warm for a minute or two but Lieutenant Hottie would spoil all the food with the heat he generated in me.

"That fish doesn't smell like fish," I said.

"It's cleaned with bleach. That way we don't have to worry about E. coli or salmonella or trichinosis. The chef will have none of his diners becoming ill," explained Andres.

"Is that safe? I'm not eating any bleach-soaked fish. Hey, does he do anything else with the bleach? How much does he have? Where does he keep it?" I asked, in a hushed tone.

Andres moved closer and whispered in his sing-songy voice. "I will take you to all of the secret places. We will make beautiful love in the laundry room, my little peach tart."

"Hey, you! Boil those potatoes. Now!" screamed the chef.

Andres shrugged his shoulders and carried the pot of potatoes to the sink and filled it with water.

* * *

As we were plating up dinner the chef shoved me out of the way and made a dash for the bathroom. The next thing I knew Andy was running in there. Apparently the attendant call button had been pressed.

I didn't want to look at the chef while he was in the potty but I felt compelled to offer aid. I stood behind my brother in the hallway, just out of the line of site. Andy mumbled a few things in there and then heaved the rotund chef into the hallway with his pants around his ankles. I quickly turned my head. Thank goodness his apron covered what I didn't want to see.

"Get the A.E.D. and call for help," Andy ordered.

A.E.D. Automated External Defibrillator. They had one on the train? I could have used that on *Big Marc*. Where was it? "Where is the A.E.D.?" I asked.

"By the fire extinguisher. Hurry!"

Andy commenced with two quick breaths and chest compressions. I raced to the end of the car and lo and behold there was the A.E.D., right next to the fire extinguisher. I opened the compartment, removed it and rushed it back to Andy. I slid it down the aisle then ran for the microphone.

"We have a medical emergency by the kitchen potty. All available personnel please respond. The chef has diarrhea and needs C.P.R."

I raced back to Andy who said, "Stand clear! Get back!" He pushed the button.

The A.E.D. zapped.

"Resume C.P.R.," said the invisible little woman inside the A.E.D.

Andy said, "Shit!" and gave him two more breaths. I leapfrogged over him and started doing compressions.

We tried the defibrillator a few more times until the battery died. I kept hollering "Help! Fire!" and nobody came. I ran up the stairs to the dining room. Where was everybody? It was as though they had evacuated the train and forgot about the kitchen help.

I ran back downstairs. "Where's your radio?" I asked.

Andy said, "Switch on three. One and Two and Three."

165

I climbed over him and positioned myself to do the rescue breathing. I pinched his nose, closed my eyes, gave him two quick breaths and Andy resumed compressions. One more series of this and I ran to the end of the car and hollered up the stairs. "Help! The chef is dying! Dead! Help!" Nobody came. So I pulled the emergency brake. Again.

The refrigerator door swung open and I was thrown inside. The door banged shut. I landed on something slimy in total darkness. The train screeched to a stop.

"We pillage and plunder drink up me hearties yo ho," said somebody in the dark.

"Who's there?" I asked.

Silence.

I was trapped in a cold slimy refrigerator with a pirate. This could only happen to me.

Chapter Twenty

My tailbone hurt so badly. I knew I'd probably broken it again. I broke it twice before. Once on rented roller skates with Dina and Al Dente on the streets of Key West. The second time same crew but at the bowling alley. I tried a Fred "Twinkle-toes" Flintstone technique. I was no cartoon caveman. But I sure gave my friends some big guffaws until they realized how much pain I was in.

"Hey. Mr. Pirate, sir. Could you please help me? I've fallen in the dark in something slimy and I can't get up."

I should probably be afraid of him but at this point I was desperate for help.

"Hello?" I asked.

"Drop on the deck and flop like a fish."

"Funny. I have dropped on the deck and flopped like a fish."

"Something is fishy in Arizona."

"What?" I asked the pirate.

"We'll take care of Donaldson," he said.

"Do you know about the murders?" I asked.

"Colonel Mustard did it in the library with a marble," said the guy in the dark.

Great. I was trapped with Deep Throat who spoke even weirder than the great Al Dente, husband of the lovely marionette of mystery.

But this guy seemed to know stuff and was willing to talk. If I could just figure out his language maybe I could get some help from him.

"What do you know about *Mini Mary Agnes* and her marbles?"

"I'll get you my pretty," he said.

"Did you kill Mary Agnes Starr?"

"Brown paper packages tied up with…raindrops on roses and whiskers on kittens."

Good gosh. Was this guy a savant or something? Drunk, perhaps?

"Soak the spot thoroughly with bleach," he said.

If my pain in my behind hadn't been so intense perhaps I'd figure out if I should be scared because I was holed up with the murderer. Or did this guy just know the murderer and was trying to blow the whistle on him?

"My name is Sandra. What is your name?"

"Sandra Dee. Flouncing with virginity."

"Well, how crude. I know that's from my Mom's favorite movie. But my middle name is Marie, thank you very much. And my virtue is none of your business."

This guy knew everything about the murders and the clues and he was playing me. Like a clown.

"What about the dog tags?" I asked.

"The one with the waggley tail," he said.

"Who chased *Tabloid Tilly*? Err…Matilda Irwin?"

"Waltzing Matilda," he answered.

"Fine. Be that way. Hey, what are you doing in the refrigerator in the dark?"

He didn't answer. I heard a soft cracking noise. It was creepy.

"Help! Somebody help me! I'm in the refrigerator and I can't get up! Help! Help! It's me, Sandra Faire."

"Captain Sparrow, bring me my rum!" he said.

I laughed. Oh did that hurt. But I couldn't help it. Leave it to me to be trapped in a pitch black refrigerator with *Peetie-the-Parrot* playing me like a fool.

"It is so good to know you are all right, Peetie. I've been worried where you got off to. What are you doing in the refrigerator?"

"What are you doing New Year's Eve?" he asked me.

I slid my hands under my head and smiled. "On New Year's Eve I'll be standing in Times Square waiting for the ball to drop. I'll count down from ten to one. Then turn to Lieutenant Hottie who will kiss me very inappropriately…"

Light filled the compartment. My eyes squinted. I shaded them with my hands.

What are you doing in here?" demanded Lieutenant Hottie.

My heart dropped to my toes. I hoped he had not heard that.

"Come on, Sandra, get up. I ought to throw you off this train. If you weren't my sister, I would. And I still will if you stop this train one more time," scolded my brother.

"Get up," said Lieutenant Hottie.

"I can't. I think I broke my coccyx. And I smacked my head

168

pretty hard, too. And I'm stuck in this sticky stuff." I noticed my hands were red. Catsup?

Lieutenant Hottie hoisted me to my feet and sniffed then licked the tip of my pinky. "Cherry marmalade."

* * *

Jimmy Tamales inflated a fluorescent orange life vest and placed it on a chair in the conference room. I gingerly sat on it, easing myself down, gripping the armrest tightly.

"Are you all right? Can I get you some ice?" he asked.

"Thanks, no ice. Where is everybody?"

"In the picnic grove. They decided to hold the session outside so the investigation can run unimpeded. There is some sort of new age spiritual expert talking to the writers. Didn't you know about it?"

"That was tonight? Shoot. I'd forgotten."

We looked out the window at the flashing lights of an ambulance and a couple of cop cars. The paramedics were performing C.P.R. as they loaded the chef in the back of an ambulance.

"I hope he makes it," I said.

"Yes. For liability purposes," Jimmy said.

I looked at him with a puzzled and jaded expression. "Nobody is going to eat that fish, right?"

"We've ordered pizzas from town. The kitchen car is sealed off. They'll uncouple it in Albuquerque and switch us out with a new one."

"Albuquerque? How close are we?"

"Not far. But we've lost our right of way on the tracks, goofed up the railroad schedule. Now we've got to let a bunch of freight trains through. Can't stand in the way of interstate commerce. We'll be there by morning."

"Can you carry a chair outside for me?" I asked.

"I don't see why not." He spun my chair around and drove me to the end of the car. I took his hand and winced as I stood. He helped me to the vestibule then hopped down the stairs. He grabbed my arm and guided me down.

"Oww. Oww. Oww. Ahh." I made it to the ground. Jimmy retrieved the chair with the life vest. I sat in it and he wheeled me over to a picnic grove beside a stand of squiggly cactus. I'd never seen such tall specimens before. These sure don't grow in Florida.

169

The air felt dry. How bizarre to me. No humidity.

Jimmy wheeled me over to the gathering. A young man with big crooked teeth had the writers enamored with whatever it was he was speaking about. He'd be cute if it weren't for his teeth. I wondered what kind of kisser he was. This trip had made me appreciate that sort of primal man-woman coupling…connection.

I thought about Andres. Was he upset about the chef? I don't think the chef was very nice to him. Andres was so funny with his German food-love talk. I was grateful to him for unclogging the toilets. I should pay him. How much did plumbers make? Eighty bucks an hour? I guess he spent about eight minutes total so I could pay him ten bucks. *Wait. I don't think my math is right…*

"What did you do to the chef?" accused *Weepy Wendy*.

I looked up at her.

"Pardon?" I inwardly groaned and flushed. Why was she accusing me of harming the cook? Oh, right, I was with him in the kitchen. Opportunity. I couldn't think of anything to say that was plausible, so I said, "Where were you an hour ago? What did you have against the chef?" I raised my voice as my chapter mates wandered over. I tried my best to turn the suspicious deaths around on *Weepy Wendy*. To deflect suspicion from myself.

Tabloid Tilly snapped a photo of me sitting on the orange life vest while *Weepy Wendy* extended her arm, pointing her finger an inch from my snoot. I smiled for the second through fourth snapshots.

"Sandra, my little bacon spaetzle. Are you in much pain?" Andres trotted over in true slow motion lifeguard form.

"I'll be all right in a few days. Andres, I'd like you to meet my friend, Wendy. She's a trauma nurse practitioner and writer of romantic comedy." I smiled. "Wendy, this is my colleague Andres. He's a lifeguard."

Andres took Wendy's boney fingers and shook them.

"Hello," she said, apparently taken aback.

"It is so lovely to meet such a beautiful friend of Sandra's. I believe nurses and school teachers are angels on earth. Come and walk and talk with me."

She did. That got rid of *Weepy Wendy*.

The editor and *Contest Carly* trailed after them. The young editor was drooling so closely that she kicked Andres in the back of the heel.

Rosemary was seated at a picnic table. Trance-like. *The poor dear.*

Pat-the-Pirate was seated at an adjacent table, flipping through a stack of files in her beat-up brown leather brief case.

Dina perched on a table top to chat with the guest speaker.

Birds sang. Wow. It had been a week since I'd heard birds singing. I looked into the cactus grove and saw my first real-life roadrunner.

Hack 'em Up Hazel was seated at a table in the back off to the side. I looked from her to Rosemary and back. Remembering what Mom and I had interrupted. Okay, so I interrupted. Why couldn't I have listened to Mom and not opened that door?

Where was Mom?

I really wanted to comfort Rosemary. I tried peddling over with my feet but the ground was too rocky. I'd have to walk.

My chair spun around. "Hello, my little marionette of mystery. It is I, Alfredo Dente, hus—"

"Al, have you seen my mother?"

"Affirmative. She is on the train in the crusader's lounge car knitting with four elegant evangelists."

"Does she know about the latest mur—death…sick person on the train?"

"Positively. The revered reverend led everyone in a little impromptu prayer for the cheeky chef."

"Have you heard how he's doing? Will he make it?"

"His fate is in the cradle of the heavens, dear marionette of mystery. It is not for us mere mortals to know."

"Al, the parrot. Peetie. Is he still in the refrigerator? Somebody needs to get him out of there."

"I am not in acquaintance with Mr. Peetie Parrot. For what reason is he residing in the refrigerator?"

I peered around him. *Pat-the-Pirate* was still shuffling through her papers. "Push me over to Pat," I whispered.

"It will be my distinct honor to assist your expedious travel to…where?"

"*Pat-the-Pirate.* The lady over there pretending to be busy with her briefcase."

Al Dente shoved my chair about half a foot before I yelped.

"Stop! I'll walk. Help me up."

He locked his arm in mine and strutted as I gingerly took little Japanese-wife steps across the grounds.

"Hi, Pat. I'd like you to meet my...best pal, Al Dente. He's in the Navy. Protecting freedom for all."

Al Dente stuck his hand out.

Pat looked up.

"Al, I'd like you to meet my friend, Pat. She's an award winning historical adventure novelist."

Pat shook hands with Al Dente.

Jimmy Tamales plopped seven pizza boxes on the table. They smelled so cheesy and yummy. My brother positioned a case of bottled water next to it and removed the paper plates and napkins from the top.

The editor, *Contest Carly*, Dina and Rosemary appeared, grabbing at plates and meat lovers' pizza.

I winced as I tried to catch up with my brother. He was walking at a good clip back toward the train. "Andy. Andy, wait up," I called out.

He turned his head and stopped.

It seemed to take me a full minute to catch up to him.

"What?" he asked.

"Well, you don't have to be so short with me," I said.

He shook his head. "Sorry. I'm just really busy. What a hell of a trip this is turning out to be."

"How is the chef?"

"Dead."

I cringed. And whimpered in pain. "Foul play?"

"The chef appeared to die of natural causes, but that's just my opinion."

"What does Hot...Lieutenant Hernandez think?"

"He has no authority here."

"Where is he, anyhow?" I scratched the back of my neck.

"Moving his things into the writer's sleeper."

"Why?"

"The crew has to relocate because they'll be cutting this car out at the next big hub stop."

"Did anyone take the parrot out of the refrigerator?" I asked. "Do you know who stashed him in there?"

Andy said, "See for yourself." He gestured behind me. The local police were loading *Peetie-the-Parrot* into the back seat of a cruiser. It looked like an evidence tag was tied to his cage.

"Look at me Sandra Dee!" he squawked.

I looked over at Pat. She shoved meat lovers' pizza into her mouth like nothing was out of the ordinary.

"The parrot was talking to me in the fridge. He was saying crazy things and I think he knows who the murderer is…"

"The parrot is feeding you clues?" Andy rolled his eyes at me. His radio squawked. He talked into it and then told me, "Gotta go." He trotted back to the train.

"So you did have your radio. Why didn't you use it summon help for…"

He was long gone.

"I saved you a slice, Sandy," said Dina. I turned to see her smiling, bearing pizza.

I took it and bit into the lukewarm sustenance. It was pretty good.

"Is *Pat-the-Pirate* acting suspiciously to you?" I asked her.

"Yes. I'm so glad you think so, too. She seemed dazed during the workshop and she's not talking or taking notes. And did you see the coppers carted off her bird?"

I shook my head. "He was in the refrigerator!"

"Who was, the copper?" Dina asked.

"*Peetie-the-Parrot*. He was talking to me. Dina, I'm pretty certain Peetie knows who the murderer is."

Her eyes grew big. "Hold that thought." She ran back to the picnic table and sprinted back, gobbling a slice of pizza. "Do tell! Don't leave one single detail out."

"All aboard!" shouted my brother.

"I'll tell you on the train," I said.

Everyone hurried past me. I moved snail-like.

Andy finally picked me up and hoisted me aboard. He retrieved the chair and life vest and launched it into the conference room.

Contest Carly stopped it with her foot. "What's up with you and the life vest and the wheelchair, Sandra?"

"I broke my tailbone."

"How?"

"When I…I fell when the train stopped so suddenly…the last

173

time."

"I certainly hope it is the last time. I had no idea trains were so dangerous. They ought to invent some better brakes," she said.

"How've you been, Carly? I haven't had a chance to chat with you. What are you working on now?"

"Oh, I'm writing a cozy mystery."

"That's a departure for you. You're doing so well in the romance contests," I said.

"I'll keep trying until I find my voice and sell." She looked past me.

I turned to see *Tabloid Tilly* by the potted plants.

"Excuse me." Carly walked down to Tilly.

I checked my wrist for Tinker Bell. And nearly cried. She still hadn't returned. The last dregs of daylight were darkening the landscape outside. I awkwardly walked back to my compartment. The light was on. I opened the door.

Lieutenant Hottie was sprawled in my bottom bunk. Typing on his laptop.

Chapter Twenty One

"I'm sorry. I must've gotten mixed up. I thought this was my room," I said. Maybe I was in the wrong car. "Did they shuffle the cars around while we were at the picnic grounds?" Thinking back, I would have noticed if the train moved. Uncoupling and coupling are pretty noisy. And I wondered if Lieutenant Hottie was noisy when he was uncoupling and coupling up. Boy was it getting hot in here.

He held one finger up briefly without ever looking at me.

All righty then. He must be engrossed in a pivotal scene as Tony O'Rourke. "You should wear a hat when you're him."

"Him who?" Lieutenant Hottie asked as he removed his flash drive from the side of his laptop and closed the lid.

"Tony O'Rourke. You should wear a hat when you write. That way I'll know not to disturb your muse."

"What kind of a hat do you suggest I wear?"

"Crown. Top Hat. Deerstalker. Not a doo-rag, please. Cowboy hat…" I flashed on *Hack 'em Up Hazel* riding Jimmy Tamales. "No, not a cowboy hat."

"I'm bodyguarding you again," he said. "You don't mind the top bunk, right?"

"I can't climb the ladder. I broke my coccyx…"

"Oh, right. Is that still bothering you? Do we need to stop the train in the next town and call an ambulance?"

"Are you being smart with me? It really hurts. Everyone who has never broken their tailbones always makes it seem like a big joke and they don't realize there really is a bone there and it really does hurt to have a broken bone especially one that you rest so much weight on."

Lieutenant Hottie slipped his laptop back into a steel case and locked it. He heaved the case up onto the shelf over the chair. And then he took me by the hand and led me to the bed. "Sit down, gently. Lie on your stomach. I'll massage…"

"Hello there, baby dumpling. Lieutenant Hernandez," said my mother. She was carrying a red and blue tote bag embroidered and beaded with the American Flag. Her knitting was tumbling out of the top.

175

"Hello, Mrs. Faire. How are you?" Lieutenant Hottie asked.

"I broke my coccyx again, Mom." I groaned as I contorted to lie on my side.

"I've told you time and again to be more careful. Were you roller skating again?"

"Mom, no. I was not roller skating on the train."

"Well, then you must've been horsing around with those chairs in the business car. Why on earth they would allow free rolling chairs on a moving train is beyond me. I'll go and get you some ice." She took the ice bucket and left the compartment.

"Let me rub it for you," Lieutenant Hottie said in his deepest erotic whisper.

I tingled from the tips of my earlobes down to the hairs on my toes. "Don't you mean you want to rub it for *you*?" I teased.

"Here's the ice," Mom said. She made up another ice pack with a cloth napkin and a plastic Target bag this time. "Roll onto your tummy, baby dumpling. Lieutenant, please assist her," Mom said.

At least Mom must have thought my moans were groans because I couldn't suppress responding to his big strong warm loving hands as he rolled me over.

"Thank you. I can handle her from here. You can run along now," said Mom.

"No, he can't. He's bodyguarding me. He's staying here."

"What danger is Sandra in?" she asked.

"I'm not sure but as a precaution with the latest suspicious death and since she was the one to discover all of the victims…"

"Andy discovered the chef. I just helped with the C.P.R.."

"Really, Sandra. Do not speak of people in such ways, it is not ladylike." She crossed her arms. "Well, this is going to be awkward. We are rooming together. Can't Andy bodyguard Sandra?" Mom asked.

"Andy is walking the train tonight. All night sentry," said Lieutenant Hottie.

"Well, I certainly can't double up on such a small bunk. I have the leg thing," said Mom.

"Leg thing?" Lieutenant Hottie asked.

"I have it, too. I thought it was just me and Mom. But then I started seeing those commercials on TV selling drugs for restless leg syndrome. So if they named it then someone else must have it," I

176

explained.

"Mom and I can't sleep together. We'd kick the bejeevers out of each other all night and wake up bruised and cranky," I said.

Mom stepped into the bathroom to change.

I lay in the same spot with my cheek pressed to the pillow. The ice pack in the small of my back had begun to work its numbing magic.

Lieutenant Hottie rummaged through his gym bag. Mom emerged from the bathroom in raspberry floral Capri pajamas. She scooted around him to get to the sink. As Mom applied moisturizer, Lieutenant Hottie stepped into the bathroom.

"I spoke with your father this afternoon." Mom sorted her lotion and dirty clothes back into separate compartments of her suitcase.

"How is Daddy? And the guys?"

"Good. Things are quiet on the beach. They haven't made any arrests in the death of your young sailor. Matt is seeing that awful Lulu again

"Lulu isn't so bad. She only dresses trashy. And has a potty mouth. And smokes. She has a trust fund and is kind to the homeless," I said.

"I told your father what that tawdry Rosemary Donaldson did to our Andy. He brushed it off! I'll never understand men." Mom replaced my ice pack, shook a blanket over me and kissed my cheek. She held her face close to mine and I kissed her back. "Now Sandra. This sleeping arrangement is a bit uncouth. Make sure you don't do anything inappropriate to embarrass us." She climbed up the ladder and I heard her snuggle under the covers. She switched the light off.

The bathroom door opened. Out stepped Lieutenant Hottie clad in thin black drawstring pants and a white muscle undershirt.

My pulse quickened.

He stashed his weapon under the bottom of the mattress, opposite where my head was.

"I guess there isn't another pillow," he said.

Mom tossed hers down. "Here. Wally always tucks his gun under his pillow."

"Thank you, Mrs. Faire. Are you sure though?"

"Oh, I took a P.M. I'll be out like a hibernating bear in three or four minutes. I won't miss the pillow."

"Thank you again." Lieutenant Hottie retrieved his weapon and stashed it under the pillow just a few inches south of my feet. Then he climbed in. We were sleeping head to toe. If Mom weren't here we would call that something numerical and we wouldn't be sleeping. Well, maybe we wouldn't.

"It sounds as though your mother over-estimated the time before her sleeping pill would kick in. She sounds like a lumberjack up there," said Lieutenant Hottie in the dark.

"Yeah, well, you should hear my grandma snore. You'd think you were at a logging camp," I said.

"None of the ladies in my family snore," he said.

I readjusted my icepack. "Well, we Savoir women are hearty. We do everything with gusto, including sleep."

"Really now? You do everything with…gusto?"

I smiled. "Maybe you'll find out someday."

"Savoir women?" he asked.

"Mom's maiden name. Savoir."

"So your mother is Terry Savoir-Faire then?"

I laughed. "Oww, that hurt."

Lieutenant Hottie sat up. He removed my ice pack and gently rubbed the small of my back. I squirmed and rolled over. "Oww!"

"What are you doing?" he asked.

"What are you doing?" I countered. I settled on my back looking straight up in the dark. I could make out the outline of Mom's bunk.

"Peetie knows things," I said.

"Who's Peetie?"

"*Peetie-the-Parrot*. I told you about him."

"Oh, right."

I could sense him rolling his eyes.

"I hope the local police have an avian expert. Peetie could sing this case wide open," I said. He was such a lovely bird.

"Sing this case wide open. You watch too much TV," Lieutenant Hottie said.

"No, I do not. I read a lot. I have this one favorite author. He writes brilliant, poignant police procedurals. Perhaps you've heard of him. Tony O'Rourke."

"Tony O'Rourke never wrote about a singing parrot cracking a case."

"Perhaps he should. The case of the…The case of the Pirate's

178

Parrot, by Tony O'Rourke."

"No. The Case of the Pirate's Parrot by S.M. Faire," he said.

"S.M.?" I asked.

"Men usually won't buy books written by women."

"How chauvinistic."

"Just the facts, ma'am."

"Now who's been watching too much TV?"

"Busted. But what else is a lonely guy to do on Saturday night?"

"Go out on a date."

"Can't get a date."

"What do you mean you can't get a date? Every single female from eighteen to eighty in Cocoa Beach would love to do you…date you," I said, blushing in the dark.

"Yeah, but I've done every single woman from eighteen to eighty in Cocoa Beach."

"Bragger. And I know for a fact you have not done every one."

"My problem is the only one that I long for is married."

"How did you find out about that? My mother didn't tell you, did she?"

"Nobody told me. I tailed you."

Boy did that evoke a mental image.

"Tailed me when? Where?" I asked.

The train was chuffing along at a nice even pace. My coccyx was barely bothering me.

"During the hurricane. I followed you to Vegas."

My heart rate pounded up a storm. I swallowed. "You did? Why?"

"Official business. Officially I was investigating racketeering involving that kid, Dente. Unofficially, I was chasing after the girl that…"

"The girl that what?"

Mom rolled over and fell to the floor. Lieutenant Hottie scrambled down to her aid. I fumbled on the wall for the light switch. I flipped it on and inadvertently pushed the attendant call button.

"She's still asleep," said Lieutenant Hottie.

"Well, hold on, help me get up. I need to check for broken bones."

He helped me out of bed. I tried crouching down but my back

179

wouldn't allow it.

"What's wrong?" said Andy. He stood in the open doorway. "What happened?"

"Mom fell out of bed."

"She's unconscious!" He shoved Lieutenant Hottie aside and climbed over me. He placed two fingers on her carotid artery. "She has a pulse." He put his cheek to her face. "And she's breathing. Does she have a concussion?" Andy performed a quick trauma exam. "No broken bones. How far did she fall?"

"From the top bunk," I said.

"Go get that nurse with the hideous hair," he said.

"I don't know which room she's in," I said.

"She's down the hall, Compartment F."

Lieutenant Hottie helped me up and out the door. I stiffly walked down to Compartment F and knocked softly. No response. I knocked louder. Nothing. I tried the door, it was unlocked. I slid it far enough to open the curtains and peek inside. "Wendy? Wendy, are you awake? My mom has had an accident and we need you.

I couldn't see her in the dim light from the hall. I felt around and switched on her room light. Wind whooshed in. It was really loud. The room was torn up. It looked like there might have been a struggle. I shivered. The window had been removed. I walked to the bathroom and knocked on the door. No answer. I opened the door. Nobody screamed at me. It was empty.

I hurried back to my compartment. "Wendy is gone. Foul play. Window is missing," I blurted. "How is Mom?"

She mumbled something and rolled over.

What a relief. She'd taken a sleeping pill. She slept through the whole thing. I tossed a blanket over her. "Don't put her back in bed. Let her sleep it off on the floor. That way we don't have to worry about her getting hurt if she falls again," I said.

Andy and Lieutenant Hottie were out the door before I finished talking.

Lieutenant Hottie had forgotten his gun. I'd better take it to him. I lifted his pillow but didn't find the weapon. Oh, maybe he did have it. I hurried down the hallway to Wendy's room. Lieutenant Hottie and Andy both had their guns drawn. The North American Passenger Railway crew chief arrived.

"Go back to your room, Ma'am," The crew chief told me. The

tone of her gritty voice made me obey. I needed to get back to Mom.

Hack 'em Up Hazel followed me down the hall. "What's going on? Which one of us did you discover this time?"

I shook my head and kept going. When I reached my room, Mom was back in bed. On the bottom bunk.

"Mom, are you all right?"

"Go to sleep, baby dumpling. This is a school night." She rolled over.

I tucked her in and kissed her forehead. I could hear Hazel breathing behind me.

I turned to her and said in a hushed tone, "Wendy's window has been removed. Her room is very disheveled. Do you know if she is neat or a natural slob?"

"I wouldn't know. I've never had her for a roommate. Where is she?"

"Missing. Apparently. Do you have any thoughts off the top of your head?"

"Well, she was always depressed. So it could be an attempted suicide."

"Do you think there is any chance Wendy could be mixed up in the murders?" I asked her, my voice trembling. "I mean, just between you and I. I don't mean to imply that her character is bad or anything, and I feel really bad for saying anything, and never mind."

We heard the horn blow through a grade crossing.

"No. I don't think Wendy has it in her. She is a lifesaver not an angel of death. That's too overdone."

"Who do you suspect?" I asked her point blank.

"I am not convinced there has been one murder let alone a series of them. It's all circumstantial as far as I'm concerned.

It was at that moment all of my doubts were erased. This was no series of unfortunate coincidences. These deaths were all linked. And *Hack 'em Up Hazel* was now on my list of suspects. Why? I'd think of a reason later. Just one of those gut hunches.

"I need to lie down now. I hurt my lower back. Good night." I practically shoved Hazel out my door before I pulled it shut.

I had forgotten all about my hurt back. Maybe most of it was all in my head. Maybe Andy and Lieutenant Hottie weren't so wrong with their taking this lightly. Or maybe adrenaline had dulled the pain temporarily. I decided to take one of my mother's sleeping pills and get a good eight hours.

I didn't have to dig too far down in her purse to locate the little white envelope. I read the drug interaction precautions and then shook one capsule—half a dose—into my hand. I popped it in my mouth got a little drink of water from the sink and swallowed. After going potty I climbed up the ladder and switched the light off.

I was aware of my injury but somehow it had numbed. I gingerly rolled around until I was on my back. Pressure seemed to help. I pulled the covers up to my chin and closed my eyes.

How many possible deaths and missing persons were there now?

In the death column, there was David Starr, one. *Mini Mary Agnes Starr*, two. *Napping Norah*, three. Dina's Aunt Beverly/Al Dente's step-momma/my step-mother-in-law, four. Chico five. The chef, six.

Missing persons: *Big Marc* Clinger but he's back at work. *Weepy Wendy*. I wondered where she was…

I tried to concentrate on the mysterious goings on aboard the train. With my eyes closed, Wendy's black and white hair swirled around in my mind and I saw Dalmatians. I remembered *Peetie-the-Parrot* had disappeared but returned and was now in police custody. And poor little Tinker Bell was still unaccounted for.

Pirates and Peter Pan and Tinker Bell and Captain Jack Sparrow and Cruella de Ville and Wendy were all arguing in my head. They were floating over an amphitheater in the rain and fog.

* * *

I woke up feeling great. Well rested. Whoops. My tail bone hurt. But more of a dull ache, not burning pain. As my eyes focused in the dim Tuesday daylight peeking in from the gaps in the drapes, I realized the train was not moving. And I really needed to go to the bathroom. I backed down the ladder and entered the potty, doing what needed to be done. I stepped out and over to the sink.

As I washed my hands and glanced in the mirror at my bed hair and mascara smeared under my eyes, I could see the bunk behind me reflected in the mirror. I gasped.

Mom was sleeping on the bottom bunk. Cuddled up to my Lieutenant Hottie.

Chapter Twenty Two

Lieutenant Hottie woke up and instinctively grabbed his weapon from under his pillow. This action tossed my mother onto the floor.

She woke up and looked at me. "Sandra Marie Faire. Why did you kick me out of bed?"

Lieutenant Hottie scrambled out of the covers. "What's going on?"

"What are you doing sleeping with my mother?"

"What?" he asked.

"What?" my mother asked.

"Exactly what is going on here? And while I was sound asleep on the top bunk!" I screeched.

I noticed a flash from the hallway. I looked out the corridor window to see *Tabloid Tilly*, snapping away. Tears trickled down my face. I ran back into the bathroom and locked the door. There had to be a logical explanation. Lieutenant Hottie must've thought it was me in the bottom bunk when he returned last night. Mom and I are clones except for her voluptuous extra thirty pounds. Surely he would have noticed. And surely Mom would *never*.

I heard someone on the P.A. system. Something about we'd arrived in Albuquerque and everyone must detrain.

Great. Just great.

Mom pounded on the bathroom door. "Sandra, let's go. We have to get off the train. Come on. I've heard the breakfasts at the coffee shops here are to die for. A friend told me about this little German place," she said.

I opened the door. "Tell me you don't have a thing going on with him."

"Him who?" she asked.

"Lieutenant William Hernandez, Homicide."

"What are you talking about?"

Lieutenant Hottie was gone. Had I imagined it all? Yes, please say it was all part of my weird dream. Okay, Sandra girl, let's go with that.

"Mom, do you have weird dreams when you take your sleeping pills?"

"My life is a weird dream. And I love it. Why do you ask?"

My brother interrupted my trying to make sense of it all.

"Ladies, please detrain now. We are scheduled to depart for Los Angeles at two P.M. You will need your identification, boarding pass and ticket to return. Take all valuables with you."

Mom opened her purse and pulled out the three items and held them up. I did the same. We returned our documents to our purses, dressed, and headed off to explore Albuquerque, New Mexico.

* * *

Much to Mom's protest we ate at McDonalds. I was starving and we weren't sure which way the German coffee shop was. I happily gobbled my sausage sandwiched between two small pancakes with syrup mixed into the batter.

Mom nibbled at a fruit cup and flipped open her cell phone. She dialed and then said, "Hey, Delores. Yep, it's really me. Sandra and I are in town. The train was a little delayed…Of course! All righty. I'll see you then. Bub-bye now." Mom closed her cell phone and checked her watch.

"Have you seen Tinker Bell? I can't find my watch anywhere. I don't feel good without her," I said and sucked down the last slurp of my small orange juice.

"Sandra, you really need to put your jewelry away in a proper case. The sterling silver will turn black if you don't keep it in a jewelry box with an anti-tarnish liner."

"So that means no?"

"No what?" she asked, chewing a cantaloupe nugget.

"Have you seen my watch?"

"No. Sorry. Where did you last have it?"

I tried to remember. "It was sometime before the last time I stopped the train."

"Sandra, you have to stop doing that. It is very embarrassing. And inconvenient to the crew. They have to walk the whole length of the train outside on both sides to inspect it. Then wait for the brakes to fill with air again. Not to mention everyone onboard being thrown around. It's a good thing the bartender is stocking pain reliever. I'll bet—"

"What bartender? I haven't seen any bartender," I asked.

"Up in the evangelists' lounge car. The very first passenger car on the front of the train," she said, as if I were oblivious. Boy did my

184

mother know me well.

"But Rosemary banned alcohol…"

"Her husband didn't. He enjoys a little snort of sacramental wine or whiskey. I've watched him."

My mind wandered away. I remembered the pile of crap the writers had brought with them. "Mom, do you know who brought the bleach aboard the train?"

"What?"

"When I was waiting to board back in Orlando, there was a big pile of odd things mixed in with the luggage. Do you know who brought the bleach? How about the kitty litter?"

"Chico did laundry for Rosemary and her husband. And that skinny nurse, Wendy, has a kitten."

"*Weepy Wendy* brought a cat? How come I never saw it or heard it?"

"I don't know. She had it in the evangelists' lounge car one night when I was giving a knitting demonstration. I tossed the cutie pie a ball of red wool and she went to town with it."

"Wendy did?"

"No, silly. Kitty did. That's the kitten's name, Kitty," Mom explained.

I didn't remember seeing a litter box in Wendy's room. But I didn't get a real good look.

"How often did Weepy Wendy commingle with the evangelists?" I asked.

"Nightly. Why?"

"How odd…"

"No, not odd at all. Everyone goes to the evangelists' lounge at night. It is a warm fuzzy atmosphere. Reverend Donaldson tells little anecdotal jokes about the funny encounters he has with his followers. And he links them to people in the Bible so that makes us all pause to realize people haven't changed in all these years. You really should come with me tonight. I'm sure you'll have fun. And they always have cheese and cracker platters." Mom wiped up the table and threw our trash away.

"How come you didn't ask me who Delores is?" Mom asked.

"Huh?" I was still trying to wrap my brain around evening storytelling and booze with the reverend. "She's one of your online knitting friends, right? And you are going to meet her face to face at

185

the local yarn store here in Albuquerque," I said. My mother was so predictable.

"Well Miss Smarty Pants since you think you have it all figured out, tell me what Delores knits."

"She knits scarves for servicemen."

"She knits stuffed bunnies for the police. They give them to little scared children who are auto accident and crime victims. You should see her web portfolio. Delores is a very talented lady."

"I'm sure I'll be seeing the bunnies really soon, in the flesh, now won't I? Where and when are we meeting her?"

"In half an hour at the Darn Yarn."

"Do you have directions?"

Mom pulled a paper from her purse. She unfolded a computer printed map.

* * *

The Darn Yarn was quite a walk for us up the main stretch of road. It was a storefront in a little strip mall which seemed to stretch on for miles. "Look at the mountains, Mom."

"They are purple," she said.

"And they are sparsely vegetated with the same one kind of scrub pine. We're surrounded on three sides. Look." We spun around.

"I prefer our tropical swamps and beaches," said Mom.

"Me too. But the Ozark Mountains were nice to chuff through. I could have avoided that bus ride of death though," I said, shuddering. Poor Chico. Rest his soul.

"I've been thinking a lot about that and Chico's death in particular," said Mom. "Why is it that he was the only one to succumb to the carbon monoxide poisoning?"

"Maybe it hits men worse?"

"I wouldn't think so. Men are usually larger than women and can hold toxic substances better."

"Such as?" Men holding toxic substances better…what was she now, a famous pathologist? Well, she was a secret Charlie's Angel in Chicago so maybe in Albuquerque she could be a secret pathologist.

"My back hurts," I said.

"I'm sorry, baby dumpling. But walking should do it some good. You really do need to be more careful. You've broken your

186

coccyx three times now. You'll have arthritis there within the next decade."

"Thanks for giving me something to look forward to," I grumbled.

"There it is!" We walked across the parking lot and into the open glass door of the Darn Yarn.

"Delores?" Mom asked the woman behind the counter. The rest of the store was empty.

"Terry? Terry Faire?"

"Yes. And I'd like you to meet my daughter, Sandra."

"Hello." I shook hands with the little old Native American lady.

Mom and Delores chatted like long lost chums. I wandered around the brightly lit store. The tops of the yarn cubbies lining the three walls were capped with stuffed animals. I walked around with my head snapped back. "Gee, you make the cutest bunnies and squirrels and chipmunks and...turtles!" They were absolutely adorable. "Do you make wolves too? I love wolves." I asked.

"I can make any kind of woodland creature or dessert creature you'd like. I'll make up a pattern and send it to you. You do knit, don't you, Sandra?" asked Delores.

"Of course. Being the only girl in a family of seven, of course I would want to spend quiet hours with my mother's attention." I grinned.

"How much yarn will I need?" I asked.

"Pick out one large skein of whatever you'd like the main color to be then some remnants for the muzzle, paws and face," She walked over and led me to the remnant bin.

"I didn't know yarn stores sold remnants," I stated.

"I've never seen that either," said my mother.

"Oh, I always say, why charge a knitter for a full skein if she only needs a yard?" said Delores.

My wolf would be white, of course. I pulled the softest white cashmere I could find first. Then I returned to the remnant bin to choose the other colors. As I dug through, Mom and Delores caught up on online knitting group gossip.

"I understand you've been on a train for a few days," said Delores.

"Yes, we're riding on the *GOOS Express* to Los Angeles," said my mother.

187

"How delightful. My Harry used to take me to the Hollywood Brown Derby for our anniversary lunch. We just adored the Cobb salad. I would hollow out my sourdough rolls and stuff the salad inside. You must eat there when you arrive," said Delores.

Mom and I had eaten at the Hollywood Brown Derby at Disney's Hollywood Studios many times. And we both knew that the original restaurant out in L.A. had long ago been torn down. Mom was too polite to point that out.

"Did you hear about poor Beverly Dente?" asked Delores.

"God rest her soul. The poor thing. All she wanted was to have the nerves in her wrists repaired and ended up dying of a staph infection. Medical misadventure. I hope her family sues the hospital," said Mom.

I found some lovely pink yarn which would work really well for my wolf's nose. There was some golden brown at the bottom. I leaned inside the remnant bin as far as I could. I scrunched my face up tight and closed my eyes expecting a sharp debilitating pain. The stretch actually felt good. Perhaps Mom was right again. How does she come up with all this wisdom?

I found the last color I wanted and paid Delores. I checked Mom's gold watch. "Mom, we've got to go! The train is leaving in twenty minutes!"

She and Delores hugged and Delores handed me a purple paper bag with raffia handles. It was really cute.

Mom and I hustled out the door and down to the North American Passenger Railway station. We made it just as Andy was boarding the last passengers.

"Where have you two been? I thought we'd be leaving you in the desert," said Andy.

We climbed on board and walked back to our compartment. It had been cleaned and the beds were folded up. No sign of Lieutenant Hottie.

"Hey, Mom. I thought Lieutenant Hernandez was supposed to be bodyguarding me."

"And so?"

"Why didn't he return to the room this morning? And why didn't he venture into Albuquerque with us?"

"Well, that's silly, baby dumpling."

"Silly?" I was confused.

188

"I was bodyguarding you," she said as she freshened up her coral lipstick in the mirror.

"Right. I forgot. You're a super-secret Charlie's Angel," I mumbled.

"I heard that," she said. "Freshen up and we'll go down to the evangelists' lounge. Perhaps Joel will play the piano tonight."

"How was I kept in the dark so long about the party car?"

"It certainly wasn't hidden from you. Everyone else found their way," said Mom. She cleaned out her purse while I brushed my hair.

I stepped into the hall. Mom shut the door and I beckoned her to lead the way.

Contest Carly was arm-in-arm with the editor, right in front of us.

I whispered to Mom, "I don't think the little lady can stand upright without support."

"Really? The poor thing. What do you suppose is her malady?"

"An extreme case of writer-suck-up-to-me-ism."

"Sandra Marie Faire. You just stop that talk right now or we are going back to the room."

I giggled.

We arrived at the evangelists' lounge and Mom told me to sit by the window. I did. I crossed my legs like a lady and set my bag on my lap. I stuffed my hands inside running my fingers through the soft cashmere and decided to knit an animal with Mom's instructions. Then I'd soon have something to snuggle with. Yeah, I know. I should be snuggling with a man at my age. But at least stuffed animals didn't break my heart and didn't care if my legs were hairy and I slept in my socks.

Something metallic tangled around my finger. How odd. I peeked in the bag and pulled out a chain. A metal ball chain. With dog tags attached.

Oh, no. Not again.

Chapter Twenty Three

I stuffed them back into the bag and then scooted over to the light. I looked around and no one seemed to be interested in me. So I bent down close to read them. There were two sets on one chain. I read the top one:

DENTE, LUIGI A.
555-99-4098
BLOOD TYPE: AB-
ROMAN CATHOLIC

Okay, I knew Al's Dad had served in the Navy during Desert Storm.

The second one pretty much floored me:

DONALDSON, ROSEMARY D.
555-55-9900
BLOOD TYPE: AB-
ROMAN CATHOLIC

Rosemary Donaldson was in the Navy? After she was married? Is she still? And she's a Catholic!

"Your mother says you are going to knit a bear," said a bubbly septuagenarian dressed in a fuchsia skirt suit. Her varicose veins didn't go well with her ensemble.

I stuffed the dog tags back to the bottom of the bag of yarn and stood up holding it behind my back. I stuck out my hand and said, "Hello, I'm Sandra Faire."

The lady had a very firm grip as she clamped my hand in between both of her age-spotted appendages. "Lovely to meet you, Sandra dear. I'm Mrs. Higgenbottom-Barnesworth. The fourth," she said, surprisingly without an air of old money.

"Nice to meet you too, Mrs. Higgenbottom-Barnesworth the fourth." I wiggled my hand loose.

"So what kind of a bear are you knitting?" she asked.

"Not a bear, exactly. More of a white timber wolf."

"Oh, now isn't that singular. I'd love to see your progress," she said.

"Sure. But I haven't started yet. I'm still waiting on the pattern. Mom has a friend, Delores in Albuquerque. We visited her yesterday. She's with the online knitting club. Are you a member too?" My mind was clicking away. I had no doubt whatsoever that *Double-stitch Delores*, dear old lady, was the one who planted these dog tags inside my bag of wool. How was she connected to the goings on? Yep, goings on was a good term for the crazy weird things which kept enlivening this voyage to the bottom of the sea. To the sea anyhow. The Pacific Ocean.

"Have you ever seen the Pacific Ocean, Mrs. Higgenbottom-Barnesworth the fourth?" What a mouthful. She still hadn't answered me about the knitting club.

"Only in Hawaii. My great-grandma-mah had a little shack on the ocean front. If you looked east, you saw the volcanoes. If you looked west, you saw the pineapple plantations. I found the black volcanic sand to be unattractive. And the water very cold..." Mrs. Higgenbottom-Barnesworth the fourth blustered on and on about "Hy-wy-yah."

Contest Carly plopped herself in the chair I had risen from. She gobbled hors d'oeuvres. No, in Rosemary's car in the front there were hors d'oeuvres. These were bonafide party snacks. Fritos, pigs in a blanket, cocktail meatballs and she even had a small bowl of chili with shredded cheddar cheese, scallions and a dollop of sour cream on top. Yum.

"Excuse me, Mrs. Higgenbottom-Barnesworth the fourth. May I get you a bowl of chili?" I offered.

"What? Oh, no dear. I am on a restricted diet. But you go right ahead," she said and smiled at me.

Another evangelist doddered up to her and they began chatting.

I moved across the car to the credenza. I couldn't decide on nachos, individually topped chips with beans, cheese, green salsa, guacamole and sour cream or a big hearty bowl of chili. So I loaded my plate with nachos and dumped chili on top. I grabbed a fork and a napkin and a can of root beer and wandered through the evangelists' lounge car in search of a perch.

I wondered what had become of old *Peetie-the-Parrot*. Had he been released? *Pat-the-Pirate* was seated at the piano. She was playing a rousing version of "Row Row Row Your Boat."

I stuffed a chip in my mouth and closed my eyes. It was that good. I wished I would have known about this speakeasy back on the first day I climbed aboard this train of ghouls.

I couldn't help myself and began singing along with my mouth full.

Andres stepped up to me. "Sandra, my little apple streusel, let me assist you." He wrestled my plate from me and carried it down to the other end of the car. He set it on the green marble topped bar. "Here, have a seat, my pretty little fräulein. Your Andres has missed your plump lips…"

I set my can of root beer on the bar and popped the top open. I guzzled a big pull of it, fizzy and sweet.

The bartender turned around. He had been hanging wine glasses.

"Gee, it's a marvel that the stemware doesn't clang together and break when the train gets a rockin' and a rollin'," I said.

The bartender grunted at me. He was Eagle the hotshot volunteer beach patrolman. And mob lieutenant. And my getaway driver. Shoot. Was I still a fugitive from justice? An escaped criminal? Nah, that was all hoo-hah. But weird they hadn't come after me. Why? Because they weren't looking for Sandra Faire. That was pretty clever of me giving them my pen name. My unpublished pen name.

Hack 'em Up Hazel sashayed up to the bar. "Hello, Sandra." Either she was blushing in embarrassment or she'd been at the bar a few times earlier this evening.

"Hello, Hazel. Did you enjoy Albuquerque?" I asked.

"Bartender, I'd like a cosmopolitan please," she said.

Eagle grunted and threw a gold-embossed napkin on the marble counter before preparing her girly-drink.

"I bought some enchanted beads from the Indians."

I tried to formulate an apology for Mom and I busting in on Hazel and fat old Jimmy Tamales with the bad knees, but I couldn't figure out a way to bring it up jovially.

Lieutenant Hottie caught my eye. He was carrying his laptop case under his arm and nodded for me to join him. Well, okay, so maybe I was imagining he was nodding for me to join him. He might have had a crick in his neck.

"Excuse me. Enjoy your Cosmo!" I glugged two gulps of root

192

beer, shoved a nacho piled high with chili into my mouth, stuffed a pile of gold embossed napkins in my pocket then took my plate and can over to Lieutenant Hottie. He was standing at the east end of the car near the restroom.

"Hello," I said after chewing and swallowing. "Fancy meeting you here. I thought you were my bodyguard." Flashes of seeing him snuggled up with Mom replayed in my mind. My face must've been screwed up something fierce.

"What's wrong? The food doesn't agree with you?"

"No, the food is delish. I just don't know *if you agree with me*," I said with a little hurt in my voice.

"Agree with you about what?" he asked.

Men. Either they are oblivious to our feelings or else they are just…men. I couldn't think of any way to have this argument with him that would be beneficial to either of us nor the audience who were no doubt perusing this hot guy from all corners of the lounge car.

"What are you writing?" I asked.

"Same old, same old. And you?"

Wow. Tony O'Rourke asked me what I was writing. "I'm trying to finish a cozy with the working title 'The Case of the Adorable Plumber.' It's set in an old Civil War town in Virginia…" I babbled and babbled until I realized I had lost bestselling police procedural writer Tony O'Rourke's attention. He'd morphed into his alter ego, Lieutenant William Hernandez, Homicide. I turned to see what he was so captivated with.

Great. *Tabloid Tilly* was perched on top of the baby grand piano, sprawled across it in her turquoise safari styled mini-dress and thong high heels. No stockings. She was singing "Once I Had a Secret Love," the old Doris Day song from, I think, the movie *Annie Get Your Gun.* The last time I heard that one performed was at a charity event I attended with Mom and Dad in Hollywood, Florida. Barry Gibb sang it. And I swooned. I had a thing for older guys. With hot voices. I wondered if Lieutenant Hottie could sing.

Reverend Donaldson had made his way into the car. He and a couple of geezer men and Al Dente. They were crowding around the piano. Eyes glued to *Tabloid Tilly's* impossibly long and chiseled legs.

Heat rose in my cheeks. She wasn't so hot. What did she have that I didn't?

Well, she had a mixed ethnic heritage that was exotic. And she was tall. And she dressed well. And she had an air of mystery…

She even had a boyfriend in Chicago. A guy in every port. I stopped short of calling her an unflattering name in my mind. Mom seemed to like her. And I never did think of a reason to dislike her. Except for that little zinger she threw on me back in the writer's parlor car the other night. *"I know what you did."* What in the heck did she mean by that? And what did I do? I mean besides stop the train. Three times. And discover dead bodies.

"Sandra. Carly wants to see your yarn," said Mom with Carly in tow.

As I crunched the chip in my mouth, I panicked. What had I done with the bag of yarn and the dog tags? I had it when I was chatting with Mrs. Hy-wy-yah. From there I moseyed over to the feeding trough. Did I set it on the bar?

I hurried over to the bar and didn't see the bag. I ducked underneath. Eagle grabbed me by the scruff of the collar of my tee and the waistband of my jeans and threw me over the bar. I landed under the piano. *That wasn't nice. Why did he do that?*

Pat stopped playing. Matilda stopped singing. Everybody stared at me. I crawled further underneath then made my way through the legs back over to the food. There was my bag. I had set it down next to the chili. I kneeled, grabbed the bag and then shuffled across the car on my knees over to Mom.

"What on earth was that all about? Are you hurt? Do you want me to kick his behind?" She asked.

I stood up and dusted off my knees. I glanced over to Eagle and saw the daggers in his blue eyes. I shivered.

"Carly, see, white, pink, brown and gray." I barely pulled the end of each skein out. "I have to go." I made a beeline back to my compartment.

As I approached the door, I heard, "Sandy, come here." Dina beckoned me into her compartment. I shrugged my shoulders and entered it.

"What's up?" I asked her.

"Exactly. I've been contemplating the disappearance of Wendy. I don't think she escaped or was pushed out the window or kidnapped," Dina whispered as she closed the hall door.

I plopped down on her sofa and set the bag in my lap. I dug through and felt the dog tags. Good. "So what do you think happened to *Weepy Wendy*?" I asked.

Dina tossed a bag of sour cream and onion flavored potato chips next to me and plopped down. "I think she is hiding. She orchestrated this big elaborate flashy disappearance so she could go underground..."

She ripped open the bag of chips. A few went flying. I picked them up and munched them. The thirty second rule applied on trains, too. If the food is on the floor less than thirty seconds then it's still germ and dirt free.

"I think she is hiding out, sleuthing out the killer," said Dina. She shoved her arm into the bag and grabbed a huge handful of chips.

"So you don't suspect her of being the serial murderer?" I asked.

"No. I think she wants to be the heroine of this excursion."

I stood up. "Well, we'll just see about that. I think not. If anyone is going to solve this cozy it's me and you. And maybe Al Dente can help a little. Well, and Mom. And Andres is handy. He unstopped the commodes you know. And he kissed me, too. Not bad," I said.

"Yes, he's pretty good," said Dina.

I gave her a look. She returned it and we laughed.

I shook the yarn bag on my lap. "New clues!" I said and fished out the dog tags.

I showed Dina the names. Al Dente's father, and Rosemary Donaldson! "And look, Rosemary is Catholic! How much does her husband know, do you think?"

Dina licked the sour cream and onion powder from her fingers then quickly rinsed them in the sink and dried them on her long jean skirt. She grabbed the tags. "This is positively fascinating. You know, it's high time we— Where are you going?"

"Off to get a fresh journal. Be right back," I said as I closed her door behind me. I hustled to the business car. Great! There were still a few journals left on the credenza. Two chocolate and one animal print. Cheetah, I think. Hmm...should I choose the chocolate leather or the animal print? Chocolate is in this season. Even in gold and diamonds— so says Mom. She gets her fashion trends from the *Have I Got a Deal for You* channel.

I decided to take the Cheetah since nothing was trendy about this investigation. If there was a trend I sure was missing it. I grabbed another gold foil pencil and turned to trot back to Dina's room. Emerging from the bathroom was none other than *Weepy Wendy*. So Dina had been right! I stood completely still hoping she wouldn't notice me since she was facing the other way. I watched her slip down the stairs to the crew quarters. She was wearing thick pink snuggle socks and they don't make any noise at all.

I heard voices approaching from the evangelists' side of the train. It sounded like Andres and...*Tabloid Tilly*? Yikes. I made a beeline back to Dina's compartment.

I slipped into her room and shut the door, locking it and pulling the drapes shut. Rubbing hard on the Velcro, I made sure the loops caught together.

"You were right!" I whispered.

Dina unwrapped a twin pack of Hostess chocolate cupcakes. She offered me one. I took it.

"What was I right about? Do tell," she said, taking a big bite.

I sat next to her and said, "*Weepy Wendy* is on the train! I saw her come out of the potty in the business car. Then she crept down the stairs into the crew's quarters." I ate my cupcake.

Dina smiled with contentment. We both stared into the mirror above the sink. We had chocolate crumbs on our lips.

I kicked my ballet flats off and sat Indian style on Dina's blue sofa. I opened the new cheetah journal and wrote on the inside of the cover:

The Case of the Body Discoverer
By
Dixie London

"Do you want me to list you as co-author?" I asked.
"Nah. Just include me in the dedication."
We smiled at one another.
I wrote at the top of the first page:

Outline for Part One

I found a dead sailor washed up on Cocoa Beach. He wore his

uniform, no dog tags and a Star of David. He smelled like bleach, felt squishy and looked happily mischievous.

It was later revealed his name was David Starr and it was a homicide.

Lieutenant William Hernandez was the lead investigator.

Gathered at the crime scene were the following suspects:

Lieutenant Hottie

Six Uniformed City of Cocoa Beach Cops

Three Copacabana Hotel Security Dudes

Eagle, the hotshot volunteer beach patroller

Andres, the Euro-blonde Lifeguard and decent kisser,

Old *Bicep Betty* in her yellow polka dot bikini and matching support hose

Various hotel guests drinking Starbucks and eating donuts.

Two guys fishing

An early jogger

Me, the Department of Public Works Employee, who discovered the body

Dina read over my shoulder. "Did you forget anyone?"

I reread the list. "Nope...Next..."

I turned the thick crisp ivory page. It was ruled in chocolate-colored ink. "Dina do you have any more chocolate?"

"Sorry. You want the rest of the chips?"

"Nah. Thanks though." I licked the tip of the pencil.

Outline for Part Two

I discovered a dwarf angel in white hanging in the bathroom of my compartment on the train. *Mini Mary Agnes Starr*. Sister of the *Star of David*, a.k.a. the first dead guy. She had been ministered to privately by her pastor, Eugene Donaldson. Sometime after he left (assuming he didn't do her in) she hung herself with the sash to her beautiful white dress, my skein of rainbow yarn and Al Dente's dog tags.

Before she died *Mini Mary Agnes* told me she had spilled her marbles near a red limousine and two muscle headed guys said "We'll get Donaldson..."

I later found a blue aggie marble behind a Norfolk Island Pine

197

potted plant in the writers' parlor car. Someone had brought the plant with them on the trip. I had seen it stacked up with all the other crap as we boarded in Orlando.

A red limousine belongs to Al Dente's Uncle Santy Claus a.k.a. mob kingpin. Said limo with Dina and Al helped me escape from custody in Missouri. Eagle, the hotshot beach patrolman was the driver. He took us back to the train.

"Who died next?"

"The chef?" Dina asked.

"*Big Marc* Clinger. He was clinically dead. Yeah, he died after the dwarf because she was the reason I was sleeping in the parlor car on account of..."

Outline for Part Three

I was in the parlor car after midnight when conductor *Big Marc* stumbled in. Now that I think of it, could he have been inebriated or on medication? Well, he smelled like root beer.

He told me about a top secret naval assignment, he had secretly refueled submarines in Rio De Janeiro, Brazil, after World War II. He also mentioned Australia. *Tabloid Tilly* a.k.a. Matilda Irwin is from Australia. Is there a connection?

The train pitched hard. He ran across and hit his head on a window, breaking it. I tried to help him but he collapsed and stopped breathing. Then started breathing. Then his heart stopped. He also had a big gash on his cheek. His right cheek. He didn't lose his cataract eyeglasses.

I could not rustle up any help so I pulled the emergency brake and woke up in Lieutenant Hottie's compartment. I told him about poor old *Big Marc*. He checked with Andy and they determined *Big Marc* Clinger was missing.

He later turned up in old *Bicep Betty*'s room handcuffed to the bed. He was taken to the hospital and later rejoined the train trip. Old *Bicep Betty* a.k.a. Old Lady Fletcher was at the scene of the first crime, too.

"I can't read her books," Dina said.

"Me either. She's too twisted. No wonder she rakes in the

royalties," I said. "Okay, getting back to *Big Marc*..."

I stretched out my legs and moved my ankles in circles.

"How is your busted rump?" Dina asked, giggling.

"I must be a quick healer. I don't notice it anymore except when someone mentions it. I did take one of my mother's sleeping pills and ever since, the pain has been tolerable."

I wrote:

Big Marc was back on the train and armed. The train allegedly had been hijacked and he was protecting us. Al Dente and Dina and I saw his little pistol. They didn't treat the hijacking as seriously as I would have thought. Who was the hijacker?

Big Marc was also in the parlor car when I chased after *Hack em' up Hazel* who wielding her poker. She outside the observation car. I found the marble on the floor there. "Was this when I found it?"

Dina had dozed off in a carbohydrate crash. I covered her with a thin white blanket and sat back down.

I turned the page and wrote:

Big Marc whistled when my mother dropped her towel. I stopped the train because Rosemary Donaldson, the preacher's wife, was holding a gun to my brother Andy. Why? The reverend said it was something to do with their son, Joel. The surly piano player. Al Dente got the gun away from her. Lieutenant Hottie detained the deranged Rosemary but Andy declined to press charges so she was released.

"Was this before or after Rosemary kicked us off the train and herded us onto a bus because her husband had revealed an affair on national television?" I glanced at my snoring pal. Oh well, I'd figure that out later. Next...

My mother drove the rental bus. We were all overcome by carbon monoxide poisoning. I pulled everyone off the bus in a cornfield. Except I couldn't get *Hack 'em Up Hazel* all the way out. I was pooped and she got stuck. I passed out. I awoke in a barn where the locals took us for triage. The sheriff of Nester County, Missouri told me I was under arrest for the murder of Chico, Rosemary Donaldson's hairdresser/pool boy/paid companion. He had died of carbon monoxide poisoning. My fingerprints were allegedly found on the tennis ball stuffed up in the exhaust pipe of the bus. Well, I yanked it out so that's how my finger prints got on…Wait a minute. If I yanked it out then it wasn't in the tailpipe so unless he or somebody stuffed it back in, that was all made up. And he said he had fingerprinted me while I was unconscious. I looked at my fingers. I never had any ink on them…Something stinks here.

I gave him a false name. Alternate name. My pen name. The sheriff took me in his car to the jail and left me in the backseat, handcuffed. Al Dente opened the door, helped me escape and Eagle drove us back to the train with Dina.

The sheriff never came looking for me again so far as I know. Not that it would have been easy for him to find Dixie London. Unless somebody told him my real name.

Eagle was on the beach at the scene of the *Star of David.* Mobster Santy Claus Dente owned the red limo. *Mini Mary Agnes,* victim number two saw the limo. So did Dina. Was Eagle one of the "muscle-headed guys?"

What did I really know about Eagle anyhow? He was a volunteer beach patrolman. He raced around the sand in his ATV startling the sunbathers. He was pretty good at breaking up fights between drunken teenagers. He was married. Never met his wife. I heard she worked as a waitress at the truck stop. Not that I knew where the truck stop was. I think if it were in Cocoa Beach I'd have noticed. He didn't talk much. He always seemed aloof and waiting to react. Why did he toss me over the bar? What was back there he didn't want me to discover?

I set my cheetah journal and gold pencil down and walked over to the bathroom. I held my breath and opened the door. And gasped.

Chapter Twenty Four

I closed the door.

"Who's dead?" Dina tumbled over, all tangled in the blanket and her long denim skirt.

"Nobody is dead. Al Dente is in there. How long has he been in there?" I asked.

"I didn't know he was," said Dina, folding up the blanket.

We heard the flush. The door banged open.

"It is I, the wandering minstrel, Alfredo Dente," He walked past us and washed his hands.

"How long have you been hiding in there?" I asked, irritated.

"Hiding? Not I. Slumber overtook me. I simply succumbed to the sandman. That sleeping pill works extra fast. Imagine that only if I had taken the full dose. I might well have slept the trip away."

"Did you get it from my Mom's purse? What did you take?"

"Alfredo Dente pays his own passage. I did not surreptitiously remove medication from the lovely mother-in-law dearest."

"Where did you get it?" I asked again.

"Over-the-counter medications and assorted toiletry items are for sale in the evangelists' lounge."

"I didn't see a store in there," I said, my mind conjuring up the piano, grub and old ladies.

"Does the lovely marionette of mystery desire an analgesic, a motion sickness elixir or a sandman seducer? Alfredo Dente would be honored to obtain whatever you require."

"Where do you get it from? A tricky French connection or something?"

"One simply inquires with the barkeep," said Al Dente.

"He shouldn't be selling such strong stuff. There are a bunch of elderly passengers. Most are probably taking handfuls of prescription heart, cholesterol and diabetes medications. No telling what terrible interactions could occur…"

I sat on the sofa next to Dina. Al Dente plopped down next to me and peeked out the window and then he picked up my journal. "May I read the deepest yearnings of the lovely marionette of mystery?"

"Sure. Whatever. Maybe you can help. Read away. I'm trying to solve the murders."

Al Dente opened the book. "The Case of the Body Discoverer..."

I watched as his lips moved following his finger sweeping across the page.

"Alfredo Dente vouches for the moral character of Vicar Donaldson. He is above murder..."

"But he's not above fooling around. Did you see the picture of him fooling around with the late Mary Agnes?"

"No. And photos can be Photoshopped. Do not believe everything you see. Who is the photographer?"

"*Tabloid Tilly*. Matilda Irwin," I said.

"Oh, the pert photographer from down under..." he said wistfully.

I rolled my eyes.

"Hey, Tilly went running out of the *Daily Planet* building in Chicago. A suit was chasing her. Mom tackled him but he got away. Somebody said he was her old flame. Must've been Mom...Perhaps he was one of the red limo guys. It wasn't Eagle. I would have recognized him. What other muscle-headed guy works driving the car for your uncle?" I asked.

"*Freddy the Ferris Wheel*. He's Eagle's partner in enforcement," said Al Dente.

"Did he ever date Matilda Irwin?"

"Neither *Freddy the Ferris Wheel* nor the pert photographer from down under has ever engaged Alfredo Dente in conversation. Alas..."

"Have you ever seen them lock lips?" I asked.

"The meandering minstrel does not spew forth gossip of a lascivious nature."

I got in his face. "What did you see? Spew, Dente."

He cleared his throat and gave us an evil grin.

"The pert photographer from down under and *Freddy the Ferris Wheel* have assumed a, shall we say, numerical position in the back of the crimson vehicle on many occasions..."

I paced to the corridor door then back to the exterior window. "I'm not convinced the chase was just a lover scorned." I looked at Dina.

"Me neither." She sipped orange juice.

"Suppose she dropped off a little disc of photographs to the *Daily Planet*. And there was something in those images that somebody powerful like Uncle Santy Claus didn't want published. Like the photograph of the reverend with the dwarf," I said.

"But why would Santy Claus care about the dalliances of Eugene Donaldson ?" asked Dina.

I paced back to the corridor and peeked out. *Hack 'em Up Hazel* was waddling down the corridor carrying donuts. I walked back to the exterior window. A freight train was passing us by.

"Maybe Uncle Santy Claus is friends with Donaldson. And he wants to cover his rump," said Dina.

"Yes, they have some sort of holy alliance and I'm not sure what it's all about. Al, would you like to shed some light?" I asked.

"It is not my secret to tell…besides, what little I do know on a need to know basis, if I spew, I'll splatter." He made a falling off a building kind of motion with his hand.

"Not even to help solve the serial murder case so that no one else will die?"

"I do not wish to be the next one embalmed. And I would be if I spewed. What are you not understanding, oh lovely marionette of mystery?"

"Fine. But if we guess it will you confirm?"

"No," he said and walked out of the compartment.

I closed the door behind him.

"Suppose Santy Claus doesn't want to cover up for Donaldson . Suppose he wants to cover for *Mini Mary Agnes*…but why?"

"Maybe he felt guilty she died," said Dina.

"Why?" I asked.

She shrugged her shoulders.

"Maybe they want to get rid of *Tabloid Tilly*! Maybe it was a real hit! It would be perfect that her lover, *Freddy-the-Ferris Wheel*, would do her in!" said Dina.

"How about…the government or the mob paid *Tabloid Tilly* to snap the photo and turn it in then they wanted to get rid of her so she wouldn't talk. They didn't want anyone to know the photograph was staged!" I said.

Dina drained the last of her juice. "I like that. Let's go with this line of reasoning…"

"So, do you remember the movie 'Wag the Dog'?" I asked.

"The President started a war to cover up...I don't remember what," she said.

"I don't remember what either but I'm thinking, what if the reverend and the mobster staged a sex scandal that didn't exist to cover up the money laundering, which I'm pretty sure does exist, from bits and pieces Lieutenant Hottie and Al Dente have fed me. Yes...this sex scandal would be a perfect cover for why the President's Special Investigator was aboard the train full of evangelists," I said.

"Ladies, may I have your attention please," said my brother on the public address system. "Due to a derailment on the line ahead of us, we will be held in this position...for quite some time. If any of you detrain to walk around in the desert, please take water with you."

"Who'd want to walk around in the desert?" asked Dina.

I shrugged my shoulders. "Snakes, prairie dogs and scorpions."

"Right." Dina stood, stretched and threw her orange juice bottle into the little chrome trash slot.

"That should empty out half the train..." I grinned.

"It's a good thing the door wasn't open. Your mother just walked by. Hey look, she's stepping off the train."

I shook my head. "Now what is she up to?" I stood up and looked outside. "Uh-oh. Rosemary is out there." I ran down the corridor and hopped down the stairs.

Mom was straightening her purple silk chemise blouse. She had a matching pair of walking shorts and little purple leather walking shoes. She started toward Rosemary with resolve in her eyes. I knew that look. Mom was on the warpath.

I chased after her. "Mom! Mom! Stop!"

She did. Mom turned and looked at me. "What is it, Sandra? I'm a bit predisposed."

"You need to get back on the train."

"Why?"

"Because...you didn't bring water."

She pulled two bottles out of her gold satchel.

"Because I need to talk to you. Me and Dina need you."

"Well, why didn't you say so? What's wrong? Is Dina in trouble? The poor dear must be grieving so for her Aunt Beverly."

204

I grabbed my mother's elbow and guided her back to the train. I turned to see who had gotten off. *Contest Carly*, *Tabloid Tilly*, the editor and Mrs. Higgenbottom-Barnesworth

Mom climbed onto the train ahead of me.

I squeezed ahead of my mother in the vestibule and led her to Dina's room. I knocked on the glass. She smiled and jumped up. I slid open the door. "Nobody is in the bathroom, right?" I asked.

"I never know," she answered.

"What's this about bathrooms?" Mom asked.

"Oh, nothing. You know, I just keep opening bathroom doors and being surprised when they are occupied."

"Sandra Marie Faire, haven't you the decency to knock before entering? Apparently not, after that embarrassing incident with Jimmy Tamales and that writer lady."

"Do tell! What happened with Tamales and which writer lady?" asked Dina.

"Sandra opened the privacy door between her compartment and that lady's. And interrupted dirty sex."

"Which lady? Who did Jimmy's Tamales?" asked Dina.

I busted out laughing. "*Hack 'em Up Hazel*...but you didn't hear it from me," I said.

"Too bad Matilda wasn't there to snap a picture," said Mom.

I looked at her, shocked. "Mom! I can't believe you'd say something like that."

"Well, Matilda seems to be taking sneaky inappropriate pictures everywhere. If one shows up of me so help me I'll..."

I remembered the towel incident in the parlor car.

"You won't have to, Mom. I'll do it for you if Andy doesn't get to her first...but I thought you liked her."

"Keep your enemies close. Don't you ever listen to me, Sandra?"

"I didn't know you had any enemies..."

"That's because I keep them in check under my green thumb."

Okay, I was really getting a headache now. The kind that made my left eye water. Severe pain in my left temple and then the swollen weeping snake eye.

"Mom, who'd you get the sleeping pills from?"

"The bartender. Why? Do you want to sleep at this time of day? Get some warm milk and some fresh Bing cherries if you want a nap," she said.

"Cherries?" asked Dina.

"Eating cherries before you sleep ensures you'll wake up with a morning bowel movement. Nature's sweet little elixir.

"No, I have one of those snake eye things going on and my head is killing me."

"I don't have any sinus medication. But the bartender might." She whipped a tissue from her pocket and dabbed my eye. Then Mom rustled through her satchel and pulled out two ten dollar bills. "Here, go on and see if he has any." She handed me the money.

"What a price gouger! Twenty dollars for a bottle of sinus pills?"

"Oh, that's just for one dose."

"What in the heck are in these pills?" I asked.

"Gold. It's going for two thousand dollars an ounce now, you know," said Mom.

"I didn't realize you followed the market, Mrs. Faire," said Dina.

"Oh, I learn a lot on *Have I Got a Deal for You.* "

"I don't have much money so if I can't pay for it in cash I don't buy it," said Dina.

"That's a very sensible attitude. Your mother must be very proud of you. Where is she now?"

"I think they are heading to Washington, D.C. now. Dad can spend three days in the Air and Space Museum. Mom favors the National Gallery of Art and the Library of Congress."

"I wish Wally would retire so we could travel. In his line of work by the time they retire they're so old that half of them die within a year..."

The snake eye was reaching the point of no return. "I've got to get some medicine." I rushed out the door with my left eye closed and my right hand holding pressure on my left temple to try to alleviate the pain. I stumbled through the cars. Two little old ladies were coming toward me in the first evangelists' sleeper. Normally I'd back up and let them pass but I really needed those pills. I shoved through muttering "Excuse me. I'm really in pain." I hustled into the next car.

Reverend Donaldson was telling an anecdote about a man passed over for a promotion. His enraptured audience packed the evangelists' lounge car. I shoved my way through and made it to the bar.

Eagle glared at me.

"I need something for a sinus infection. Pressure, pain, runny eye and an occasional full faucet drip from my left nostril."

He muttered, "Twenty Dollars," and pulled a key ring from his pocket. He unlocked a metal box, the kind you use as a fireproof box for your valuable papers…and things you want to hide from your mother.

I pulled the tens from my pocket tossed them on the counter and he handed me a small white envelope. I couldn't read the label at all on account of the snake eye thing. "What is the dosage? How many? How often?"

"Two pills every four to six hours. Take with a full glass of water and food," he said.

"Water. Now." I ripped the envelope open and shook a pill into my hand. I shove the envelope into my pocket and the pill into my mouth. He gave me a glass of water. I guzzled it. "Food. Now."

"There are pretzels on the credenza. You need to take the other pill."

"Nah, I never do. One works for me." I shoved my way over to the credenza and shoveled pretzels into my mouth. Then I took as many as I could hold and pushed back through the crowd with my handful of pretzels over my eye and on my head. I can only imagine what the holy people must have thought about me.

As I passed through the business car I blurrily noticed Tony O'Rourke pounding away on his keyboard. Normally I'd stop and gush and try to read over his shoulder. All I wanted to do was sleep this snake eye off.

"Hello, Sandra, I've been thinking about you. I have an erotic scene I'm trying to write and I need some input from you. Come on over and read what I've written so far," he said in that deep testosterone voice that sent blood pooling in all my lady love areas.

I stopped and plopped into a chair across the table from him. Well, near as I could see, I was across from him about four chairs down. The chair spun and so did my head. I kind of felt like I had when Al Dente and I slurped the blue Jell-O shooters.

I slumped down in the chair and my head flopped onto the back of it. I closed my eyes and covered them with my arm.

The train pitched and the chair and I sailed backwards until we hit the wall. My legs splayed wide open.

"I love it when you are submissive," he whispered and evidently walked over to me. "I'll read it out loud. Would you like me to talk dirty to you?"

"'*Type Dirty to Me*' by Dina Devers. That book has been written," I said. But my voice sounded kind of funny. Like it was coming from someone else's mouth.

"Exactly what I need you to help me research. So I can realistically type dirty...to you. This chapter will be foreplay at its finest. Before the couple is interrupted by an unfortunate turn of events. The hero slips his hands underneath the heroine's form fitting white tee shirt and she of course is not wearing anything else. She gasps for air as he kisses her fervently. His dominating lips won't let her break free. As his long fingers pinch..."

That's all I heard before my world went dark.

Chapter Twenty Five

This dark place was warm and comforting. I couldn't see or hear but I could smell and feel.

I was aware of Lieutenant Hottie examining me. I knew it was him by his touch and by his scent. His deodorant was so manly. He wasn't the type to wear cologne or after shave lotion. And it was Lieutenant Hottie, not bestselling author Tony O'Rourke. How did I know this? Because I was in love with Lieutenant Hottie. His take charge of the crime scene. His domineering attitude. His swagger. His firm and demanding touch. His pheromones. His muscular body. His heart, buried somewhere very deep. Very protected.

I could feel the locomotion of the train. I was lying on a hard surface. Lieutenant Hottie's fingers were on my neck. His cheek was pressed to my nose and lips. His hands were running the length of my limbs and then pressing my abdomen.

His arm slipped around my back and under my legs. I felt the ascension as he lifted me. The blood rushed to my head. He must have thrown me over his shoulder again. I wished I were awake.

* * *

"Sandra, wake up. Wake up, Sandra," said Mom.

Darn it. What happened to my Lieutenant Hottie? Where did my lover go?

"Sandra Marie Faire, wake up. Wake up this minute." I could hear the irritation in her voice.

I stretched and squirmed.

"Come on and open your eyes," she said.

I did. I saw Mom's Hollywood hoop simulated diamond earring. Her hair was pulled into a ponytail. Her ponytails always were tighter, neater and higher than mine. No matter how long I fussed with my hair my ponytails were always loose and sloppy. I didn't inherit the ponytail making gene.

"How are you feeling?"

"Ponytails," I said. "My little pony. I want a pony. Mommy can I have a pony for my birthday?"

"Your birthday was last week. Where would you keep a pony in your apartment? Your father and I gave you a lovely potted banana tree for your balcony. Didn't you like it?"

"Banana bread. Yes, please may I have another slice of banana bread? And a glass of milk with a bendy straw?"

"Sandra, what's wrong with you? Have you been drinking liquor? I sent you to the evangelists' lounge for headache medicine. Did you drink tequila instead? That will only give you a worse headache. I don't know why people drink that wormy stuff."

Wormy...Worms crawling on the sidewalk after the morning rain. Dried worms. Dead worms. Death...

Corpses...the dead sailor's bloated body on the beach...*Mini Mary Agnes* hanging in the bathroom...*Napping Norah* stinking up the room...The chef with his pants around his ankles ...Chico dead in his sleep...me dead on a train...

"No! No! I don't want to die!" I screamed.

"Sandra, it's all right. You are not dying. Wake up and open your eyes again," said Mom.

I tried really hard to open my eyes but they wouldn't cooperate. *Weepy Wendy.* I needed *Weepy Wendy* to come and help me. I needed a shot or something. What was wrong with me? My head hurt so bad. My face hurt so bad. My mind was so soupy. I needed a shot to find the killer. Before he killed again. Before he shot me...

I must save the others. I must save Mom and Andy and Lieutenant Hottie and Dina and Mrs. Higgenbottom-Barnesworth and Al Dente. Why did he come last? I was still mad at him. He ruined me. Without ruining me. He tricked me into getting married for some stupid secret reason. So that made me an old maid. Matron. Took me out of circulation. Took me away from my Lieutenant Hottie...

* * *

I rolled over and opened my eyes. To Al Dente's enormous nose. I pushed myself back.

"Greetings, marionette of mystery. What is the status of your comeliness? I, Alfredo Dente, your valiant minstrel of melody have been distraught with dire worry. Are you unwell?"

"My head stopped hurting," I said and sat up. It felt good to smile. I looked around the compartment as the train gently rocked back and forth. "Whose room is this?" I asked.

"It is the rolling command center of the muscle bound magistrate. Would that we were on steady ground, I would whisk you away to my castle in the sand."

I remembered Al Dente's sand castles. "Will you build me the one with the turret?"

"As you wish, lovely marionette of mystery."

"And will you build me a moat full of alligators to keep all the dead bodies away?"

"I protect the gates of Hell for you, my beloved marionette of mystery. Nevermore will the demons escape to haunt you."

"Al, aren't you scared of them?" I asked.

"Terrified. Yet it is my duty. I was born to protect and serve. I shall guard the gates of Hell until it is time to pass the fiery torch to the next chosen spirit."

The door closed. "So it's true!" said Dina. "You know where the gates of Hell are?"

"Hi, Dina. Did you bring me anything to eat?" I asked.

She pulled two packs of Smarties candies from her pocket and handed them to me. I sat up and unwrapped the first pack. As I sucked the sugar in the first yellow candy I tried to wrap my mind around Al Dente and Dina's bizarre paranormal enthusiasm.

"*Mini Mary Agnes* has been visiting me," she whispered, giggling.

My pulse quickened. I pulled Lieutenant Hottie's blanket up over me, hugging it to my shoulders. It smelled wonderful just like him. "Where is Lieutenant Hot—Hernandez?"

"I don't know. He came by my room and got your mom and then she came back when Al took a turn sitting with you," said Dina. She crunched a handful of Smarties.

"So, is *Mini Mary Agnes'* ghost naughty or nice?" I asked. Not really believing she saw it. But believing she thought she saw it because I adored my friend.

"She's tormented. She's mad because she said there was a mix-up in her paperwork and they sent her down under." Dina tossed a pack of Smarties to Al Dente.

"To Australia? They buried her in Australia?" I asked.

"No. That's not what I meant. She went to Hell," said Dina, matter-of-factly, as if it was a common occurrence, people whining about going to Hell in their afterlives.

I checked my wrist and sniffed. "Has anyone seen Tinker Bell? I'm lost without her.

"You still haven't found your watch?" asked Dina.

"No. And she was special. Her pixie dust got me through some stressful times," I said, frowning.

"When were you last comforted by the wee fairy's pixie dust?" asked Al Dente.

"I guess it was the first time I worked in the kitchen. The chef made me take it off and stow it on the shelf. I don't remember strapping it back on and when I looked for it the next day, it wasn't there.

Dina closed her eyes tightly. "I'll see if he took it with him."

"What do you mean?"

"Shh…"

"Spirit of artisan food, please show me the chef…" chanted Dina. I tried not to giggle.

"Ladies, may I have your attention please?" My brother's voice came through on the public address system. "The toilets in the evangelists' lounge car are backed up. Please do not flush anything but human waste and the railroad issued toilet paper. You may use the restrooms in the business car and writers' parlor car as well as in your rooms."

Al Dente said, "I shall endeavor to return your beloved Tinker Bell, lovely marionette of mystery."

Dina opened her eyes and frowned. "I couldn't see him. Sorry."

"I should look in the refrigerator," I said. "When *Peetie-the-Parrot* went missing, that's where he turned up. On top of a crate of cherry marmalade."

"Why would a crate of cherry marmalade be refrigerated?" asked Dina.

"You know, that is weird. After a jar is opened, I can understand. Why would a full presumably unopened case be chilled?"

"Are you up to standing?" Al Dente offered his hand. I took it.

"Let's go down and look for my watch and crack open the case of marmalade," I said.

We walked like connected ducklings through the train. Al Dente first, with me holding the back of his belt. Then Dina behind me with her hands on my shoulders to catch me if I fell.

I still felt a little woozy but not hung-over like on my wedding night. That reminded me. "Al, I want an annulment."

"That pains me to hear. Alas, that cannot come to pass. It is impossible at this point of the mission," he said as we descended the stairs.

"What do you mean mission? What mission? Are you still laundering money? I thought the feds are onto you. Are you stupid or what?"

"I wish to assure the marionette of mystery that her faithful husband, Alfredo Dente, is most definitely not stupid. The Laundromat is closed. It ceases to exist. The one in Florida anyhow."

"In there. This is the refrigerator." I pointed to the door. "Then as soon as your trial is over we can get on with the divorce or annulment or whatever, right?" I asked.

"The minstrel of melody will not be tried for any crime," he said.

"What do you mean? Are you going on the lamb?" I asked.

"*Au contraire*, my *chère amore*. There are no charges filed against me."

"But Lieutenant Hot—Hernandez told me you were the scapegoat and that's what the meeting between him and the Special Investigator was about, using you to take the fall for a year then relocating you to Iceland..." My head felt kind of like a sugar rush. I decided not to eat the other pack of Smarties yet. Dina was still rustling open packages and snarfing them.

"Okay, somebody isn't telling me the truth here. Maybe the Lieutenant doesn't know the whole story? Then what is your mission that is preventing our eminent divorce?" I asked.

"I am not at liberty to discuss the details and you cannot force me. Just be assured that I, Alfredo Dente, am protecting the world from the most hideous of demons."

"The terrorist who commandeered the train?" Dina asked.

I opened the refrigerator door. And Screamed. *Weepy Wending* was sitting on the marmalade crate, naked with her feet on her shoulders. Some sort of yoga position.

Chapter Twenty Six

I couldn't tell if she was humming or if it was the condenser. Al Dente and Dina shoved me into the refrigerator. Al Dente had cocked his head to the side obviously to take in the view of the skinny nurse with the scary hair.

"Is she dead?" asked Dina, her voice brimming more with curiosity than compassion.

Why is it always me who has to feel for a pulse? Fine. I tiptoed over to Wendy with my face scrunched up and my own pulse pounding. I inhaled the scent of cantaloupes. Not death. Good sign. I touched her wrist. And felt a weak pulse. I stuck a finger under her nose. I felt her breath. "She's alive."

"Wendy. Wendy, honey. Are you all right?"

No response.

I gently shook her shoulder. Her very cold shoulder. Her eyes were closed and she was trancelike.

"Let's get her out of here and warm her up," I said.

Dina held the door open.

"Come on, Al Dente, get the fettuccini over here and carry her out. He diverted his eyes and skulked over. Making several spastic hand movements, it was obvious he couldn't figure out where to grab her.

I eased her legs down from behind her neck and she flopped straight out. As Al Dente grabbed her arms, she flashed green eyes and ran screaming out of the refrigerator. Like a banshee. However a banshee might sound and whatever a banshee was. I followed her up the stairs and through all the cars until we got to the end of the train and she flung herself out the door. I yanked some drapes down before I joined her.

I said, "Wendy. It's me, Sandra. What's wrong, honey?" I wrapped the drapes around her shoulders.

"The gates of Hell have opened…"

"No they haven't. You just had a bad dream or ate some bad fish or something." I tried to calm her down. I've never had to talk down a crazy person before. I didn't like this job. Why me?

"I offered the Devil some clean souls to steal…"

214

She was creeping me out. I wanted to wash her face. The dark circles of mascara under her eyes…oh, good, they really were green. I didn't see the flash of monster eyes back in the refrigerator after all…

"Wendy, honey…what do you mean you offered the Devil some clean souls?" I held my breath.

"I eased some souls into the hereafter."

"How?"

"I treated their symptoms by giving them life everlasting…"

"In Hell?"

"Of course."

"How did you treat their symptoms?" I remembered how Mom was dead to the world after taking a sleeping pill. And Al Dente and me with the sinus medication…I'd bet everyone from *Mini Mary Agnes* to the chef had taken her deadly doses…Wendy was a trauma nurse practitioner. She could prescribe all types of drugs and knew their potencies…

"The Devil needs to bring my daddy back. I want my daddy!" Poor Wendy launched into a tirade which morphed into a child-like temper tantrum.

I stepped back and let her fall to the floor of the observation deck. She pounded the metal with her fists.

I looked inside the window and saw Dina, taking notes. Al Dente was big eyed, no doubt enjoying peeking at a naked woman. Mom, Lieutenant Hottie, Andy and Eagle had joined them. I kept covering Wendy with the drapes and she kept flinging them off.

"Wendy, honey, it's all right. Everything will be all right. Get it all out. Let your anger out and then you'll feel much better."

I turned toward the audience and threw my hands up. I wanted to help poor *Weepy Wendy* but I wasn't a shrink or an exorcist or…I saw Eugene Donaldson through the window.

I opened the door and whispered to Mom, "Go and get your robe. Hurry. And send Reverend Donaldson out to help me, please."

Mom nodded and took off.

I turned my attention back to Wendy.

"I read your letter, Daddy. I sent clean souls to the Devil and he didn't set you free! The devil didn't set you free! I need you, Daddy!" She rolled into the fetal position.

Reverend Donaldson stepped out onto the observation deck.

"What's wrong?"

"We found her naked in the refrigerator. She's been missing for awhile. The exterior window in her compartment was broken out. But I saw her skulking around downstairs yesterday. Anyhow, she keeps saying she sent clean souls to the Devil but he won't open the gates and set her daddy free. Can you do an exorcism or something?"

We looked at Wendy. She had stopped moving. Her eyes were fixated on the railing. Her vacant eyes. Oh, no…not another one.

"Wendy, are you all right?" I asked.

"Wendy, are you feeling better?"

No response.

I stuck two fingers on her carotid artery. No pulse. I rolled her onto her back. I screamed. Blood trickled from her eyes, nose, ears and mouth.

I cringed, shut my eyes tight then opened them. My little Yiddish advanced first aid instructor whispered to me: "She's dead, that one. Cover her up."

I opened her airway and put my face near her nose. I didn't detect any breathing. Her chest wasn't rising. I looked at Reverend Donaldson and said, "Get the defibrillator."

He dashed inside.

Andy, Lieutenant Hottie and Eagle emerged. "Go inside, Sis. We'll take care of her."

Go inside, we'll take care of her? Can I be hearing correctly? I'm relieved of trying to revive the dead? Yes!

I stepped behind Lieutenant Hottie. Why did he always have to look so darned good?

I pushed through the crowd.

"She's clinically dead," I choked out.

Rosemary helped me to a seat in a leather arm chair. "You tried your best. Thank you for being there for her," she said in her nasal voice. Today Rosemary was dressed in gray leather boots with buckles all over them. Black and white striped socks up to her trim thighs. Black ruffled mini skirt. And a crisp white blouse with the collar turned up, unbuttoned down to there.

"I'm…I'm very sorry about Chico…" It occurred to me that I had never talked to Rosemary since the carbon monoxide poisoning on the bus. "I know he meant a great deal to you. He did such a good job with your hair." Come to think of it her hair looked a whole lot better since Chico had passed away. She had just been brushing it no elaborate Puerto Rican prom doos.

"Thank you. Thank you so much, Sandra."

I hugged her. She hugged me back. Very tightly. Tears welled up in her voice. "Thank you," she repeated. "You understand. Chico was my best friend. I don't know how I'll go on without him."

"I'm here for you. If you ever need a friend I'm here for you, Rosemary..." I said.

Her long orange nails dug into my back.

I looked around the writers' parlor car. Reverend Donaldson ran through with the Automated External Defibrillator.

Mom paced, clutching her pink chenille robe. Dina was making a cup of hot chocolate at the credenza. *Big Marc* was talking into his train radio/phone thingy. Al Dente sat in the far corner softly singing. It sounded like Glory Hallelujah. He could even make a hymn rock. God he was a talented musician. I wished all the best success for him. My friend since kindergarten.

Hack 'em Up Hazel and *Contest Carly* stepped into the car.

"I'm sorry, ladies. We have a possible death here. Please go to the evangelists' lounge car if you need refreshments," said Conductor *Big Marc.*

"Who died this time?" Hazel asked.

"That skinny girl with the crazy hair," he answered.

"Wendy?" asked Carly.

"I don't know her name. Please return to your rooms or the evangelists' lounge car." He shooed them away.

Mom folded her robe and draped it over one arm. She pulled a travel packet of tissues from her pocket and walked over to me with purpose.

I grabbed tighter to Rosemary, bracing myself for the catfight of the century.

Mom shook out a tissue and dabbed Rosemary's eyes. Rosemary turned me loose, accepted the tissue and said, "Thank you so much, Terry. You have raised a lovely daughter...I don't know what I'd do without her. She and I are going to be spending quite a bit of time together now...Sandra, I'd like to offer you the position of my personal assistant."

"She'd be delighted to take the job," said Mom.

"Wait one minute. I didn't say I was looking for a job."

"Oh, Sandra, you just have to. You just have to. You are the only one that understands. I need your friendship," pleaded Rosemary.

So she wanted me to be her new Chico. That was so funny. If only she knew how lousy I was at making ponytails. And I flunked swimming lessons so I would be a terrible pool boy. But the paid companion part, I could do that…and I had mailed my letter of resignation to Igor…

"What does the job entail?" I asked.

Rosemary blew her nose. "You move into my guest house. It's two thousand square feet fully furnished with a kitchen, great room, two bedrooms, theater room, sunroom and three bathrooms. You can eat all of your meals in the mansion with our family if you'd like. You travel with me wherever I go.

"I'll pay you two thousand dollars a week," said Rosemary, straightening her mini skirt.

"I'll take it!" I agreed. After all, poor Rosemary needed me.

The North American Passenger Railway crew chief and Jimmy Tamales walked through the car. They opened the observation door.

Reverend Donaldson, Lieutenant Hottie and Andy came inside, the chief and Jimmy left.

The reverend said, "May I have your attention please?"

The car fell silent.

"We have lost another soul. Let us bow our heads." We did.

"Dear God all mighty. Please rest our tormented sister Wendy's soul and give peace to the ones she left behind. Amen."

We ran "Amen" around the car.

"It's finally over now," I blurted.

"What do you mean?" Mom asked.

"The serial killings. It's over," I said.

"How can you be sure?" asked Lieutenant Hottie.

"Sit down, everyone," I said.

Mom and Rosemary sat. *Contest Carly* snuck in and stood in the back."

"Al, go and get Carly, Pat and Hazel."

He did.

"Please, sit down." The guys firmly planted their feet and stood around the room. Lieutenant Hottie and Andy blocked the observation car door. Dina rubbed her hands together, smiled and sat next to me.

When Al Dente returned with the writers they took seats on the round couch.

Somebody was missing…and Eagle was slowly making his way toward the other cars. *Tabloid Tilly*. Where was she and what was she up to? I caught my brother's eye and nodded toward Eagle. Apparently I had also caught Mom's eye because she tossed the robe in the air and lit out after Andy did, hot on Eagle's trail.

"Excuse me, one moment please. Lieutenant Hernandez, will you please make our guests comfortable and make sure they stay until we all return? Thanks!" I trotted through the cars searching every unlocked compartment. I didn't find *Tabloid Tilly*.

When I arrived in the evangelists' lounge car Andres was strumming his guitar. An elderly couple drank wine at a little table. Andy had Eagle handcuffed behind the bar.

"You should be ashamed of yourself. Wait until I tell your mother. We go to the same nail salon, you know. You'll be in really big trouble when she finds out…" said Mom.

I almost felt sorry for him.

"What did you find, Andy?" I asked.

"His drug box. I won't know until it's analyzed but I suspect these over-the-counter drugs are really narcotics," my brother said.

"I suspect a lethal dose of chloral hydrate. The stuff they use to slip someone a Mickey Finn," I said. "Bring him back to the writers' parlor car…Please."

I walked over to Andres. "Have you seen Matilda Irwin?"

He stopped strumming and smiled at me. "Hello, fräulein. Have you come for another passionate kiss?" He set his guitar down and stood up.

"Maybe later." I meant that. Well, if things didn't work out with Lieutenant Hottie. "I need your help again. I need a big, strong, intelligent man."

"I am always at your service, you sweet little apple streusel."

The elderly couple clinked their wine glasses together, toasting us.

"Find Matilda Irwin. Fast. The exotic Australian with the camera. She's all mixed up in the murders. Bring her to the writers' parlor car as fast as you can. I don't care if she's dead or alive."

219

The old lady gasped.

"I mean…you know what I mean. Just find her! Quick." I ran back through the train to the writers' parlor car.

* * *

"May I have your attention please?" Everyone politely looked at me. *Pat-the-Pirate*, *Contest Carly* and *Hack 'em Up Hazel* finished whispering to one another.

"The murders are over. Yes, murders, not deaths. It seems as though our long time Global Order of Scribes chapter mate, Wendy Devlin, poisoned us. With malice of forethought. She brought dangerous, lethal drugs with her, packaged and sold as safe over-the-counter remedies, by her accomplice, Eagle."

There were a few gasps.

"I had nothing to do with this. Well, yeah, I did sell the pills but I didn't know they were poison. I swear, I'm innocent," said Eagle, emphatically.

"A judge will decide that," said Andy. He pulled Eagle to a chair near the observation car door by the potted plants. "Sit," ordered my brother the cop.

Eagle sat.

Andy glanced out the window. Lieutenant Hottie moved over and stood on the other side of Eagle with his arms folded in front of him. Looking mean. I loved that look on him. So darned alpha male sexy…

"But drugs only explain poor Norah's death," said Dina. "She died in her sleep."

"Well, it's still just a theory and before the police start arguing with me I'll say toxicology tests need to be performed on all of the apparent death victims starting with David Starr, the sailor I found on the beach," I said.

"Chloral hydrate and morphine were found at lethal levels. He also had drinks with Wendy Devlin, she was the last person he was seen with," said Lieutenant Hernandez.

"Does anyone know if Mary Agnes Starr, Chico or the chef took any over-the-counter pills before they died?" I asked.

"Chico had a terrible headache. I bought him pills from…that monster!" Rosemary pointed to Eagle.

Her husband held her back and spoke calming words.

"Chico was the only person on the bus trip to succumb to carbon monoxide poisoning. I'm guessing it's because he ingested lethal drugs," I said.

"What about the little lady who committed suicide?" asked *Hack 'em Up Hazel*. After she had dirty sex with you?" Hazel walked over to Reverend Donaldson and wagged her accusing finger at him.

Hand in hand, Andres and *Tabloid Tilly* joined us. What the heck?

"The wee one did not have dirty sex with the reverend. I doctored those photographs," *Tabloid Tilly* proclaimed, smiling.

"Well, then why did she hang herself?" *Contest Carly* asked.

"More than likely it was staged by the suspect. Wendy Devlin," said Lieutenant Hernandez.

I noticed Rosemary didn't seem relieved or surprised to hear that her husband hadn't cheated on her. She was still glaring at Eagle.

"Eagle, did the chef take any over-the-counter drugs prior to his death?"

"I sold him antacids to settle his stomach. But I did not know they were poison…" said Eagle.

"Yes, I thought the fish was bad. I wouldn't eat it or serve it." said Andres.

"Did anyone else take any medicines bought from Eagle?" asked Lieutenant Hernandez.

Me, Mom, Al Dente and Big Marc raised our hands.

"Well, then your theory is all manure, Sandra," said *Contest Carly*.

"Mom and I only took half a dose," I said.

"As did I, Alfred Dente, wandering minstrel of melody…"

"I took two analgesics, the full dose," said Big Marc. I got a little woozy but they didn't take the arthritis pain away. I normally need to take a higher dose of everything because of my size. I'm glad I didn't this time."

The train stopped. I looked out the windows. An old man seated atop a ladder painted the overhang at the station.

"Everyone please remain on the train until the possible death victim is removed. You will have a two hour layover in San Bernardino, California. We will advise you when you may detrain…" said Andy.

"Can we go back to our rooms now?" asked *Pat-the-Pirate*.

Lieutenant Hottie said, "Yes. Stay in your rooms until you are told you may detrain."

"Way to sleuth, Sandy!" said Dina with a huge smile. "I'm going to pack a few things." She headed out through the vestibule to the rest of the train. The other writers followed.

I walked over to Mom. "I'm so proud of you," I patted her shoulder.

"For what?"

"For setting your anger aside, well founded as it is, and being compassionate with Rosemary," I said.

"Why wouldn't I be compassionate? The poor dear lost her best friend. To murder no less." Mom looked out the rear window. I did too. They had zipped Weepy Wendy into a body bag. She would weep no more.

"But you were so mad at her for holding Andy at gun point,"

"Oh, that. The gun probably wasn't even loaded. She's a great actress."

"What?"

It was all staged. Her husband hadn't cheated," said Mom. She crossed the car to chat with Andy.

But I distinctly remember the reverend had said that Rosemary was upset about their son, when she pulled the gun on Andy, not that she was mad at him for cheating on her.

* * *

I was alone in the writers' parlor car with Reverend Donaldson. I asked him, point blank, "Why did you stage a sex scandal?"

The media will have a field day with it for weeks. Hopefully by the time it fizzles out I'll have found a source of private funding for our special project," he said.

"But reverends do not survive sex scandals."

"I'm not worried about surviving the scandal. My wife knows the truth. She was more than willing to help out."

"What truth?"

"We were diverting funds from a shell mortgage company to fund protection of…"

"Protection of what?" Why wouldn't he just spit it out and tell me?

"It is not my place to tell you. I can only tell my wife. Nobody

222

involved can tell anyone but their legal spouse. Because everyone has to tell someone. You cannot live with such mind blowing knowledge and not tell someone."

"Does Alfredo Dente know?" I asked. After all he was my legal husband.

"That is not for me to say."

"Fine. So what about the shell company? If it's a shell so be it."

"We thought it was a shell. It was supposed to be a shell. Unfortunately not being able to explain things to the employees we had to hire for the cover, they did their jobs loaning money to down on their luck borrowers. People who couldn't afford to pay them back. They were foreclosed upon and lost their homes. But we had to protect the secret."

"What secret?"

"Exactly. There isn't a secret. We never discussed anything…"

* * *

I cornered Al Dente in my room and locked the door. I opened the bathroom and no one was there.

"Spit it out. What in the fettuccini is this big secret that everyone is protecting? It has to do with the Navy. And Reverend Donaldson told me the people guarding the secret can confide in their spouses. Hence, I am your lawfully wedded wife, more or less. So spit it out, Al Dente. What is the big secret?"

"Lovely marionette of mystery. I have long waited for the day I could share this with you. Firstly, this is the reason I needed to marry you. In great haste. You were the only woman I could trust. I could not marry my step-cousin so that left me you."

"Yeah, yeah, yeah. I'm leftover. So spit it out."

"And you were slightly compensated for your spousal role. The automatic deposits. I hope you have enjoyed the extra pay?" he asked.

"I haven't touched it."

"Why?"

"Why should I? I'm a big girl. I have a job. Had a job. Hey, I've got a new job. Rosemary's P.A. I get to live in her guest house."

"But I thought the marionette of mystery enjoyed beachcombing and sleuthing…"

"I hate discovering dead bodies. I hate picking up garbage. And I hate slathering on sunscreen three times per shift. It's probably loaded with carcinogens."

"The money is yours. Do with it what you will…follow your dreams, sweet wife."

"Speaking of which, there was a huge error on the last statement. It was a hoot to stare at."

"No error. Final payment since I finished my tour of duty."

"Millions?"

"Yes."

"For me?"

"Yes."

"How about we split it?"

"Only if you insist, my comely wife."

"I do. Once we un-do the marriage."

"Impossible," said Al Dente.

"Why? What is the big secret? Why were you, *Big Marc* Clinger, Rosemary Donaldson and your dad all in the Navy?"

Al Dente cleared his throat, smoothed his black tee shirt and whispered, "We patrol a specific longitude and latitude of the area popularly known as the Bermuda Triangle."

"Why? To keep other people from stumbling over it and disappearing?"

"Au contraire my chère amore. To keep people from stumbling out."

"What?"

"The Bermuda Triangle is the portal to Hell."

Chapter Twenty-Seven

I didn't laugh. I just collapsed on the floor and lay my head on my arms absorbing the revelation. Holy revelation. Holy smokes. Holy Ghost. Holy guacamole.

"Did Wendy's father ever guard it?"

"Yes."

"He left a suicide note. She found it. And killed people. She thought if she gave clean souls to the devil, he'd resurrect her father. The devil would release him…"

Al Dente knelt down and cradled me in his arms. "Marionette of Mystery, but if not your mother had taught us to take half doses of over-the-counter drugs, we would be the clean souls Wendy offered to the devil…"

The door flew open and hit me in the head.

"Oww!"

"Oh, pardon me," Mom said. "I'll leave you two lovebirds alone. Don't let me interrupt now. I'm looking forward to spoiling my grandbabies." She backed away and slid the door shut.

"Are you terribly injured, my dear sweet marionette of mystery?"

I sat up and rubbed my head. "No. It didn't really hurt. I just have 'Oww!' on autopilot. I've been banged up so many times on this train."

"It would please the wandering minstrel immensely if you would share your inside sleuthing information. How are you so sure that the skunk haired nurse poisoned all of the pure souls?"

"My gut. Just a feeling. And Lieutenant Hernandez seemed to corroborate some of it. And my brother rapidly assessed the situation at the bar with Eagle and the pill box. So I'm figuring the cops were on the same trail. We just reached the rainbow at the same time."

I stood up and looked in the mirror. My hair was a mess. I grabbed my purse and fished out a hairbrush. As I tried to detangle and fluff, Al settled on the sofa and crossed his gangly legs.

"Let's go look around *Weepy Wendy's* room. If it's not taped off as a crime scene. Even if it is." I shoved my brush back into my purse and fished out nitrile gloves. I tossed two to Al Dente. "Here.

Let's roll."

"What clues will we be seeking to uncover?"

"Dog tags for one. I kept finding dog tags with the names of the keepers of the gates of Hell or whatever on them. Was Rosemary one of the chosen ones?"

"Affirmative. The skankily dressed holy wife and I shared duty a few times," he answered as he shoved two fingers into one hole.

My gloves were on. I grabbed his hand and fixed his.

"Everyone who guards the gates is Catholic?" I asked.

"I don't think so. The vicar's wife and son are not," said Al Dente.

"But the dog tag said Rosemary was. So did yours"

"When did you read my dog tags?" He pulled the chain from inside his black tee shirt and examined them.

"Have you had these in your possession the whole time?"

"Yes. Regulations. I always wear them. I am a dutiful sailor."

"So the tags I found are fakes. Wait a minute. Rosemary's son is guarding the portal to Hell too?"

"Alas, he was up for the next tour of duty but reneged by way of hijacking the train."

"Joel Donaldson was the terrorist?"

"The holy one's offspring did not believe in the mission. He was a conscientious objector and chose to show his surly disenchantment in a flamboyant style."

Well that explains the low key ending of the hijacking. And Rosemary flipping out with Andy. "Let's go." I slipped open the door and peeked out. It was quiet. Most everyone must have gotten off the train to see sunny beautiful San Bernardino. California at last. And I was skulking around a train with my husband whom I would never procreate with. Poor Mom. No large nosed Dente grandchildren for her.

We tiptoed down to the late Weepy Wendy's room and slipped inside. Al Dente closed the door behind us.

There wasn't any police tape. The window had been replaced and the room had been tidied up.

A loud meow emanated from under the chair. I dropped to my hands and knees and pulled a little black kitten from her litter box.

"Hello, little kitty. Don't be frightened. Has anybody fed you? Are you hungry and thirsty?"

Al Dente plugged the sink drain and squirted water in it from the faucet. I set the kitten on the stainless steel counter and she dipped her head down and lapped the water with her tongue.

I peeked under the sofa. "Ah ha!" I pulled out a step ladder. "So this is where it disappeared to! She used this when she trussed *Mini Mary Agnes* up on the shower rod in my bathroom—to stage a suicide." I looked at the door to the next room. I pointed to it. "That was our room! She was able to get in unnoticed. Why, I'll bet she knocked and poor *Mini Mary Agnes* welcomed her heathen soul inside. The poor trusting...angel."

"Step-cousin dearest has implied the dainty dwarf is no angel. She was sent down below."

"You guys creep me out with that supernatural hoo-ha some times." I grabbed a crumpled up bag from under the sofa. I smoothed it out. Pets Mart. Inside was a receipt for pet ID tags. "Shazam. Am I good or what? Wendy had the tags made at the pet supply store. She was gas-lighting me. I'll bet she sent the bleach too. Wait... What does bleach have to do with the deaths?"

"The skinny skunk haired one must have been throwing a red herring your way. Trying to implicate my family laundry. Or perhaps the departed butler boy of the vicar's wife? Did he not cleanse laundry aboard the train?"

"Or the chef. He used bleach on the fish. Carry the litter box back to my compartment." I picked the kitten up and petted her as we exited the room. No one was in sight. I closed the door behind Al Dente.

By the time I talked Andres into opening a can of tuna fish for the cat, I heard my brother greeting the passengers as they returned. Great. I had missed my first chance at California dreaming. Oh, well. We would reach our final destination in a couple of hours.

I returned to my compartment and fed the cat. Al Dente lay back on the sofa and his eyes blinked a few times then stayed closed. I covered him with a thin blanket and kissed his forehead.

I plodded down to the parlor car.

"The writers are all in the business car having a meeting. Why aren't you with them?" asked Big Marc.

"Nobody told me. How are you feeling?"

"My eyes are dry. I think I have an abscessed tooth. My shoulder aches. I've been having this pain in my gut—"

"I hope you feel better. I must join the others. I'll check in with you later." I trotted off to the business car.

Rosemary was recapping what we'd learned.

My gaze wandered to *Tabloid Tilly*. She was fondling a large portfolio this time. She seemed to be cameraless. How odd. I slipped into the chair next to her. As *Hack 'em Up Hazel* congratulated Carly, I whispered to *Tabloid Tilly*, "Just what did you mean the other night when you told me *'I know what you did?'*"

"I read your journal. I know what your book is about."

Before I could let out a string of *How dare yous*, Rosemary said, "Matilda would like to show off some little surprises she has worked very hard on."

All eyes turned toward the young Aussie photojournalist. She opened her portfolio and held up a large photo. Applause and laughter filled the car. I glanced at her creation. It seemed to be a book cover. *The Case of the Adorable Plumber by Dixie London.*

"Dixie London is the pseudo Sandra is using," beamed *Tabloid Tilly*.

I looked closer. Hey, that was me pictured on the cover. Kissing Andres! In the bathroom. And she Photoshopped in a toilet plunger. So that's what she was doing with all of those seemingly compromising snapshots...

As she passed the cover art around I realized I was the heroine pictured in three other books. Mom was even in one. And Al Dente was on the cover of Pat's latest pirate trilogy.

* * *

By the time I got all of my crap packed up including a plastic trash bag to stow the litter box in, the last shuttle had left the Los Angeles North American Passenger Railway station. What the heck, I decided to spring for a cab. After all, I was a wealthy woman. If the last deposit in our joint checking account was for real. And if it were, I knew exactly how I was going to spend it. My half of the whole enchilada.

I opened the rear door of the yellow taxi and tried to heave my duffle in. The cabbie jumped out and popped the trunk. He tossed in my duffle and reached for my plastic bag. I declined and instead stuffed it onto the back seat. The kitty and I climbed in.

"Where to?" he asked.

"SunTrust Bank."

I clicked on my seatbelt and leaned toward the window, enjoying the southern California view. I don't know why I was surprised to see that California pretty much looked like Florida. Except for the hills.

The bank was only two blocks away. We arrived abruptly.

"Please wait for me," I told him. I ran into the bank with my purse and cat in tow. Instead of joining the queue at the windows I walked over to the desks. The first lady to acknowledge me smiled. "May I help you?"

* * *

The cabby dropped me and Kitty at the Hilton Hotel across from Universal Studios. Rosemary had made reservations for us all. I gave my name and showed my driver's license to the desk clerk. She handed me my room key and said, "Your husband has already arrived."

Rosemary had me rooming with Al Dente? Oh, well. Why the heck not? It wouldn't be any different than rooming with Dina. And much better than rooming with Mom.

As I crossed the lobby, I passed Reverend Donaldson. He was hanging up the house phone.

"I have something for you." I dug through my purse and handed him an envelope. "It's a cashier's check. For the real estate company. You know, to make the debts good so the poor folks don't lose their homes."

He peeked inside the envelope. "Where did you get so much money? I mean, I know it's good. It's a cashier's check. But where on earth—?"

"It was my final payout from the government for the secret program my husband is in…" I whispered.

"That is impossible. We can barely fund that project with private donations. There are no government stipends."

"Shoot! That darned Al Dente. It's mob money. Shoot, shoot, shoot!" I huffed.

I spun around in a circle and then shrugged my shoulders. "Take it. Money spends. I wash my hands of it all. I hope it does some good. Bless you, Reverend."

"God bless you, Sandra."

* * *

I entered room 8117. I heard the shower running as I plopped the litter box and suitcase down. Kitty ran around the perimeter of the room, sniffing. I set up the litter box and stowed my suitcase in the closet. It was a standard hotel room, two queen beds, a desk, chair and ottoman, armoire with TV and a nice city view.

I picked the remote up off of the nightstand and clicked the TV on. I flipped from the hotel info channel to the news. I smiled as I gazed out the window looking down at the street life below. Convertibles and pretty people everywhere. I couldn't wait to walk a couple of blocks to Grumman's Chinese theatre. I wanted to find Lucille Ball's foot prints. And Donald Duck's. And Johnny Depp's.

I knocked on the bathroom door and it sprung open. I screamed. The shower curtain was clear.

As he pulled back the curtain, I stood immobile staring at the soap slithering down his perfectly chiseled body.

"May I help you, Mrs. Dente?" asked Lieutenant Hottie.

I opened my mouth to reply but words wouldn't form.

"There is something for you under the pillow," he said. "I'll rinse off and be right out."

I backed up, pulled the door shut until it clicked and ran to the first bed. I tossed five pillows onto the floor. I didn't find anything but sheets.

I whirled around to the bed near the window. Under the first pillow was a cute little green polka dotted gift bag. I pulled some tissue paper out. And Tinker Bell! I smiled with my whole body as I shook her Pixie dust and then held her to my ear. She tick-tocked to me.

Lieutenant Hottie walked out of the bathroom with a towel covering his parts that I would never again need to imagine. He was indelibly etched in the red silk sheets of my brain.

"I know how much you like your watch. I noticed the crystal had cracked so I slipped it off of you during one of your unconscious moments. I sent it out to a jeweler and had it forwarded here to the hotel. Did you even know it was missing?"

"Yes. Thank you so much! I could kiss you…"

"I hope you'll do more than that…someday."

The news channel had moved onto the weather. "A category five hurricane is headed straight for Cocoa Beach, Florida. NASA has battened…"

Lieutenant Hottie's cell phone rang. He slowly walked over to the desk and removed the battery. It stopped ringing.

"But that might have been work calling you in…"

"I'm not making that mistake again…"

The End

Made in United States
North Haven, CT
22 March 2024

50324552R00127